MW01537745

THE PEARL OF ALL BRIDES

INFILTRATING THE TON BOOK 2

SARA ADRIEN

WWW.SARAADRIEN.COM

Better an ounce from the ground than a pound from the roof. ~ The Talmud

For my Mami

CHAPTER 1

⌘

*L*ondon, 1813.

It was an unusually chilly April in London, and Arnold could nearly smell the snow in the air. The goldsmiths had left early and, too cold to work in the workshop, he'd decided to string the pearls in the lush green drawing room of their family's stately home. Aunt Eve and his younger cousin, Lizzie, were huddled by the fire.

"April wears a white hat." Lizzie got up and stepped to the window, pushing the peridot-colored curtains aside.

Through the fog, Arnold could barely see past the manicured bushes of their back gates to the bustling street overlooking Green Park. It was about a two-minute walk to St. James Palace or Pall Mall, or another three minutes in the other direction to Piccadilly, where he hoped he could earn a spot for his jewelry business, a flagship store for his family. If he could somehow manage that, and his cousin Fave and Uncle Gustav won the competition for the king's crown jewels, they could infiltrate the ton, London's aristocratic gentile society. The ton would be swayed by Prinny and certainly covet everything the new crown jewelers would sell. And if the Pearlers earned the privilege of this place on Prinny's side, they would have infiltrated the ton from the head down. Until then, they would continue holding their breath, hoping the gentiles wouldn't sniff them out.

It had taken his aunt and uncle decades to establish their clientele among the aristocracy. There was no way the noblesse would accept them if they knew they were Jewish—unless the prince led the way, maybe if they won the competition. George IV had become regent only two years earlier and had taken the reins of the competition. An outstanding, extravagant collector and builder, George IV, also called Prinny, had selected twelve competing families to present jewels at his winter ball. The winner of the competition would become the crown jeweler and earn a place at the king's side and the admiration of his followers, including the ton. It was a risk, Arnold realized. The Pearlers would stand in the spotlight at the royal court and could be uncovered as Jews. He was constantly trying to remind himself that this was England, not continental Europe, so they were citizens and had nothing to hide, but his gut told him otherwise.

"My flowers..." Aunt Eve mourned. Usually composed, with an ever-ready smile, she furrowed her brows at the dark clouds blocking the sunlight. Odd for this time of year, although English weather was unpredictable.

Lizzie shivered and pulled the green shrug from the settee over her shoulders. "Are you quite sure that this is a spring ball, not a winter festival?"

Eve joined her by the window. She'd been planning a reception to welcome Cousin Fave's new wife into the family. Arnold's cousin had married a sweet Jewish girl, and Eve's special welcome ball for her new in-laws was a ruse to introduce them to the ton. Eve had spared no expense for the occasion. Arnold knew the splendor of the ball would distract the aristocrats—it always did.

"Whatever you call it, Aunt Evie"—Arnold was the only one permitted the privilege of calling her Evie—"invite me some pretty widows, please." He smirked, but Eve gave him a scolding look.

"You won't find yourself—"

"A good Jewish bride... I know." Arnold sighed. They'd been over it a million times before. The only so-called 'good Jewish brides' were in London's orthodox community. And they, he was quite certain, wouldn't be found within a mile of his rakehell reputation *or* the ton. He wanted a partner for life, a smart girl, not a doll to prance around with during the season and toss aside over the cold months. Like cousin Fave's new wife Rachel—or had they been found for each other? Arnold shook his head, that was another story.

He wanted someone he could talk to, wrap into his arms in the cold English winter, and... Arnold wanted real passion. His desires were bubbling up now that Fave was busy with his bride. They rarely emerged from their chambers before dinner. Arnold was happy for them, of course, but he felt a pang of loneliness. Usually, work perceivable differences between the pearls were land-marks to his expert eye.

"The order really makes a difference. You arranged them to align...how shall I put it?"

"It's called evenly matched," Arnold said. He liked tutoring Lizzie. She was a quick learner and looked up to him. If she'd been a boy, she'd have made a better jeweler than he'd ever been. She was the dearest girl, and he loved her like a sister.

He handed his knotting tool to Lizzie by the wooden handle. "Hold it here."

She followed his instructions.

He opened his left hand to reveal a row of pearls on a red thread.

She inhaled sharply. "Where'd you hide these?"

Arnold only blinked at her with a boyish grin, proud of his stringing tools. "This is the awl"—he pointed at a thin nail that was tip up—"and this the yolk." He shifted a metal piece upward. "This pushes the knot close to the pearl, like so."

Lizzie's eyes twinkled in amazement and he felt pretty good about his contraption.

"Necessity is the mother of invention." Lizzie grinned, always ready with a saying.

Arnold nodded and wrapped the silk thread Lizzie had picked up around his index finger and thumb; then he swished his middle finger into the loop and hooked the tool.

"And voila, the nod is tight against the pearl."

"That's brilliant!" Lizzie beamed and took the tool from Arnold. "Now let me try."

Arnold felt it was good for Lizzie to participate in the family's business. It was terribly unfair to leave her out only because she was a girl—especially these days, when they could use every helping hand.

"Do you have enough pearls for the competition yet?" Lizzie asked without lifting her gaze from the strand in her hands.

"Not yet. I'll speak to Pavel and find out if he has a new supply," Arnold said, playing down his concern. He didn't want to alarm Lizzie yet, or Aunt Eve, but there had been no new shipments of pearls or gems recently. Hopefully, Pavel, their supplier at Piccadilly, could explain the hold-up.

"You'll need some evenly matched pearls like these for the crown jewels," Lizzie said, absorbed with the shiny beads in her hands.

Lizzie's knotting wasn't as tight as Arnold would like, but he decided he'd restring the pearls after she left. No need to discourage her.

"The pearl is the queen of gems and the gem of queens," she mumbled as she strung some more. Proverbs bubbled out of her like water from a fountain.

Lizzie was nearly twenty now and in her first season, poised to marry some gentile aristocrat. It was a terrible plan to ground the Pearlers among the ton but, to avoid muddling their bloodlines, Lizzie was to remain childless. The mere idea of such a union made Arnold's stomach turn, but that was a matter he couldn't focus on right now. He needed to help the Pearlers win this competition and earn his place in the family. He didn't want to be their charity case, the orphan who tagged along.

His father had died of lung fever when Arnold was four. Less than two months later, his mother had died of a broken heart. His maternal uncle Gustav had taken him in, and Aunt Eve had become his second mother. Grandfather used to make up for all the love the family thought he'd lost as an orphan. His cousin Fave was only eight weeks younger and they'd grown up like brothers. In all those twenty years with the Pearlers, they'd always treated him as one of them, but at four and twenty, Arnold wished to make himself indispensable for reasons other than familial affection. It was time to prove himself.

CHAPTER 2

*A*cross St. James' Palace, a short walk from Trafalgar Square, was London's Great Synagogue, Hannah's beloved home. Even though it was located in the heart of London, a few streets away from the British Museum to the northeast and Pall Mall to the southwest, the immediate quarter around the Jewish temple appeared like another world.

"Why would you read Debrett's? There's not a chance in hell you'll ever dance at one of the ton's balls!" Esther, Hannah's fourteen-year-old sister, lacked tact, a trait Hannah had desperately tried to instill in her since their mother had died.

Debrett's was a peerage reference book for the haute-couture of London, and Hannah knew she wasn't a "peer" in the strictest sense—or any other sense for that matter—but wasn't it the duty of an open-minded citizen to know what the nation's leaders were up to?

She rolled her eyes and closed her text. "Such

language, Esther. *Tate* wouldn't approve." Hannah resorted to her father's authority whenever she needed extra firepower in educating her younger siblings.

"You shouldn't be reading this; it's not our place," Esther said.

"It takes a certain finesse, you know, to deliver a blow. Yours is all too obvious." Hannah packaged the scolding in her best teaching tone, but she was hurt. It bothered Hannah more than she cared to admit that she was a spinster in her sibling's eyes, the reliable egg that would sit in the pantry and never emerge to the salon without an apron tied around her waist.

"Whatever do you mean by a blow? I'm a girl. I can't deliver anything but *food*... argh!" she said angrily, her brows furrowing in the middle as she did. Esther was fuming but Hannah was secretly pleased, for her little sister's frustration with the subdued role of girls was her influence. She saw herself as her sibling's tutor and one thing was for sure, she would not let her sisters be obsequious.

Hannah smiled. Maybe her sister was learning a little from her after all: the injustices between sexes, between religions, between social classes... Hannah was fascinated by both the unspoken boundaries *and* the lure of breaking through them. Even as a girl, Hannah had studied the Torah and knew more than most men. However, as a girl, she was bound to domestic duties. It was just that her mind and heart could not embrace the limitations of household duties. She knew she was destined for more.

"Aristotle said"—Esther interrupted Hannah with an indignant exhale—"No, just listen to me! He said that the aim of the wine is not to secure pleasure but to avoid pain." Hannah lowered her voice to wrap up her lesson, hoping her recitation from the greatest of philosophers would appease her little sister.

"Shakespeare said, 'Hell is empty, and all the devils are here,'" Esther said, brimming with pride at her retort.

"Touché! Well done! But don't be ungrateful for what you have. A likely impossibility—"

"Is always preferable to an unconvincing possibility, I know, I know."

Esther really had to stop interrupting people; it was most unbecoming. And yet, Hannah admired her sister's feistiness, even though she constantly felt a sense of underlying doom for her and for the prospects of all orthodox girls. For them, the future was limited to the home. It was a girl's duty to become a mother, and it was a mother's duty to instill pride in their traditions for the next generation. And yet, she could manage this *and more*. Except she'd not been able to explore what this "more" might entail because she'd never seen anything beyond the margins of their community.

All in all, time had stood still for the orthodox community in London, while people all around them participated in a more modern way of life. Hannah Solomon, the Chief Rabbi's oldest daughter, was something of a princess of the community, in plain sight for the Jews and yet invisible to gentiles if they happened to pass through the orthodox quarter. Here, the men wore black wide-brimmed hats and long black coats. Women kept their hair hidden under scarves and their opinions to themselves. Except for Hannah.

Giving her opinion had become her vocation. She was the sole author and editor-in-chief for the *Community Circular*, a small weekly newspaper. Hannah fancied herself a self-made investigative journalist, passionate about publicizing untold stories of Jews who'd overcome incredible obstacles. She hoped women would find inspiration in her writing and gain the strength to stand against the paternalistic environment that marked their time. Despite all her domestic duties, Hannah's mind painted strokes of freedom and equality for Jews, especially the poorest among her community. She thought it her humanitarian duty to shape her community's opinion in an educated and critical manner. To her father's chagrin, she knew her writing was frequently denounced as risqué by the elders of the temple—all men, of course.

Her father had—before his responsibilities had gotten the better of his time management—spent uncountable hours teaching Hannah to interpret the Torah. As the spiritual leader of the largest community in Great Britain, Rabbi Solomon was a respected scholar, and he'd taught Hannah everything he knew. Now, Hannah was teaching her younger siblings, who weren't allowed to attend the best, albeit non-secular, schools. Her younger brothers and sisters missing their education was out of the question as far as Hannah was concerned. Her sense of fairness, justice, and equality was the driving force behind her bottomless energy and devotion to her siblings—along with her big heart. She dearly loved each of her three little brothers and four little sisters, and she wanted the best for them.

. . .

LATER THAT DAY, Hannah chewed on the end of her quill and reread her closing lines before she handed her latest issue to her father, who was seated behind his desk. The next best thing to nourishing her siblings' minds was doing the same for her community. And so, over the past few years, Hannah had turned the *Community Circular*, the synagogue's news pamphlet, into London's only Jewish newspaper. She had two thousand subscribers, which barely paid the printing cost—but she didn't care as long as people read her columns.

YET ANOTHER JEW converted to Christianity and became a member of parliament this week. Is it not heartbreaking that our kind is reduced to conversion to become eligible politicians? Let us not forget that the Mishneh Torah is our goldmine, our guidelines for virtuous lives of love, humility, and compassion. As such, dear members of the community, let us search deeply within ourselves for the strength to find acceptance in our circles. Together, may we prevail and seize control over our fates. Since Maimonides, we have had time to adapt to our challenges...

"YOU CAN'T WRITE THAT!" Rabbi Solomon put his daughter's draft of the *Community Circular* aside. "I won't send this to the printer. It's too political and ... you can't speak up against Baron Stone!" he said, slamming his fist on the desk—a functional oak desk with an inkwell salvaged from the Jewish school at Kenton before its renovations. The hand-me-down desk seemed right at home here, with the cracked ceiling, the large wall clock, and the shelves full of reference books. Hannah had always thought her father's office, tucked away behind the sanctuary's doors, resembled an old schoolroom.

"It's the truth, *Tate.*" Hannah crossed her arms and stood firm before her father.

"It is, my *zis tokhter*, sweet daughter, but nobody wants to *hear* the truth. Treason on religion is one of those truths..." He leaned over the desk and put his hands on her cheeks. She felt the roughness of his burden.

"*Tate*, the members of our community are in a rut. They're pious but sometimes ... if they can't breathe, they might try to escape."

She saw her father closing his eyes. Why was it that he seemed to brace himself for a blow when she spoke of her observations? "They don't know why they do what they do and why we are so different."

"*Channi*"—he used her Yiddish nickname to draw her closer—"we are no different. Like the English, we bleed when we are cut, we breathe the same air, we drink the same water."

"And yet, we don't eat like the English, we don't dress like them, we don't even love like them!" Hannah bit her lip, fearing that her final analogy had gone too far. "You preach of virtues and belief, but we need to educate our community to truly internalize—"

"There is nothing to internalize; it's *in* our blood. How much deeper do you want it to go?"

"If people understood, then..."

"They will not lift themselves out of poverty, *Channi*.

They barely have the strength to hold on to what they have."

"Some rise above. Some use skills to escape poverty. What about Pavel?"

"What about Pavel?" her father mumbled.

"He's the richest Jew in London, *Tate*."

"He's not. There are others much wealthier than him." His hand trembled in the air for emphasis. Hannah recognized that he spoke of *that* family—the Jews who were in the ton. To her, it seemed an unspeakable combination.

"You're hiding them from me. You go in and out of their homes and I don't get to come." Everyone knew of them, but only her father knew their identity. He'd officiated at the wedding for one of them less than two weeks ago—a clandestine affair. Hannah had been specifically forbidden from running a story on the secret Jewish wedding on the margins of the gentile aristocracy. Whoever they were, those secret Jews were exciting and mysterious, and hiding in plain sight of the ton. Their camouflage had become legendary, for nobody knew exactly who they were. Hannah imagined them hanging from roofs, wrapped in bat-like wings, watching like gargoyles from their palatial perches near the Royal Palace.

"You said they had renounced their religion. That's what I fear for others who see no future in the orthodox ways." Hannah knew that she was overstepping, but she said it anyway.

"Not exactly. I said they don't submit to *all* our customs," her father said.

Hannah sniffed. *Potato, potahto.* All the men she knew

wore the yarmulke, the head cap. The women wore a *sheitel,* a wig, and they all ate kosher.

"I just want to do the right thing. The community is suffering." Hannah inclined her head and gave her father a bottom-up glare. With a few more winks through her eyelashes, she'd have her newspaper printed.

"At times, doing the right thing may diminish one's character. You imply that Judaism is a burden, and I disagree. It's what you make of it, a calling, a privilege…"

"*Tate,* spare me the sermon on moral attrition. Look at me!" Her hands were ink-stained, and her old dress had been mended so often she'd essentially refurbished it like a tapestry in the British Museum. Since her mother had died, Hannah split the household and familial duties with her aunt, Rivkah. Unfortunately, Rivkah was slow and Hannah nimble, so Hannah did a lot more in a much shorter time. "I dress like a peasant girl, not a scholar. What am I to make of that?"

She knew this was a low blow. He'd spent uncountable hours with her, studying all the leather-bound volumes on the shelves behind him. He'd told her that even though she was a girl, she was a peer, a scholar to him. A rabbi was, after all, ordained by another rabbi, following a course of study of Jewish texts, such as the Talmud. Her father had been ordained when he was three and twenty, but he'd told her that she was ready now—if only she wasn't a girl. She couldn't be ordained or called to any greater purpose beyond the stringent bounds of society, and the rules for orthodox girls were stringent, indeed.

Hannah batted her eyelashes, forcing a tear to add to

her argument. Her father's eyes sank at the corners, his signature resignation, and she knew she had him.

"I'll send this to the printer, but mark my words, you're no Joan of Arc."

"Nor would I want to be, *Tate*. She was burned as a heretic!"

"I just want to make sure you have no aspirations to play a heroine."

"Don't worry. I don't need a holiday named after me." Hannah grinned, knowing all too well that her sly comment bordered on blasphemy. And yet, even in her victory, she felt a pang of discomfort, for she wanted to make a difference to her community and recently, the *Community Circular* had started to seem insufficient for accomplishing her goals.

CHAPTER 3

*H*annah walked up the stairs in the back of the synagogue. Their modest home was tucked away behind the sanctuary. It had the Rabbi's office, a small corridor connecting to the kitchen on the ground level, and then the small salon and bathroom on the first floor, and the tiny bedrooms under the roof that they shared between the ten of them: her father, aunt Rivkah, Hannah, and her seven siblings. Whoever had designed the synagogue had clearly valued the spectacle in the sanctuary over those responsible for putting it on. It was another of society's friction points where expectations and values didn't necessarily align. She'd heard of a bare-knuckle prizefighter who earned more in a boxing match than a doctor did in a year. Hannah sighed, and then froze.

What was that?

Something dark with a long pink tail scampered past her. She shivered and hurried to the warm parlor, where her brothers and sisters were playing and reading in front of the only fire in the house besides the kitchen.

"*Tate* said that we're going to see the new baby soon," Lenny, her seven-year-old brother, said brightly.

Hannah smiled. Her sister Leah, only eleven months younger, had married a Rabbinical student in Birmingham less than a year ago. Leah's husband seemed nice, but just like every other man she knew, he had a beard and *peyot*—sidelocks—that made him appear much older than he really was. Their first baby was due soon, and Leah had sent notice that there was no mohel in town. *Tate* was going to have to perform the brit milah—ritual circumcision—if the baby was a boy.

Hannah knew it was a tremendous honor, especially because it would be Rabbi Solomon's first grandchild. But it had been years since he last performed a *brit milah*, and he was wary; he'd told her as much last Shabbat when they went for their weekly father-daughter walk. Leah and Hannah had grown up like twins. But after their mother had died, Leah had married and moved out of the house. Hannah didn't want to worry her and assumed all motherly duties in addition to her tutelage of Esther and Alma, her sisters aged fourteen and ten. Now, with little ten-month-old Ruthie in tow, Hannah had no time to write to Leah as often as she'd wished.

Hannah looked around the salon, the same room in which her life had taken a dramatic turn less than a year ago…

* * *

MOTHER WAS SITTING on the wobbly kitchen stool, her belly stretching forward. It was a Friday morning. The challahs had to be delivered to the twenty needy homes in their community—some single parents, some elderly, and the blind Mrs. Markovitz, a former opera singer from Moscow. Hannah always brushed extra egg wash on her challah, so she could feel the shiny golden goodness with her fingers.

"How good of you to write with Leah and Esther. You're such a good egg, *Channi.*" Mother always called Hannah her good egg, as if she hadn't hatched yet. Hannah liked it. She felt cozy, safely nestled under her mother's care. *Tate* had been so busy since he'd been appointed Chief Rabbi, and she rarely saw him except on their Saturday walks and when he studied with her. All the same, those moments were always organized, and always treasured. Somehow, her parents made time for each of their children, no matter what else was going on. They had the uncanny ability to find more than twenty-four hours in a day

"Can I bring you a glass of water?" Hannah asked when she saw beads of sweat running down her mother's temples. This was a late pregnancy; her mother was almost forty, and Hannah knew the risks. At the same time, she had heard her father's prayers and thanks for the blessing of another child at the *bimah,* altar, on Saturday mornings. Her mother looked exhausted, but Hannah didn't have the heart to dampen *Tate's* enthusiasm for baby number eight.

"No, I'll have to go back upstairs to the chamber pot if I drink water again. I can't face it," her mother said, breathless. Mama had told her that her urine was frothy, like foam on a beer. She seemed busy with the chamber pot more than during her other pregnancies.

"I'll braid the challah as soon as—" Her hand cramped over her heart, and her eyes rolled backward, disappearing under her lids.

"Mama?" Hannah dropped the quill, spilling the ink on her column draft.

Mother stared at her, frozen. Hannah rushed to her side and wrapped her arms around her. "Mama?"

Her mother didn't seem to be breathing. She crumpled in Hannah's arms, and sank to the ground.

"Mama?" Hannah said, lips trembling

No response.

"Mama?"

Silence.

Hannah let go of her and sprinted down the stairs, two at a time. "*Tate! Taaateee!*" she shrieked in horror. She felt like her life was unfolding before her, like the stairs would never run out in this terrible nightmare. She staggered down to her father in a panic.

By the time Hannah and her father returned to the kitchen, mother had rolled into a ball, violently throwing her arms against the box of flour, her skin splitting open against the wood.

"Ruthie!" *Tate* turned her around.

Hannah's heart dropped when she saw the foam around her mother's mouth. *Tate* lifted her upper body, but Mother was shaking uncontrollably. She spasmed and stretched her arms and legs as far apart as her body allowed, her round belly pointing into the air.

The door opened and Lenny came in, and then froze. "What's—Mama?" He grimaced and tears of shock welled up.

Tate got up. *"Lennikush"*—he used his Yiddish nickname, his telltale method of softening a blow—"run to Pavel. Tell him to come with Dr. Stuart. Run as fast as you can and tell Pavel it's life or death. Now!"

Lenny darted away.

Hannah stayed by her mother's side, holding her like a child, but the shaking didn't stop.

The moments stretched into eternity and Hannah felt her mother's tremors weaken. Alma and Esther came and went—*Tate* didn't let them stay. Esther brought a bowl of hot water and some clean linen rags.

By the time Dr. Stuart arrived with another man, a big leather bag, and a stack of cloths. Hannah couldn't see her mother's chest falling and rising anymore, she looked puffy but limp.

Pavel came and whispered something to *Tate,* but Hannah couldn't hear any more. She felt as if she were stuck in a dark tunnel, pushing with her soul. She knew she was hatching.

Someone grasped her arm. Pavel helped her up and took her downstairs.

"What is happening to Mama?" Hannah asked, afraid to hear the answer.

"They're going to try to save the baby now. It won't be long," Pavel said.

Hannah's eggshells shattered around her and splintered into a bleak future.

As she and Pavel stepped into the sitting room, where

her siblings were waiting, in silence with solemn faces, Lenny sobbing and gurgling silently on his tears, they heard the cries.

First, a loud wail, probably her mother's pain at being sliced open. Then a yowl and whimper from *Tate*. Some voices mumbling in English. Finally, a baby's first screams. Esther got up and took Ephraim and Simon, the five-year-old twins, by the hands and walked to the court-yard with them. She, too, had hatched, Hannah thought. It would be her duty to care for the younger siblings now. Hannah was the oldest; she would raise the baby.

The helper Dr. Stuart had brought came to the room, holding a screaming bundle of bloody cloths in his arms. "Which of you is *Channi?*"

Hannah stepped forward, her arms limp, her lungs constricted with pain.

Pavel put his hand on the back of her head. *"Ti virst es kenn tin, klig maidale."* You will manage it, smart girl.

And so unfolded the worst day in Hannah's life, when she became a mother to her little sister at the same time as she became a half-orphan. By the time Dr. Stuart had left, *Tate* had arranged the funeral, painstakingly following every Jewish custom to honor his beloved wife. It was late afternoon, and a body had to be buried before sundown, before Shabbat.

Hannah wasn't allowed to come; she had to stay home and hold the little bundle that was Ruthie, sleeping in her arms. A rosy and wrinkly little darling, unaware that she'd been named after her mother, whose body was barely cold.

If she was completely honest, Hannah had always been

secretly relieved that she'd missed the funeral. She couldn't imagine throwing a shovel of dirt on her mother's body wrapped in linen, the age-old custom of returning the body to the earth. What if her mother woke up again? Hannah had spent uncountable nights awake pondering this question, never reaching an answer. Some customs were greater than she could comprehend. She'd seen funerals from afar, but she'd never been to one. One was considered a child in Jewish tradition for as long as both parents were alive and children—tradition dictated —didn't belong at funerals. She hadn't said goodbye to her mother, and yet she had a piece of her in her arms in the shape of baby Ruthie.

* * *

HANNAH BLINKED and surveyed her siblings with all the love in her heart. In moments like these, with the baby sleeping on her chest, heavy against her, doom wasn't really so bad. She'd call Ruthie her "good egg" and not let her hatch too soon. And so far, Hannah had protected her siblings' shells as best she could, which made her feel proud. Yet, as she looked back down at the baby's sleeping face, she thought of something Esther had said to her not so long ago—"You'll still be here at forty, by the time we're all married and hatched." And somehow, despite her love and devotion to her family and the community, Hannah had never pictured this to be all her life would hold.

CHAPTER 4

The city seemed quieter than usual as Arnold stepped out the front door of the Pearlers' four-story townhouse. Although it was springtime, a chill ran down his back and he rubbed his hands together. He'd finished restringing the pearls and decided to deliver them himself. Of course, they had people in their employ for deliveries, but Arnold had learned it all from the bottom up, and he liked to take care of some aspects himself, rather than always sending an employee.

He'd just decided to take the shorter route, cutting through St. James Park and then along Pall Mall toward the synagogue, when a man called, "Ehrlich!"

A young man of middle height, with dirty blond hair, and a somewhat large nose walked up the stairs to Arnold's home. His coat was as bulky as Arnold's, lined with the finest shearling, just visible around the hem.

"What are you doing out in the cold?" Arnold asked,

recognizing his Oxford classmate, Baron Gregory P. Stone. "Isn't it warmer in the House of Lords than out here in the street?" He patted him so hard on the shoulder, Gregory almost stumbled on the Pearlers' front steps.

Arnold had to remind himself that most men of his age weren't as strong as he was. Arnold and Fave didn't overindulge in unhealthy habits. They preferred to fence, ride, and run in the early morning hours, burning their energy until their bodies burned with exhaustion. But recently, Fave's athletic energy had been redirected to his new wife, and Arnold felt a bit superfluous. He loathed his sentiments and kept them to himself because he was so happy for Fave and Rachel, and yet, he missed his best friend, his cousin, the only and dearest brother he'd ever had.

"I came to speak to you," Gregory said sternly and Arnold shifted away.

Everything had changed since they'd returned from Oxford. Gregory was technically of Jewish lineage, but his father had been baptized before Gregory's birth. He never had to hide as much as Arnold and Fave had to get a gentleman's education at Eaton and Oxford. If anyone had known the Pearler boys were Jewish, they'd have been expelled because Jews weren't admitted to the highest and most prestigious educational institutions. Despite his parents' conversion to Christianity, Gregory had remained an ally to the Jews, privy to the Pearlers' secret —one that few among the ton knew. Arnold appreciated Gregory's loyalty. For years, a former patroness of Almack's, Lady Carol Bustle-Smith, had extorted and blackmailed the Pearlers. She had threatened to expose them, and by extension, endangered their livelihood as the haute-couture jewelers of the ton. Gregory wasn't like that.

Arnold straightened before his old friend, "What can I do for you?"

"I think the question is what we can do for each other," Gregory said.

Arnold inclined his head expecting Gregory to explain.

"I know you're running in the competition for the crown jewels"—Arnold nodded—"but the rules are changing."

"How can the rules change?"

"It's Prinny"—George, Prince of Wales, the eldest son of George III, and Prince Regent since 1811—"His father rarely emerges from his chambers, he's lost his mind, so Prinny's in charge of the competition and you know how—"

Arnold groaned and kicked the stone steps. "He's not playing fair, I've heard."

Gregory tilted his sideways as if he had a hard time dislodging the right words. "He's a devout supporter of the arts."

"Hmpf," Arnold muttered.

"I wouldn't disregard that if I were you. He's generously commissioning architects, poets, musicians…"

"You mean we have to sell him jewelry as an art form to garner his support?" Arnold asked.

"That's why I came to see you."

Arnold nodded appreciatively. "The street's not the right place to discuss business."

"Certainly not."

"Would you like to join us for *Shabbes* tomorrow? We can speak freely after the ladies retreat. Fave and Gustav will be there."

"I'm afraid I have dinner plans, but I can join you for a drink later in the evening."

"Alright." Arnold turned, ready to hire a hack.

"One more thing." Gregory put his hand on Arnold's shoulder. "My sources tell me that Prinny wants pearls—lots of them."

"Prinny's Pearls. Preposterous." Arnold sneered.

Gregory laughed. "If I were you, I'd get as many as possible. And then more!"

Arnold eyed him incredulously. "It's not about quantity when it comes to—"

"Pearls, I know. But my sources tell me that pomp will sway the jury in this competition." Gregory's face wrinkled. "See you tomorrow then."

Arnold closed his eyes and inhaled as he watched Gregory walk down the street into bustling Piccadilly Circle. He knew this competition meant everything to Uncle Gustav, and Gustav and the Pearlers meant everything to Arnold. It was their chance to earn a place in the ton. Arnold tasted acid at the thought. As if they hadn't more than earned their place already—many times over. The difference now was the competition was judged by Prinny alone, so the Jews stood a true chance. Their regent had a reputation for being eccentric, and also unbiased. If they won the competition, their position would be founded in merit on the side of the monarch. With his pearls, Fave's original designs, and Gustav's business sense, they were unbeatable. Whatever complications Gregory could throw at them, Arnold's resolve was unshakeable. He'd do everything in his power to help the Pearlers win.

CHAPTER 5

$\mathcal{B}$ig Ben chimed loudly, its bells resonating through the cold April air. Arnold felt the vibration in his stomach, so raw had his exchange with Gregory left him. He was blinded by the desire to win the competition at all costs.

It was only two in the afternoon. He could walk over to Pavel's shop in Piccadilly Circus and order a batch of pearls for the competition and still have time to drop off the delivery for the Rabbi.

Pavel was more than twenty years older than Gustav, and one of the most respected jewelers in the city. An orthodox Jew, he had half a dozen sons. Pavel had traveled the world with Grandfather Pearler, and the families had trusted each other implicitly for decades. For as long as Arnold could remember, Pavel had been their importer of gems and pearls. His sources were legendary. And most importantly, he was honest and trustworthy—a rarity in their business.

Arnold walked briskly to Pavel's store. When he pushed the heavy door open, a little bell rang above his head. Pavel, as usual, was nowhere to be seen. He always made people wait for his grand entrance and cordial greeting. If Pavel wasn't a master of his art, Arnold would eat his sword.

And then Pavel appeared. Pavel's eyes seemed droopier than usual, and his shoulders were slumped.

"Arnold Ehrlich, *meyn ingel, vus brengt dir aher in der kelt?*" My boy, what brings you here in the cold?

Arnold reached out to greet Pavel and noticed the older man's hands were trembling.

"*Ikh bin do vayl...* I'm here because of... the competition," Arnold said. With Pavel, the only way was the direct approach.

Pavel nodded grimly, pulled a stool to the counter, and leaned against it. Arnold had never seen him do this before. Why did he suddenly seem so frail?

"Two of my sons were attacked last night."

Arnold gasped.

"Gideon. He was with Caleb." Pavel knocked three times on the wooden stool. It was a superstitious signal of gratitude that Gideon and Caleb had survived, but Pavel drew his lips in as if he wanted to hold back bad news.

"Is he alright?" Arnold asked as he swallowed the uneasy gut response to the act of violence against his friend, a fellow Jew.

"We hope so. His left eye is swollen, and we don't know if he'll be able to see again." Pavel looked down at the counter. "Imagine"—he forced a hard laugh through his beard—"a jeweler who can't see…" But the laugh sounded more like a cry.

"Can I do anything?" Arnold offered.

"I'm afraid this is only getting started, my boy. The port authorities didn't come to help. Gideon and Caleb must have looked Jewish to them, and the guards didn't want to save Jews from criminals. We lost our last shipment of pearls and diamonds." Pavel sighed. "We haven't been getting shipments from France. It's been months since anything came via Spain. The Dutch have stopped doing business with Jews. It's just that…before long, I'm afraid that—"

"Your supplies will be depleted." Arnold understood immediately that their participation in the competition was in jeopardy. With the materials drying up, the jewelers would be like fish without water. Pavel had joined forces with him and Cousin Fave when he gave him a rare emerald to cut for the jewels, but with the increased demand for pearls, there might not be enough to complete their entry.

No, Arnold wouldn't let this chance slip away. He was determined to win this competition for Gustav, Fave and all the Pearlers. It was his big chance to earn his place, not merely to occupy it.

Pavel stared at him now, with warm eyes that spoke of sorrow and fear. "I raised six sons, six jewelers. I never thought … without the materials…"

"I understand." Arnold dropped his head. This was awful.

. . .

SPRING LOST its vigor under the cold afternoon fog. Since Pavel gave him such terrible news, Arnold seemed to feel the cold more acutely. Without raw gems, Cousin Fave would have nothing to cut and set in his intricate designs —an artist without a canvas. Without pearls, Arnold would have little to sell. And without a whole lot of jewels, they had no chance in the king's competition.

Arnold kicked a stone. His mood curdled, but he wasn't prepared to lose hope. There had to be a way to get what they needed for the competition. Giving up wasn't an option.

He could have walked to the synagogue to make the delivery, but it was so chilly the birds had stopped chirping, so Arnold hired a hack instead. He wouldn't be long, and a one-horse carriage would suffice for the trip down Haymarket and along Pall Mall. He'd never been to the Great Synagogue, or any synagogue for that matter. The Pearlers lived on the margins of the Jewish community, doing business with other Jews, but no more. They were assimilated among the gentiles and lived an unprecedented lifestyle, as if they were English aristocracy.

Except that they weren't. Evil tongues like the dowager Bustle-Smith and her daughter, Allison, who'd married Arnold's nemesis from Eaton, Marvin Thompson, never missed an opportunity to remind them. The Pearlers were neither here nor there, but that was alright, for they had each other—and now Arnold's new sister-in-law Rachel and her family. Fave's wife had brought a burst of fresh air along with her little brother, Sammy, and her parents. Arnold had taken an immediate liking to her, and they had become one big family of clandestine Jews.

At twenty past two, Arnold stepped down from the hack, brushed off some invisible dust from his immaculate coat, and eyed the unimpressive Jewish quarter and its inconspicuous temple. He climbed the stone stairs to the double front door, which stood in the middle of the arched synagogue entrance. It was a Thursday, so he had no reason to expect anyone there. Uncle Gustav had instructed him to turn left into the hallway after the *bimah*, the Rabbi's podium in front of the Torah cabinet, so he strode in, his leather soles clacking on the floor tiles. It smelled of old books and moist wood.

Even though the outside was rather plain, the inside left Arnold awestruck. Economist and philosopher Adam Smith had said, "Outside hostility breeds inside solidarity," but oh my, how the Jews had taken the approach of inside over outside to heart. There were at least five hundred seats on wooden benches oriented toward the Torah, the scrolls holding holy Jewish texts. Luxury seemed to be reserved for the inside in less of a British understatement but rather a precaution against antisemitic attacks. A combination of awe and defensiveness overcame Arnold. Yet, his heart warmed with the sense that he belonged among the people who gathered here, even if he was never there to participate.

Arnold hadn't seen one of the precious hand-written Torah scrolls since his Bar-Mitzvah, his coming-of-age ceremony at age thirteen. Nonetheless, Grandfather Pearler had instilled a sense of belonging and pride, and thus being so close to the Torah cabinet stirred something within him. He stepped through the benches and tried to read the Hebrew lettering on the worn prayer books in the front pockets of each seat. Arnold knew that synagogues were rarely as intricately adorned as churches—and he'd been to plenty of those—but the tall arched windows and wrought iron chandeliers impressed him immensely. How would services be run here? How would it feel to be part of hundreds of like-minded souls *davening*, swaying, in prayer together? Arnold had never been part of something so big. The thought gave him goosebumps.

A screech came from the *bimah* and a light flickered from behind a side door. Startled, he walked towards the noise.

"Where's your *kippah*, your head covering?" asked a female voice, and he glanced around, trying to spot her. "You are in a sacred place! Cover your head."

He caught sight of a tiny figure in the shadows.

"I… ehm… I'm sorry, but I don't have a *yarmulke* with me." Arnold never carried the little brimless cap with him. Why would he risk being found out with the telltale Jewish head covering? He'd been raised to carry the respect for his people in his heart—not as a cap on his head.

"You're a Jew? Without a *kippah*?" A slim girl—no, a young woman—stepped into the light. She was modestly dressed, with her neck covered up to her chin. The woolen dress had the sensible air of being easily mended.

"I am, I'm afraid. Arnold Ehrlich, at your service." He was already holding his hat in hand, so he brought it to his chest and bowed deeply.

How liberating to start a conversation by introducing himself as a Jew. He'd never do that near St. James or Piccadilly Circus, where he spent most of his time with gentile aristocrats. Arnold's mood immediately lifted now that he could be himself, a Jew with another Jew. They had a common denominator. The girl was too far away for him to offer a kiss on her hand. She also seemed a bit snappish, and he was unsure that the ton-style greeting befitted the situation.

"Did you finish the pearls, Mr. Ehrlich?"

Arnold blinked, surprised. She knew about the pearls?

"And who are you?" he asked as he eyed her.

She came closer. The candlelight allowed him to scan her face. He tilted his head sideways to see better. Her eyes were almost black, rimmed with long dark lashes, like bleeding ink on a wet sheet of paper. Despite the loose updo, Arnold noticed streaks of copper in her thick brunette curls.

She wasn't beautiful in an obvious way, and yet she took his breath away with the quality of a rough gem.

Her woolen dress seemed like a shroud, as if enveloping a delicate figurine to keep her warm and safe. She was pale and slender, yet brimming with freshness. Her innocence was palpable. As his eyes passed over her narrow figure, Arnold felt instantly dirty by comparison. His sour mood was replaced with the all too familiar heat in his mid-section. He was mesmerized, as if this girl were a twinkling star far above his head, in a world parallel to his own.

"Why are you here alone?" he asked, for he felt a young lady should be chaperoned, especially around him.

"Oh, I'm not." The hint of an answer glistened in her eyes, but she spoke no more.

Her gaze made the hairs stand up on his arms and back. Arnold had forgotten why he was here, and yet it seemed there was nowhere more important to be but here. He felt her hungry eyes down to his bones. Arnold, the rake, the ever-smooth talker and manipulator of the ladies of the ton, was dumbfounded. No woman had ever affected him so.

"My father told me to count the pearls when the messenger brought them."

Ah, the pearls. Yes, of course. Arnold removed the linen pouch from his coat and handed it to her.

"Where's the box?" She took the pouch and opened it immediately, sinking onto one of the benches to count. "The jeweler didn't put the pearls in a box?"

"I'm the jeweler, not the messenger. And pearls need to breathe, they'd lose their luster in a box," Arnold said matter-of-factly, as if everyone ought to know how to best care for pearls.

The girl didn't look up, engrossed in the counting, but he saw a tinge of red creeping up her smooth cheeks. Then she tugged the strand. Arnold flinched; tugging a silk strand of pearls was like petting a cat against the direction its fur grew. He should have opened and restrung the section Lizzie did earlier, just in case.

"Why are there so many knots?" She peered at him.

At the sight of her lips, Arnold's tongue felt dry, stuck in his throat. He swallowed, willing his voice to return. "Each knot prevents the pearls from rubbing against one another. They're freshwater pearls, you see"—he walked closer and picked up the end of the loop that hung from the girl's hands—"the luster is quite sharp."

The girl looked up to him. When her eyes met his, his stomach flipped. His clammy fingertips left tiny droplets of condensation on the pearls he touched. He started to sweat like a green boy, even though it was freezing in the great sanctuary.

"H-how do you know they're freshwater pearls?" asked the girl with the mesmerizing eyes.

Arnold's world spun, his heart thumping as he stood frozen before the beauty, both of them holding on to the strand of pearls.

"There's barely any blurring around the edges of the light reflections." He leaned down to point at the tiny white points of light reflecting on the pearls. But his eyes never left hers. She was so close now that her breath blew on his cheek. She even smelled innocent, like fresh cucumbers in a summer breeze.

She raised her eyes from the pearls to his. When she fluttered her big brown lashes, Arnold's gut shot ripples of longing through his body.

"I don't think I have… I mean…" she began.

Her proximity blasted his self-control and he was consumed by the need to touch her. His lips dropped to hers via a magnetic pull, swelling with desire when he closed the distance between them. He caught her mouth mid-syllable, but it didn't matter. Nothing mattered but his thirst for her. Arnold leaned in further, nudging her lips gently with his. She was soft and radiated warmth but her kiss was adorably clumsy. An innocent. *So precious.*

The intensity rushing through Arnold's body caught

him by surprise. He couldn't remember an experience like this—ever. This was a cleansing kiss. Chaste but lovely, hot and deep, but pure. Her lips fit perfectly on his.

He deepened the kiss, and she parted her lips in ... passion? No. Delight?

CHAPTER 6

*T*he tall stranger stood squarely in Hannah's way, holding one end of Mother's pearl strand. His broad shoulders emitted strength like a redwood soaring toward the light. Hulled in a thick dark coat, he looked warm yet pliable, and Hannah was oddly curious how he might feel if she touched him.

Tate had given Mama's pearls to Hannah for her twenty-first birthday. She clearly remembered *Mamale* wearing them in services before her last confinement. She couldn't wait to show them to her little sisters. They were their only family heirloom, and she'd wear them proudly as the eldest daughter. Except she had no elegant gowns to pair them with and nowhere to go to wear them. The best she could manage was a sensible lace blouse that she often wore under her dark gray pelisse. She probably looked at least ten years older than she was—something she'd never felt as acutely as in this instant. This gorgeous man had intruded on her daily routine and caught her off-guard.

He leaned toward her, and she saw the coat bulging around the shiny horn buttons on his chest. His neck was barely covered by the stiff collar, and his Adam's apple was jumping as he swallowed. She could smell him now, could almost taste the citrus notes. There was something else, too. Pine, or rosemary? And the salty ocean wind. Yes, exactly! He smelled like a lemon needle tree on a windy beach day.

Nonsense, Hannah admonished herself. Lemons did not grow on needle trees, and she wasn't at the beach. He couldn't possibly be Jewish, even though he'd used the Yiddish term *yarmulke*. He seemed too beautiful to be real, too crisp for a sleazy jeweler and the rest of his bad reputation among the Jews in town. Clearly, gossip had distorted the truth about him and Hannah knew instantly that her prejudice had clouded her judgment. With every whiff of his perfectly polished elegance, she felt smaller and smaller. She felt an odd heat pool within her body.

The hurt from Esther's sideways comment that she'd be here at age forty still stung. Her nostrils flared at the thought of it. She'd dwindle in the corridors behind the sanctuary like a candle on Friday night. *Pah!* How had her life taken such a turn? She felt doomed, trapped in a shabby house dress.

Where would she go anyway? She didn't fancy a single man in the community, much less find someone she'd be willing to submit to. They had their heads stuck in prayer books, without understanding what they were reading. They weren't just in a rut; they followed traditions, empty-headed, as if it were the rules to a macabre game. When Hannah thought about how little most orthodox

Jews understood of the ideologies and philosophy of their great religion, she was ashamed on their behalf—but it was impossible to say so, especially as a girl, and even more so as an unmarried daughter of the Rabbi. He preached and taught, she wrote and explained, but the community remained deaf.

Her heart went out to them because the Jews had turned obstinate through fear. The authorities never quite stood up for them; the gentiles overcharged or underpaid them. About twenty thousand Jews were scattered around England, trying to stay afloat rather than thrive. And how could she blame them? She was doing no more. She lived day by day, swimming in chores and keeping her siblings in check and well-loved, while *Tate* made sure they were warm and fed.

She supposed the handsome man who had lost his way in their sanctuary knew no such sentiments. Women must swoon before him, fanning him with feathers, and feeding him grapes in beds of burgundy satin. He looked like a chiseled Roman statute at the British Museum—the same one with the fig leaf that she never told *Tate* she'd seen. But oh, she had! And she could only imagine that a fig leaf would do this man a terrible injustice.

He'd come into the holy temple without a *kippah*. She knew the sort; she'd heard about the family of traitors who hid among the ton to amass wealth. *Tate* knew them and ensured their worlds wouldn't mix. The Jews and the ton were like oil and water. They coexisted in neat strands atop each other in the vacuum of civilization they called London. Was this man one of the rich mysterious Jews who knew just how to shake up society so the Jews could infiltrate the ton?

Oh, how the vacuum around this man sucked the air out of her lungs. He was unlike the men in their *shul*, the synagogues community, unlike anyone she'd ever spoken to. He had an uncompromising presence she'd never seen before. His face looked taut and creamy, like a dollop of whipped custard Hannah wanted to lick right off the whisk. She blushed at the thought.

And then he was close. His eyes met hers and the beauty of his irises cut off her breath. They were drawn in lines of blues, blacks, and teals—a complicated and hypnotic pattern that lured her in. In that moment, Hannah felt as though she was waking up to a new-found beauty. She was awake, of course, but with him nearby, her senses were heightened. The air grew thinner, and she parted her lips to gulp.

"I don't think I have... I mean..." She fumbled for words, lost in imagining how his mouth might feel. If she were a mouse, she'd climb into his coat pocket and nestle into the exquisite masculine strength she imagined in his chest ... and then she didn't need to imagine anymore. His lips touched hers, and his scent enveloped her. Hannah gave up—*or she gave in?* Whatever it was, she reveled in the delicious sensation of his lips on hers. One of her hands came to his rest on his chest, while the other still lingered on the pearls.

She trampled on her proverbial cracked eggshells, and she no longer wanted to be a good hatchling. She wanted this! He felt so good that she let out a little moan. But maybe he didn't hear it because he pressed his hot lips onto hers, deeper, harder. Was that his ... oh, it was his tongue! She opened her mouth slightly, allowing the barest invasion of her lips. With his every intimate swish, her heart sailed through her chest. She felt his hands in her hair like the wind on a ship. She'd set sail for a new adventure, and she wanted to stand on the bow of the ship to experience all of it first and fully. This was something she'd take just for herself, just this once she wasn't a replacement mother, she was a young woman in the arms of ... of... she couldn't describe the beautiful prince but she wanted to drink him in nonetheless.

Hannah melted onto the spot, wondering whether her feet would sit in a pool of wax like a burned-down candle. Then he touched her cheek with one of his hands, the softness of his touch a contrast to his implicit strength. As he slid his fingers deeper into her hair, cradling the back of her head, his other hand found hers. She was still holding the pearls, and he walked his fingers along the strand, wrapping it around his fingers, pulling her closer to him, luring her with them.

Just when she gasped at his tender embrace, he broke the kiss. Hannah felt the loss of his lips like a brutal tear from her soul. She wanted him back right away. And then the oddest thing happened. He smiled. A warm and toothy smile. His eyes crinkled most deliciously. And Hannah twirled like a sycamore seed spinning down, down, deeper into ... his embrace.

Her eyes darted to his. He was still close and came closer until his mouth was back on hers. She tasted his warm smile as if he could wrap her in a cocoon of his exquisite scent.

And then the moment was stolen.

CHAPTER 7

❧

"*C*hanaaaah!" someone shrieked.

Hannah jumped back, still holding one end of the pearls, while the man held the other. The silk strand tore, and the pearls tumbled onto the floor. Each bounced in another direction, scattering the floor with pearls.

Startled, Hannah bent down to gather the precious beads. Arnold joined her.

Aunt Rivka grabbed her arm and pushed her onto the moist wooden bench. "What happened here?" she screeched.

"The pearls … ahm … they came off and we're…" Hannah stuttered, unable to tear her eyes off Arnold. *Aunt Rivkah had seen them.*

"Chanah," said her aunt's voice, deep and forbidding.

Hannah had no retort. She had the sinking feeling that this sycamore seed would be nagged by a chickadee named Rivka, for those were the dee-dee-calls she made when she was piping mad. Like right now.

Arnold remained on all fours, counting pearls as he gathered them in the linen pouch. Hannah couldn't understand a single word of her aunt's high-pitched rant because she was focused on Arnold's behind sticking up from under the benches as he bent down. His white breeches would surely get dirty from the sanctuary floors. Hannah had to look twice, his crisp behind bulged up like two ovals under a tissue. His thighs stretched the white fabric to the maximum. When he squatted before her, she saw even his crotch was somehow ... swollen? Over-stuffed? Whatever the right word she was lacking, she was intrigued.

"*Soli* will make you! You know it!"

When Hannah heard her father's nickname, her eyes shot to her aunt's. "What do you mean?"

"What do I mean?" The last word peaked shriller than any before. Rivka was clearly beside herself, and Hannah was growing impatient with her aunt's hysteria.

"You are compromised. You are a ... fallen girl," her piping aunt whistled and wagged her hand before Hannah. "You have to marry him." Rivka planted her hands on her hips.

Arnold rose and straightened his coat, his face blank.

"You can't tell *Tate!*" Tears pricking Hannah's eyes. Her cheeks flushed because Arnold was now focused on her and frowned.

Rivka sat down beside her, took both of her hands, and lowered her voice to a serious tone, "*Channi*, you are compromised, dear. There is no other way."

"What's this all about?" Arnold grimaced.

Hannah took her hands from Rivkah's grasp; she couldn't bear her touch.

"She says"—Hannah tsked, it was really too absurd —"that I have to marry you now." Ashamed, she couldn't even make eye contact. How could she have been so reckless? She was stupid, a pawn in a bad joke. *What did the Rabbi's daughter say when a handsome Jew walked into the shul...?*

Surely, he wouldn't even have her, the dumb girl in the old woolen sack of a dress. She was still herself, except that her virtue had shriveled to a blemish, like the rot of an apple. She swallowed as realization sank in. Rather than being wide awake, she wanted to crawl under her covers and never resurface.

CHAPTER 8

The sanctuary grew darker with the progression of the late afternoon. Arnold wished he could drown out the chubby woman's angry whistling like a ruffled bird. He was watching Hannah, hardly taking in anything else around him. The girl he had kissed sat still, crimson-faced, her gaze lowered to her hands. Arnold didn't know how much time had passed.

Then a door creaked and closed and footsteps sounded on the tiled floor like on sand.

"Ah, Mr. Pearler, how good to see you." The Rabbi offered his hand to Arnold.

"Ehrlich, Arnold Ehrlich. My uncle and cousin are Pearlers." Arnold bowed his head to the Rabbi as he shook his hand.

"My apologies, Mr. Ehrlich. I remember you, of course. I hear you're quite the inventor. Pavel speaks most highly of the … um … stringing devices you built for him."

He took off his hat, revealing a *kippah*. Then he

stepped toward Hannah and gave her a fatherly kiss on the cheek. Next, he greeted the other woman whom he called Rivkah. Oh no. Arnold was in the political and cultural hub of European Judaism, where he'd kissed their leader's daughter *and* gotten caught? Arnold's intestines cramped, giving him a stomachache. He needed to sit, but his legs were frozen.

Hannah said, "Papa, I have t-to—"

"They're getting married," Rivka blurted.

The Rabbi's head snapped to Rivka so quickly he nearly stumbled. "I beg your pardon?" His friendly expression turned into wrinkled anger.

The girl with gorgeous dark eyes stared at him. Her rosy lips puckered, and she drew some air in and then deflated. No words emerged.

"Hannah Solomon," Arnold said to himself. He'd kissed Hannah, Rabbi Solomon's daughter. He'd gone after her like a randy bear searching for honey, and now the bees would sting him.

"My eldest daughter," the Rabbi said, presenting Hannah to Arnold. "Now tell me what I just walked into. *Channi?*" He waited for a second and then turned to Rivka.

"I came to see … and then I saw … oh my eyes!" Rivkah poked her eyes with her fleshy index fingers as if they'd been burned with acid.

How melodramatic. It had been the best kiss of Arnold's life. *Surely* Rivkah had a low bar of what would hurt her eyes. "I apologize, Rabbi Solomon. I believe what she's trying to tell you is that—"

"I kissed him, *Tate.*"

Hannah's honesty startled Arnold but then he warmed to her courage. A brave and beautiful girl. Arnold felt his body hardening again.

THE RABBI LED Arnold through a narrow corridor into his office. Arnold felt as if he were summoned to the headmaster back at Eaton. But the Rabbi's office was so much more modest, a small windowless room that smelled of mold. Behind the Rabbi was a series of leather-bound volumes, sequentially numbered, posing as the focus of the shabby bookshelves on either side of the makeshift desk. It seemed more like an outdated schoolroom table with a quilted writing mat and an ink well than the office of a distinguished religious scholar and community leader.

Solomon signaled Arnold to take a seat.

"I prefer to stand." Arnold assumed his biggest, proudest stance and felt twice as tall as the elderly man standing before him.

"I thought the job was quite clear, son. You restring my late wife's pearls. They are a present for my eldest daughter."

Arnold nodded. "I did." He retrieved the pouch of pearls. He'd have to restring them again, of course. He felt like a schoolboy caught without homework even though he'd done it.

"Don't interrupt me." The Rabbi held up his hand signaling stop. His eyes grew darker like a stormy sky. "How. Dare. You!" he thundered in a low gurgling voice.

Now, Arnold felt rather small. His latest achievement

had been to compromise the Rabbi's daughter, a new low even for him. "In my defense, I didn't know she was your daughter."

"How's that a defense? You compromised a stranger then? In a temple?" The Rabbi's question hung menacingly in the windowless room. With nowhere else to go, the accusation clung to Arnold.

The Rabbi's temple pulsed and he cracked his neck. "*Channi!*" the Rabbi yelled.

Arnold's eyes grew wide. He felt like an ass.

Within a split second, the beauty opened the door and sheepishly peeked in. Her gaze was low and heavy. It struck Arnold that she seemed tired from carrying an invisible weight, a burden.

"Shut the door," the Rabbi roared.

She stepped in and did as she was told.

"It was just a kiss, *Tate.*" Her voice quivered.

Just a kiss? Is that what she thought? It was the best bone-melting earth-shattering kiss Arnold had ever had, and he knew the domain! He'd have to do better and knock her off her feet the next time. Arnold flinched at the idea of a next time; it was against his rules to drink from the same fountain twice.

The Rabbi exploded, "May I introduce, Ms. *Channi* ... ehm, Hannah Solomon. Mr. Arnold Ehrlich. Your husband ... ehm... soon to be."

Hannah's eyes remained stuck on the stain on the faded carpet she stood on, but Arnold felt as if he were losing his footing. He tugged at his collar; it was hard to breathe. If this were a half-decent play, he'd be caught by a flying carpet and swept away. Except that this was real, and his life was about to take a turn.

"You're jesting, I'm sure," he said but he couldn't muster as much as a placid smile. The air grew sparse and he loosened his cravat.

"No," the Rabbi grumbled in a most unfriendly tone.

"But I only kissed … I barely touched her."

Now both Hannah's and the Rabbi's eyes shot to him. He felt like an ambushed dog cowering in a corner.

"I don't have time for this. You're both old enough to live with the consequences of your actions." The Rabbi sank into his desk chair.

"There are no consequences to a kiss! She willingly—" Arnold started, but Hannah shot him a death look, so he fell silent.

Speechless, Arnold waited for Hannah to protest. Her father remained motionless.

Arnold shuffled his feet. "How can you entrust your daughter to a stranger? You don't even know me!"

"My boy, you are no stranger to me," the Rabbi said without even looking at him.

He was in his late fifties and had grey hair on the back of his hands, folded on the desk. His shoulders were bony. "Gustav and I went to school together. My father, may he rest in peace, married Gustav and Eve in 1787 right here in this temple."

Arnold crossed his arms.

"Mr. Ehrlich, Arnold, my son. I knew your parents."

Arnold's muscles went limp. A frisson traveled down his back. "Y-you knew my parents?"

"Of course, son." The angry father before him, a man

of authority for the community, suddenly softened at the mention of Arnold's late parents. The Rabbi was hardly a stranger to the Pearlers but Arnold had usually escaped his scrutiny—until this day.

"I barely remember them," Arnold whispered, upset that Hannah could hear the sorrow in his voice. Over time, the memories of his father had dwindled, and his mother became just a faint figure who'd kissed him good night. He remembered the mellowness when he drifted to sleep under her careful watch but not much more. Not anymore.

"Mr. Ehrlich, I've known your family since before you were born. Your grandfather brought your father … sorry, your uncle here for his bar-mitzvah. I arranged for a Torah to be brought to your home for your and Fave's clandestine Bnei-mitzvah. Even before I took office—"

"I…" Arnold was at a loss for words.

"You, my dear, are an apple from a very large tree that stands quite firmly in moral and virtuous Judaism." The Rabbi now leaned on his elbows.

"With all due respect, I don't see how this justifies a marriage to your daughter." Arnold stood tall, his head high, trying not to allow his posture to betray his emotions. He wasn't a pawn in a game of chess that could be traded in a sly move.

"You were caught, my son." He shot Hannah a look of rapprochement across the room like an arrow from a bow.

"I can't marry her. I don't know her."

"Custom dictates. You can. And you will." The Rabbi's

words seemed final, but he didn't know the fury and rebellion imbued in Ehrlich's blood.

"You knew her well enough to kiss."

"No," Arnold declared with an apologetic glance to Hannah. Her gaze was still fixed on the stain on the floor. He didn't want to hurt her, but he was not willing to give his life and fortune for a kiss—no matter how bone-meltingly beautiful the potential bride.

The Rabbi ignored him.

Arnold was at an impasse. Did this deranged man think he was going to marry the girl only because she shared the most amazing kiss he'd ever experienced? He longed for more, much more, but that had never been a reason for matrimony. He wasn't going to let it become a reason now.

Arnold still stood agog while the Rabbi turned to his correspondence. Although he was irritated by the rabbi's audacity to order him around, Arnold hadn't fully recovered from the kiss—or was it Hannah's presence so close to him? She'd dislodged something within him, and he felt like a phaeton with a loose wheel, unable to move for fear that it would break at the axle.

"*Channi*, it is time." The Rabbi's voice fell as he grabbed a bag from under the desk and nodded toward the door. He held a small piece of paper.

Hannah stormed to him and placed her arm on his. She read the short letter in his hands sideways.

"I'll take the children with me, but somebody has to stay."

"I'll stay, *Tate*."

What were they talking about?

"Rivka cannot remain. We need her help. Surely Lenny can stay with you."

"Where are you going?" Arnold was confused by the change of topic.

"To my younger daughter in Birmingham. She's giving birth soon," the Rabbi said. "There's no *mohel*, so I'll perform the ritual circumcision if the baby is a boy."

Arnold closed his eyes. The poor baby. Better to stay in the womb.

"I'll look after Lenny. We'll be alright, *Tate*," Hannah said, wringing her hands, seeming unconvinced.

"The roofers are coming this week, *Channi*. Have Lenny tell Pavel when they're here. They won't listen to a girl."

"What does Pavel have to do with your roofers?" Arnold couldn't follow the connections between repairmen, gem dealers, and the Rabbi who was also a mohel. Everybody seemed to work double duty.

"We, er … have some trouble with the roof. It's leaking," the Rabbi explained.

"How old is Lenny?" Arnold asked Hannah.

"Seven," Hannah said.

"My eldest son," the Rabbi said proudly.

"Where's your mother?" Arnold was afraid of the answer, but he had to ask.

"She died when Ruthie was born," Hannah said.

"And Ruthie is…" Arnold circled his hand, nudging Hannah for an explanation.

"My baby sister. She's ten months old."

He put it all together: Her mother had died, the synagogue building was falling apart, and the hysterical aunt helped out with the baby and the horde of younger siblings.

"How many children do you have, Rabbi?" Arnold asked.

"I don't count my blessings," he said grimly.

Hannah lifted both hands ever so slightly and folded two fingers in. Arnold's eyes grew wide. Eight children?

"So, you're going to Birmingham for at least a week, leave a girl in a building full of roofers with only a seven-year-old to chaperone her?" Arnold wanted to make sure he had all the facts before his heart could melt anymore. He was fully aware of how men might treat an unchaperoned girl like Hannah. He didn't even want to imagine it.

"I have to leave tonight. Rivkah's packing the childrens' trunk already." The childrens' trunk. Singular. One trunk for six children.

Arnold sighed. "I'll stay."

CHAPTER 9

Hannah saw her father's eyes nearly pop out of his head. She turned to Arnold, perplexed, or was that emotional sting something else? Something unfamiliar. He didn't want to marry her, but he wanted to protect her. Surely the stranger who swept her into a searing kiss was unfit to chaperone? But at that thought, she felt the warmth return to her belly and began to hope he would indeed stay.

"I can't stay alone with him, *Tate*," she said, her make-believe shock unconvincing.

Her father rubbed his beard, which had grown rough and unkempt since mother died. In the presence of this well-groomed Prince Charming in white breeches and a black coat, both *Tate* and she looked shabby. Hannah inspected her rough fingertips, her ungroomed nails, and sighed. When had her life derailed so badly? When did she fall so low as to be pushed onto a stranger? Oh, but she wanted to be pushed. Irritated with her loose self, she was intrigued nonetheless.

"I'm perfectly capable. I'm an adult." She loathed depending on others.

Arnold and the Rabbi exchanged glances as if they'd devised a plan behind her back. Her father sat down and glanced at the wall clock, a painted metal one in a wooden frame topped with foliate carving. She followed Arnold's gaze to the clock and back to her father. Then his eyes met hers. He probably thought her a foolish, naive.

"If I may interject, Rabbi." Arnold stepped forward and inclined his head to her. "It would be my honor to oversee the roofers in your absence."

"You've already proved you can't be trusted around my daughter, Mr. Ehrlich. You must promise not to touch her!" the Rabbi said.

"I can't do that." Arnold smiled.

"I don't like what I'm hearing."

"I shall touch her only if she needs my assistance. I'll be a perfect gentleman." Arnold looked like he enjoyed having the Rabbi cornered. It was a trifle compared to what the Rabbi had done to him by trapping him in an engagement, but it was a small victory nonetheless.

"Don't do anything Lenny wouldn't do." That was strangely good advice.

"I'd never hurt her," Arnold said.

At his touching gaze, Hannah's stomach folded and shrank like a mimosa. He was going to protect her, not chaperone her. A spectrum of possibilities gaped between the notions of just two little words and lightness spread in her chest.

* * *

THE RABBI RUBBED his forehead and paced the room. He sniffed then turned to Arnold and said, "Lenny will stay. No funny business while I am gone."

"Never," Arnold said with the hand to his chest but that only earned him another harrumph. The Rabbi shook his head, his wide-brimmed hat firmly on his head like the antlers of an East Anglian Red Deer. He stood before Arnold, majestic and foreboding, the spiritual leader of Europe's Jewish epicenter.

"Hannah, it's safer with a man in the house," the Rabbi said solemnly. "Mr. Ehrlich, er, Arnold, ... you must understand that I am a father of several young girls. Hannah is my eldest, she is my..." his hand trailed through the air as if he was trying to catch the right word.

"I understand, Rabbi Solomon. I'll keep her safe," Arnold promised.

"My eldest son shall remain with you here," the Rabbi added.

Great, Arnold was babysitting this weekend. But he nodded chivalrously.

"If Leah wasn't *shvanger*, pregnant, I wouldn't leave."

"Of course not." Arnold pitied the single father, torn between his daughters and dragging a nursery full of children along to Birmingham.

The Rabbi's eyes were commanding, curious. Arnold felt as if his very soul were undergoing medical examination. But he stood still, having nothing to hide. He knew his family had a reputation within the orthodox Jewish community, but he wasn't a traitor. And Hannah needed help.

"I won't be able to make wedding arrangements until after my return, Mr. Ehrlich," the Rabbi said.

Hannah gasped.

"That won't be necessary," Arnold said, but the Rabbi shook his head and sat down slowly.

"That, we shall see upon my return."

Arnold turned to Hannah, suddenly aware that he could ruin her with a rejection. He didn't mind looking after her to protect the gorgeous girl with the bambi lashes, but marry her? He didn't even know her. And yet, she had stirred something in him, something basic and earnest that knocked him out of his orbit.

CHAPTER 10

The evening came and went, and the Rabbi left. Hannah's reluctance to part with her baby sister shook Arnold to the core. She clutched little Ruthie to her chest and kissed her tiny button nose with a tenderness that unsettled Arnold.

She gulped, clearly holding back tears, and told Arnold she'd never been away from Ruthie for more than a few hours. How could a girl so beautiful, who'd never been kissed before—he was sure of that—be like a mother to so many little siblings? He was certain of her virginity and yet she was mature as if she'd skipped a few beats on the way to adulthood. Arnold's heart warmed at the love Hannah gave so freely to her family, but he was also sad for her. She'd been deprived of something—he couldn't quite ascertain what it was—but he wanted to fill in the gaps for her.

After, the Rabbi departed with the children and the piping-mad aunt, Hannah showed Arnold Lenny's room.

He took in the modest surroundings. When he'd left home to see Pavel and deliver the pearls, he'd only planned to be gone for an hour. A lot had happened in a short period, and he found himself buttoning up his wool coat to combat the painful draft in the synagogue's corridors.

"So, what now?" Arnold asked Hannah and Lenny, the cheeky but friendly seven-year-old who was missing his front teeth. Only a few little white cusps showed of his adult teeth. His hair was unkempt but silky. He was just a little boy, most certainly unable to protect Hannah from randy and possibly coarse roofers.

"Are you staying for a sleepover?" Lenny asked.

Arnold chuckled, "So it seems."

Hannah blushed. "Are you hungry?" She shrugged and gave Arnold a sideways eyelash flutter.

Before Arnold could answer, Lenny ran to the kitchen, "I get the marrow!"

Arnold walked beside Hannah through an unlit corridor to a kitchen that had seen better days. Twenty years ago. A few unmatched chairs circled a raw wooden table. The Pearlers' servant kitchen looked a hundred times better than this. His stomach growled. Hannah must have heard because she bit her lip and her cheeks twitched.

"Did he say marrow?" Arnold asked.

"Yes, I made soup earlier today," Hannah said.

"With ox marrow dumplings." Lenny beamed. "My favorite!"

Arnold's empty stomach twisted into a knot.

"Everyone's gone, so there's more for me!" the little boy declared victoriously.

Arnold was willing to give him his if there was *anything* else to eat. Marrow did not sound appetizing to him. Not even a little bit.

A few minutes later, Hannah took the heavy pot from its hook over the fire—this kitchen was truly outdated. As thin as a match, she looked as though she might snap under the weight of the kettle. Arnold swept in, grabbed it from her hand, and held it high to prevent Lenny from getting burned. "Where shall I put it?"

Hannah signaled to the wooden table, which was even more worn than the workstations at his family's workshop. Arnold put the pot down and watched as Hannah scooped Lenny up and hugged him before putting him on one of the chairs. They seemed remarkably oblivious to their poverty. The kitchen was free from knickknacks and ornaments, empty of luxuries—and yet they were so at ease with each other. It was very different from his world, a happy one, not at all obsessed with material wealth like his home—only half a mile away but so distinct.

Hannah put three chipped wrought iron bowls on the table and some clean but frayed linen cloths folded into rectangles. Then she stepped on a wobbly stool, with a tarnished copper ladle in hand.

"I want all the *lokshen*," Lenny said, calling dibs on the noodles.

"We have a guest. We have to share them." Hannah gave him a warm look despite her reprimanding tone.

"You can have mine, Lenny. I am not so hungry." Arnold smiled, but his stomach growled, and he knew Hannah must have heard.

After she filled their bowls, Hannah climbed off the

stool. Her apron was tightly wound around her waist and accentuated her perfectly narrow figure. Arnold imagined untying the apron string and squeezed his eyes shut. He could not recognize himself in her presence, so drawn was he to her and unable to suppress the attraction. She was too short to see over the rim of the heavy kettle without a stepstool, yet she navigated the modest kitchen as if in charge. She probably was, and she behaved like a mother to Lenny.

Arnold sipped a spoonful of the hot soup. It warmed him going down. Then it burned. He coughed. Tears streamed. "What's in this?" He coughed some more.

"Er, the usual—marrow *kneidlach*, the dumplings, and some celeriac, cabbage, parsley, carrots, and horseradish." Hannah took another sip, oblivious to the sharpness of her broth.

"Horseradish?" Arnold nearly choked at the fire in his throat.

"Yes, I found some growing on the side of the road along Pall Mall," Hannah said. "I saved the roots for the *Seder*, but it would have been a waste to let the greens wilt." She spoke so freely about the first night of Passover —the Jewish holiday remembering the exodus—that Arnold realized how little freedom he enjoyed among the ton. When he was among gentiles, he never felt safe to mention anything relating to his beloved holidays. Somehow, Hannah was free despite her poverty, while he felt stifled by the expectations and obligations associated with his wealth.

Arnold was still coughing so hard he could barely breathe. "A little warning would have been nice."

Lenny and Hannah laughed.

After the spicy hot soup, the three eyed each other as if waiting for the sequel that hadn't arrived.

"Are you still hungry?" Hanna asked.

"Famished." Soup usually wasn't a meal for him, only an appetizer. He gave her his most wolfish-toothy smile, and his eyes darted to her breasts. It wasn't just food he had an appetite for after the burning soup. The fire in his throat had rekindled the other one, low inside him.

She blushed, and he suspected she knew his mind.

"I want *blintzes*," Lenny said—cheese-stuffed crêpes with raisins. He tugged at Hannah's apron and pulled her to the pantry.

"We just had meat!" Arnold knew she was protesting against the kosher infraction of mixing meat and dairy, but it was for show; she'd already retrieved some eggs from the pantry and cracked them into a bowl.

Impressed by her felicity around the burning stove, Arnold admired Hannah's skills in the kitchen. He'd never stood by watching a lady prepare food before. It was humbling and sensual to think she was going to all this trouble just to make him something to eat. He swallowed and clenched his jaws—he was going to put the little rolls of pastries that she'd touched in his mouth. Unable to go fencing with Fave to set his mind straight, Arnold searched for something to do.

He handed her the kitchen towel when she had a small spill of the batter. "Milady..."

"I'm not a lady," she said nonchalantly, avoiding his gaze as she dripped a ladle full of the liquid batter on the hot pan and expertly swiveled it to spread the crêpe.

"I beg to differ," Arnold said and took the hot pan from her hand as he set out to wash it for her.

She continued to make one after the other little round sheets of dough. Arnold marveled at her dexterity and in no time, there was a thin pastry that she turned over with one flip of her wooden spatula. An admirer of good handiwork and the expert use of tools, the jeweler in Arnold was delighted with her swift maneuvering of the hot pan. She must have noticed that he was outright staring at her but he admired Hannah in a way that he had never experienced with a young woman before. And the delicious vanilla scent of the sweet pastries enveloped him, alerting his senses to the aroma of her movements. He was unprepared for the effect she had on him but he let it spread warmly in his chest.

CHAPTER 11

Throughout the scrumptious meal of *blintzes*—a delicious treat—Arnold was as chaste as could be. But he wished it were otherwise. The occasional flirt emerged like a reflex in the presence of such a beautiful girl. And oh, Hannah was beautiful... informal, undone, domestic but sensual, clean, and seductive. He marveled at her elegance when she cut piece after piece off the rolled-up cheese dessert, eating as elegantly as any lady at the ton —and better. He never knew if their lip color would rub off, or the powder from their faces would stain his clothes.

Hannah was real and true, brimming with honesty and raw, natural beauty that he found superior to any of the rich ton women. He liked her down-to-earth appearance so much more than the stuck-up debutantes with fake hairpieces. The vain flattery and passionless consummation of his regular and boring flings seemed so far removed from Hannah's world. Arnold was grateful to have insight into her *vie quotidienne.*

Arnold enjoyed the quiet evening. There was no need to mind any eavesdropping servants or to linger for hours with dinner guests who'd bore him senseless.

After they'd cleaned up the kitchen, Hannah brought out an old box, a chess game. "Time to practice."

Lenny rolled his eyes and moaned, dropping onto the settee.

Chess was one of Arnold's easiest ways to impress, for he'd played for years with his grandfather and cousins Fave and Lizzie. Strategies, business acumen, and inventions to improve the practicality or efficiency of a tool came naturally to him, and the skills required for those endeavors translated effortlessly to the board game. He took a problem, examined it from every angle, and found a solution. If only he could apply this approach to his own life.

"This is where the rook goes and he moves like so," Hannah explained to Lenny while she slid the pieces across the checkered board.

Arnold couldn't stop admiring her long lashes and sharp eyes. But she spoke unlike a big sister would, she truly was a mother to Lenny, invested in his education and logical thinking. She was coaching him.

When Lenny rubbed his eyes, Hannah wrapped him in a blanket and let him rest on the settee. Arnold watched her warm motherly demeanor—it pleased him like a premonition of a brighter future. She tucked the blanket around Lenny and kissed his forehead. The lucky little boy curled up on the settee, turned his back to them, and fell asleep.

* * *

"YOU'RE QUITE AN OPPONENT," Arnold said.

But it was Hannah who was amazed by his chess moves. They were still sitting on the floor in the small salon, the same one where she'd hatched less than a year ago. But right now, it was cozy, with the flickering light and her view of the softest and most glowing features she'd ever seen. He was strategic, smart, and patient. And he smelled, oh, so magical—like an exhilarating fantasy. When Hannah closed her eyes and took a whiff of him, she felt as if she was standing at the park amidst fresh leaves lifting into the air on a curl of wind and dancing to tickle her nose. Her nose twitched, and she opened her eyes to find Arnold staring at her with dreamy dark eyes, too beautiful for a man and yet masculine enough to make her insides flip.

"I was hoping this would be a friendly game, I have yet to thank you for staying with us," Hannah said.

"Having a worthy opponent doesn't exclude the element of friendship," Arnold responded.

But was he a friend? Hannah was disappointed by his choice of words. "I imagine you don't have many friends," she mused.

"Why would you say that? I happen to be very well known at Almack's and Whites if you must know." But he turned away as if he'd rehearsed the mechanical response a thousand times.

"Possibly well known, but few see you for who you are." Hannah immediately bit her cheek when she heard the words get ahead of her wit.

Arnold's eyes darted to hers. He gave her a most quizzical stare, then his mien softened. Hannah had the impression he'd held a whole other conversation in his head that she wasn't privy to. He was so perceptive and bright that shyness rose within her. She froze to her spot on the worn threadbare carpet.

"Who taught you to play like a chess grandmaster?" Arnold asked teasingly, ever the conversationalist with years of ton expertise.

Hannah recognized that he was changing the subject, but she was willing to let him lead while her pounding chest paralyzed her mind, hypnotized by his attention. She'd written herself off as a spinster until he trotted into the sanctuary just hours ago, and she'd been strangely willing to let him uproot her. A minute must have passed, and he was still waiting for her answer, his brooding eyes fixed on her mouth as if the words were stuck.

"My father, he taught me everything he knows, he says. He'd call me to the rabbinate if I wasn't a girl." Hannah dropped her gaze onto the board, resigning herself to her fate as the subdued gender.

"I happen to like it quite a bit that you're a girl." Arnold gave her a gleaming smile and she felt her eyes fall to his beautiful teeth, a welcome contrast to the evening shadow of his dark brown facial hairs. They twinkled in his slightly scruffy face, like the bright moon on a clear sunset. She quite liked the unkempt wilderness that had spread across his chin and cheeks during the day. If he'd remained as polished now as he did when she first laid eyes on him, she wouldn't have the courage to sit with him such.

"I'm stuck," Hannah surprised herself with the honest declaration. She hadn't told anyone that before. "I mean … I'm here for everyone and it's my pleasure but … er…"

"I understand, you don't know how to find your place if everyone else keeps you busy," Arnold said.

She was amazed at how insightful he was. He had depth beyond being an exquisitely pretty package. He seemed to understand even the most awkward of phrases she uttered about her situation. An odd heat warmed her stomach, and she'd fan herself if she weren't so queasy and stiff.

"Then how can you waste all this time on the gossip sheet?" Arnold asked, seemingly innocent about how much his question stung her.

"How do you know about my newspaper?" Her daze lifted as her mind returned to the subject of the newspaper.

"Ah, the Community Circular. It's not a newspaper if you print it on one page." Arnold folded his hands open, miming an open book.

"It's front and back! It's folded in the middle." Hannah dragged her index finger along the book spine that his hands mimicked.

Before she could withdraw her brazen touch, his hands clasped hers, as if she were a thin page of paper deliciously captured by his strong binding.

Arnold chuckled. Her spirits returned and she was

finally able to remove her gaze from his mouth. His eyes were smoldering, his pupils wide in the dim light.

"My cousin, Lizzie, reads it. She's your biggest fan," Arnold said, but he stared down at Hannah's hand in his.

"See, it's not a waste of time," she said.

Arnold raised his eyebrows.

"Outside hostility breeds inside solidarity. And yet people lose themselves in politics even within a single community," she explained.

He folded his hands into a round hollow that kept hers safe. She allowed it, feigning ignorance of their intimacy while the conversation continued.

"There are so many members in our community with so little. I need to give them hope and inspire them, although sometimes it seems like a fruitless endeavor." Now she had to look at her hand completely immersed in his.

"It's courageous of you to identify where people are lacking and to offer solutions." He unfolded his hands and turned her hand to face up. The back of her hand felt his strong but soft skin. His were not worker hands, clear of calluses and with clean, well-shaped nails. He truly had magnificent hands. Hannah imagined the intricate jewels he must make with them.

"Then you're the only one, I'm afraid. Most people find my observations impertinent and ungrateful."

His index finger traced the lines in her palm, while her hand rested in his other hand.

Arnold frowned. His eyebrows were big and dark but soft and groomed. She wanted to touch them but didn't dare move her hand.

"People tend to silence their common sense when they act… *en masse!*" Arnold shifted his weight and she saw his muscles bulge under his shirt.

"But it's the masses who need leaders," Hannah added.

"And do you want to be such a leader?" Arnold asked as if it were possible. Nobody else had even considered the opportunity.

"I'm a girl." She shrugged sadly.

"Yes, you keep saying that." He dropped his glowering to her chest. Maybe she had a stain there from making the blintzes earlier?

"I didn't know the assimilated Jews read my circular. I… er … didn't know…"

"That we care?" Arnold read between the lines. Hannah felt a pang of remorse. Curious how she could hurt him so with her clumsy prejudice against his family, yet he was still there. Her heart sank. She really shouldn't hope that he'd forgive her rudeness, yet when she looked at him, all she saw was understanding and softness. He seemed fluffy and bright like snow, but she feared that she'd catch a chill if she immersed herself for too long.

* * *

THIS BEAUTIFUL GIRL had quoted Adam Smith, his favorite author. She was surprisingly intelligent. But she was an innocent. He could tell by her stiffness, and she hadn't responded to his flirting. She'd been the most interesting conversationalist, yet he thought she was prejudiced against him. He'd read her little newspaper. She loathed Greg and called him a baptized Jew. And Arnold was fully aware that the orthodox community considered his family traitors. For them, the Pearlers had sold their souls for wealth. What a pile of superficial nonsense.

"You think I'm betraying my people to do business with the rich and famous?" Arnold asked, eager to rectify her impression of him. Hannah dropped her gaze. Ah, an admission.

Arnold had stumbled into the kiss with her, but he'd rise to the challenge of protecting her and Lenny over the weekend. He had an unshakeable sense of obligation toward Jews—they were a small community and grandfather had always said they'd help one another. Surely, his support this weekend wouldn't be misread as courtship. He was just trying to do the right thing—or wasn't he? It felt as if he'd gone astray, navigating an ocean without as much as a map. His only point of orientation was this effervescence deep inside. It was more than desire for the forbidden fruit that was the Rabbi's daughter, he'd kissed her before he knew who she was. There was a pull toward her as if he were nothing but a flower stem pulling water from the earth to feed it to her blossom.

Obviously, they were from different worlds. They could never mesh. If he took her into his world among the ton, she wouldn't fit in. Or maybe she could with a little training? But then she couldn't return to her world, and she'd have to leave behind the family that she adored and a community that needed her. He couldn't do that. If he pursued her, he'd be chasing her into his dangerous web of ton intrigue. She'd get stung with the venom of the aristocracy and wiggle until she'd exhaust herself and resign. It hurt Arnold's insides to think of this spirited girl submissive to the ton. Alternatively, leaving his family wasn't viable. They'd taken him in when he was left alone in the world. He was a Pearler in every way except for the one—and if he could help them win the competition, he hoped this insecurity would go away. He wasn't a foundling, he was family, but he wanted to be so much closer. He reciprocated their love but couldn't understand it.

Arnold would step away and let Hannah live her life. It wasn't his modus operandi to mingle with the virginal type, particularly not the Jewish ones. Thinking about it, he'd never had a Jewish girl. The only one he knew was cousin Lizzie. But if what Fave had told him was true, the sensual peak was unlike anything…but what did Fave know? He'd only ever been with Rachel and was stuck on this mythical idea of innate compatibility. He'd always been a dreamer. Whereas Arnold was a master of the art of seduction, a Machiavellian strategist. *Veni, Vidi, Vici.* Come, see, conquer—and never look back, as the Romans said.

He was a rake, but only when permissible. When it counted, he was a true gentleman. It wasn't permissible right now, and his body urged him to defy what he knew was right. A true gentleman would never have kissed this girl and compromised her.

He flushed with remorse. She confused everything he'd known. And now she was pouting. How could she do that? Did she know the effect it had on him? Then she swallowed with lips pursed. Arnold watched her throat muscles clench and release. No, he couldn't possibly pursue this attraction. And yet, he was drawn to her with a force of an avalanche rolling down a mountain.

He gave her hand a gentle tug. She'd let him hold it all this time and let him pull her toward him. Hannah's upper body moved like a cork popping off a bottle. Arnold leaned in, but she hesitated. Her eyes darted to Lenny. The boy had his back turned to them and the blanket pulled over his head, deep in sleep. Arnold smiled at Hannah when her eyes returned to him—his mouth specifically.

So, he leaned in. He uncrossed his legs and stretched them out. Then he leaned back to welcome her closeness. When he propped his body up on his elbows, he pulled her chin gently toward his with the other hand. She leaned closer and touched his bulging chest muscles at the same moment as she parted her lips. He told himself this was only her second kiss, he had to be gentle. But his breath caught in his throat when he felt her exhaling onto his mouth.

They kissed. This time, it was slower, more chaste. Arnold took his time. But he moved the chessboard aside, knocking a few of the figures over.

"I was winning," Hanna said into his mouth.

"I'm winning now," Arnold said and deepened the kiss. "Checkmate." Arnold put his hand on the low of her back and pulled her onto his lap.

CHAPTER 12

*H*annah didn't know what she'd been missing until she laid eyes on Arnold. Whether she was lucky, brazen, or stupid to kiss him while sitting in his lap, she didn't know—nor did she care right then. She took the liberty to explore, trailing her hand up his arms to his shoulders and over his chest. His upper body was wide and solid, he radiated strength and heat. He still wore his coat, and the thick wool stretched over the polished horn buttons when he flexed his muscles. She unbuttoned them and slid her hands into his coat, reveling in the warmth. She fit well into his arms as if she'd been made to snuggle up right there.

Weak and cold, she badly wanted him to hold her. She'd been a speck of dust drifting through the air, passively waiting for something to land on. But he'd make her glow in his light and find another reason for her existence. She had an inkling he could give her a hook for rebellion against life's injustices.

· · ·

LATER, Arnold carried Lenny to his bed. Hannah was grateful because Lenny had grown heavy over the past few years, and she could barely face bringing him upstairs. Arnold had carried him with such ease that she found it humorous.

Arnold went to the cot on the floor of Lenny's room.

"Don't you want to sleep in the girls' bedroom?" Hannah had asked when they'd walked past her sisters' empty room. "Surely you want some privacy and an actual bed?"

But Arnold had peeked into the room, painted dusty pink with frilly curtains and a crochet bedspread. He'd smiled warmly at Hannah, and said, "I belong in the boys' bedroom."

Hannah suspected the girly decor wasn't the reason Arnold shied away from taking the girls' bedroom.

Arnold shook his head and took his boots off. "I promised my new friend a sleepover," he said, but she noticed his eyes estimating the length of the cot, clearly much shorter than he was. But he wouldn't fit into the twin's bed either; it seemed so small next to him as if it were a doll bed.

"Time to sleep, beautiful." He blew out the candle and pushed her out the door.

For a few minutes, Hannah stood in the hallway, discombobulated and giddy at the same time. Had Arnold just called her beautiful *and* exiled her from her brothers' room? She smiled with glee, but her stomach flipped. She was nearly sick but not in a bad way, albeit terrifyingly new.

Lying awake in her bed, she felt a pang of something.

Not only loneliness—this was the first time she could sleep without watching over Ruthie. And yet, she was hot and cold at the same time. She knew babies could die in their sleep, and she'd only half-slept for the past ten months, fearing the baby her mother had entrusted her with could drift off without noise. Every hour or so, Hannah checked on her. It had become a habit, almost mechanical. She didn't mind, for she loved her baby sister as if she had come from her own womb.

Hannah's last thought, after she'd closed her eyes, was that she couldn't believe how *nice* Arnold was. He'd volunteered to watch over her and Lenny, to supervise the roofers. There was the matter of their betrothal, of course. Hannah's insides churned as she considered the matter, entirely unsettled and completely embarrassing. This flirtation with him wouldn't last, how could he want her and her shabby little life? Esther was right—she'd be stuck in the back of the sanctuary forever, watching even Ruthie grow up and spread her wings while her own had been clipped. So, if she was doomed to being a spinster, she wouldn't stop his advances.

He wasn't at all like the reputation that preceded his family. Of course, she'd never met any of them, but the community talked about those rich Jews at St. James. She was surprisingly smitten with him. He acted with honor and dignity. Hannah felt like a small fool for believing the rumors even for a minute. Maybe she needed to look beyond the familiar to inspire her community.

Tonight, she'd been elevated by his kiss. The cracks on the ceiling, the drafty windows, not even the rats scritch scratching inside the walls bothered her. She was tucked in cottony glows of delight at Arnold's tender touch. This was exactly what her father had warned her not to do, but it felt so wonderful she stopped caring.

Hannah had pulled the lumpy down-comforter over her neck and hugged herself. Her hands and feet were cold, but her middle was hot. It had been all day since Arnold handed her the pearl strand. How could he affect her so?

CHAPTER 13

A shriek woke Arnold. Falling asleep with his cock in his hands wasn't an option, not with the child in the room, But his mind trailed to the luscious honey hair that smelled like cinnamon and raisins when he'd kissed Hannah after their chess game. Even though he'd only just met her, he recognized her exceptional intelligence. She had a big heart, sacrificing her future to look after her siblings. And the Rabbi was her father, the most respected and allegedly the wisest man in the community, who was so protective of her. Arnold suspected it wasn't mere altruism that he'd volunteered to guard her and check on the roof repairs, he'd seized a chance to be close to her.

Arnold turned and searched for Lenny, but his bed had been pulled straight. The weak sun that shone through the window made the specks of dust twinkle in the air. He'd slept in his coat to supplement the flimsy blanket ... who could sleep in this cold daily?

He pulled out his pocket watch and saw that it was only six in the morning, Friday. Arnold truly missed his hot bath. His bones hurt from the cold night and his back was stiff from the small cot.

Another shriek. Hannah!

Arnold stormed down the stairs and found her in the kitchen, cowering on a chair and clutching her white apron. She was even more beautiful in the morning.

Lenny was holding a bucket and calling out, "Here little mousy mouse, come on here … I have a bucket for you."

"A mouse?" Arnold asked as he combed his hands through his hair.

Hannah gave him a brief look and he thought he should have checked himself in a mirror before storming downstairs. Then her eyes went back to the corner under the table. Arnold followed her gaze, trying to curb his gurgling laughter. He was sure something terrible had happened when he heard her scream, but she was just terrified of a mouse.

A FAT RAT scurried across the kitchen floor.

"Oh dear, that's not a mouse, Lenny. Let me deal with that." Arnold bent down to see where it went.

Lenny ran out of the kitchen and returned a minute later swinging a wooden toy sword like a pirate in battle. Arnold laughed. "That won't do."

Hanna was still standing on a wobbly chair. "How can you laugh at such a moment?"

"A very grim moment, indeed. One of the two million

rats in London has made it to the Great Synagogue. Tsk, tsk, tsk." Although he mocked the sweet damsel in distress, he was secretly happy that the rat chase distracted him from the indomitable erection he was hiding under his coat.

Hannah was just so adorable standing on the chair, ready to shriek again any second. He loved a squirmish girl, especially such a gorgeous one in a virginal white apron. He imagined swooping her into his arms away from the dangerous wild beast that had stormed her kitchen. Arnold enjoyed seeing her less than composed, so at odds with her usual stiff self. After a night of imagining what he could do to discombobulate her, he'd woken up oh so frustrated on the tiny cot on the floor. He couldn't stop thinking about her delicate features, the pointy chin he'd taken into his hand to pull her into a kiss.

"Do you have any glass bottles? From wine or milk maybe?" he asked.

Hanna nodded in the direction of the pantry.

"Lenny, do you have any cement or gypsum?"

Lenny darted off to the door to retrieve it, but Arnold stopped him. "Wait! We also need a bigger bucket, some water, and a shovel."

Lenny ran off excitedly, as if Arnold had put him on a mission to assist in the battle against the notorious rat monster. Arnold didn't mind the rat and its sad fate at all. This was fun. He cherished Hannah's watchful gaze, sensing that she ogled his behind every time he turned. Primal instincts kicked in, and he wanted to impress her.

Arnold took two bottles from the pantry. He smashed them on the floor.

Hanna jerked back, shaking in terror. "What did you do that for? You're making a mess with the shards!" She admonished him, still on her perch, clutching her apron.

"Trust me?" He held out a hand to help her down from the chair. She shook her head, and he noticed the curly strands that came out of her bun glimmering in saffron-ginger hues. She blew them away and held his gaze.

He grinned at her, unable to speak the words in his mind. He'd never complimented a girl and meant it with such devotion. His mouth dried up when he thought of something to say. He had no words that would do her beauty justice. The shape of her face was unusually elegant, and the loose strands tucked behind her ear let lovely bangs hang over her forehead.

* * *

ARNOLD ACTED a bit arrogant in his industrious attempt to block the rat's hole in the corner. He was obviously putting on a show for her, but Hannah was secretly grateful he'd saved her from having to chase the rat away herself.

Arnold wiped his hands on a rag and brushed some dust from his white breeches. "This will dry, and we can lean back and have a cup of tea now," he announced.

Hanna frowned wistfully.

"What is it now?" he asked, rolling his eyes ever so slightly.

"Esther and I usually deliver challah to some of the elderly members of the community on Friday afternoon," Hannah said.

He sat on one of the chairs and grabbed an apple from the bowl that Hannah had set out earlier in the morning, just before the rat appeared. Arnold chomped the apple. His teeth were white—and strong, Hannah knew from the intimate contact she'd had with his mouth only the day before. Astounded, Hannah observed that his bite was enormous. He'd eaten half an apple with only one bite.

"How nice that you bring challot to the community, so sweet." He polished off the apple and reached for another.

Hannah noticed that he'd used the correct plural form of challah, challot. It reassured her that he showed respect for their faith. The ritual bread was an important part of their Shabbat holiday.

"You can use my carriage to deliver the challot. It's too cold to walk outside." He ate the second apple in no time and surveyed the room for more food.

Hannah guessed he was probably used to lavish breakfast spreads in the palace he called home.

"Where shall I send my driver to pick the challot up?" Arnold asked naively when he poured himself a glass of water.

She liked his willingness to help. It was more than just being a gentleman—he cared. But despite being helpful, he was unsuspecting of her duties within the community.

Hannah wrung her hands as Arnold's eyebrows popped up. "Ahm … The driver doesn't need to pick them up." She rubbed her palms on her apron uncomfortably now.

"So, when will the challot be delivered then?"

That made her smile. They were from completely different worlds despite living in the same city. He was a prince, with a driver, a carriage, and probably white horses that matched his white breeches and beautiful dark hair. She couldn't find an explanation for his attention to her except that he must be so very, very nice.

"They won't be delivered." She avoided his glance, not knowing why. Perhaps she didn't want him to see her baking twenty-four challot and dealing with the heat in the kitchen this morning.

Half his cheek raised into a boyish smile—he'd understood. But he remained silent, the perfect gentleman.

"I usually bake them with Rivkah and my sisters," she finally admitted. Resignation and duty sprang to her gaze.

Arnold closed his eyes for a moment and sighed as he rubbed his temples. "So, you'll have to talk me through this because I've never baked a challah before."

Hannah's heart leapt, and something clicked into place. She wasn't sure what, but his reaction took her off guard most pleasantly.

CHAPTER 14

⁂

The small kitchen smelled strongly like yeast, but as soon as Hannah removed the first batch from the oven, the room warmed with a delightful fresh bread smell. Lenny left to play upstairs.

Arnold tried to follow her directions, but he was distracted every time her hair fell to her face and she blew the wispy strands away. It was such a girly thing to do and yet entirely unladylike. No woman at the ton would do anything so raw, and Arnold wondered what else she might do that was raw and wild.

"Two up, one in the middle, two up, one in the middle. See? You try!" She smiled at him and moved over, handing him two strands that she held above the others.

Arnold took them, brushing his fingers ever so slightly against hers. He was much more interested in a chance to kiss her again than to braid two dozen challot.

"So, one up, two in the middle?" he asked with his most flirty tone.

"No, no, no, two up, one in the middle," Hannah said as she tapped his hand with the imaginary strand on it.

"Then you switch sides?"

"Yes, you start on one side and then go to the other." She focused on crimping the ends of the braided loaf together.

"That makes no sense," Arnold joked, waiting for her eyes to meet his. But she didn't bite and carried on with her endeavor to feed her community with love—for the smell of her challot could only be described as such.

"Yes, see, two up, one in the middle." She carried on.

He could only think of two tits up and something else in the middle ... and then switch sides...

"Are you paying attention?" She had the next set of four strands ready for him.

"Not to the bread, no." He tried harder with his smile. Ah, this time she blushed. Very good. She wasn't immune to his charms after all.

"So, when is four number one?" He couldn't wipe that smile off his face when she was bashfully focusing on the challah and avoiding his gaze. "Show me!"

She gave him a lump. The dough was surprisingly soft and squishy, Arnold realized as he kneaded another large glob for Hannah. It was a sensual experience, watching her lean over the wooden table and mix flour, water, and yeast to make something so elementary as challah, a relic of tradition with such a sweet nurturing aroma. When she gave him one of those sideways smiles of hers, only half her mouth lifted. She had some flower on her chin and he wished he could clean it off for her. But her glance fell to the clock every so often, and he knew she was in a rush to finish. Hannah had already made about a hundred strands that she thought he should somehow knot together to form braids.

Then she did the sweetest thing. With her fingers covered in flour, she wiped the tip of her nose and twitched.

"It's just a hair, let me..." Arnold tucked the stray strand behind her ear.

Their eyes met and the air crackled between them. Flakes of flour glimmered in the sunlight that filtered through the wooden shutters. Arnold held her gaze but then dropped his smile when he shivered, his body craving her touch.

As if their souls had connected and conversed above their heads like parents making decisions for their children, Hannah responded to Arnold's unspoken desire.

"Braiding is the best part," she said, taking his hands and laying them on hers. Arnold froze for an instant as a memory of his late mother flashed through his mind. When he was little, she laid his hands on hers when she played the piano. He missed her so much that he never touched a musical instrument after she passed. But somehow, Hannah's instructions were different. She was nurturing, instructive but not motherly to him. She emitted a warmth unlike any he'd experienced before.

"Maybe there's something even better," he said, soaking in the beauty of her eyes as he leaned in slightly. He wanted nothing more than to sweep her off the wooden stool and take her mouth with his, but suddenly he didn't dare. His cock twitched but he ignored the impulse. For the first time in his life, he thought a girl was too precious and too beautiful to be devoured like a custard pastry with a raspberry on top.

He tried to be helpful in her charitable baking and diligently made a few globs of dough. "What is so special about challah?" he asked, thinking out loud.

"Are you truly asking me?" Hannah asked as she turned to the oven to remove another batch.

"I'm not sure. It smells good and instantly turns a house into a home, doesn't it?"

Hannah smiled at him with a sheet of three shiny loaves in hand.

"There's more to it." She unwrapped her hands from the rags that protected her from getting burned after she slid the batch into the oven. "It goes beyond nourishment. Challah is a symbol and represents the idea of taking something physical and elevating it to the spiritual."

* * *

HANNAH SAW ARNOLD WAS STUNNED, as if he'd stared at the mouth of a hunter's rifle. He had a feral strength about him, majestic and vulnerable at the same time. Hannah had a shifting sensation in her chest that she wasn't good for him, that she'd disturb the natural order of his life. And yet, she couldn't stop every thought circling back to him. His sparkling eyes were like two crystal balls showing her an uncertain future she was longing to explore, but that didn't thwart the desire to close the distance between them.

"When we share challah, we don't simply provide physical sustenance, but we spiritually nourish those who eat it with the thoughts and blessings and good intentions of making our challah." She wiped her forehead with the back of her hand then continued to braid another set of four strands with renewed vigor, even though she was physically exhausted.

Hannah brushed more egg wash over the two challot on her tray and slid them into the oven. She dug her hand into the flour sack, retrieved a handful, and spread the soft white powder on the wooden table. She made a wiping motion, expertly swiping the flour to the places where she would roll out yet another lump of dough. She whispered something as she parted the lump into two and then into four as she set off to knead each one.

"What are you saying?" Arnold asked.

"I beg your pardon?" She'd been in a daze, desire bubbling in her belly.

"You mumbled something as you parted the dough," he said.

"Oh, that's just declaring the dough challah." Hannah shrugged as she drew her attention back to the moment.

"What else would it be?" Arnold mocked.

"It's ancient really. This *halachic* principle that gives Jews the rules to live by is called *daato lechalka*, the intention of the person mixing the dough is to divide it, which exempts the dough from the requirement to separate challah."

"Why would you want to exempt it?" Ouff, didn't he know anything about challah? She was getting annoyed.

"Did your mother never make challot with you?"

He shook his head. "No, she died when I was five."

"Oh." Hannah stopped with her hands on a roll of dough and looked at him with sad eyes. "I'm so sorry."

She changed the subject and returned to her lecture on the *mitzvah*, the good deed of baking and sharing challah. "It's a tremendous *mitzvah* for anyone to separate the challah. My mother always emphasized this and let us girls do it, so we may find a spouse with the same ease that we separate the challah." At that, her eyes darted to Arnold and she froze. "It's a bit superstitious," she followed up, realizing she'd touched on the embarrassing fact that he'd compromised her, and her father wanted them to marry post-haste.

"Maybe it works," Arnold mumbled and her heart fluttered in response.

She pinched a piece of dough from a lump before her and formed it into a small ball and handed it to Arnold.

"I … er … what's this?" He took the little ball of dough, seemingly unsure of the custom.

"My mother used to kiss it goodbye and throw it into the fire."

Arnold couldn't hide his confusion. "Why?"

"It's a sacrifice but it *is* food, so you send it off with respect. We discard the separate challah and hope we'll never lack food."

Then she opened the oven door and signaled Arnold to throw his piece in. He smiled, and she suspected he was so rich he'd never had to worry about having enough food.

* * *

THE HEAT from the oven hit him in the face, and he blinked tears away. The ritual of baking so early in the morning, the beautiful explanations and ancient blessings that this gorgeous girl recited caught him entirely off guard. He couldn't take his eyes off her wispy strands of hair that came loose. It took every bit of his willpower not to brush all her hair away, take her face in his hands, and kiss her senseless. Aching with arousal, he longed to lay her on the table so he could cover her with his entire body.

Arnold watched as if in a trance. She made something magical out of simple ingredients. Her spirit carried his soul away like a river, bumping into his preconceptions and experiences but washing them away with the stream of her glow. Engulfed in her duties, her energy sprang from what she wanted to accomplish. Her amazing symbiosis of obligation and drive made her irresistible. But Arnold couldn't move, couldn't interrupt her doting over the dough. She wasn't just bringing nourishment to her community; she was the nourishment. It had taken less than twenty-four hours for Arnold to realize that her innate strength could bring others into a trance and lead to dependence. He had a sinking feeling that he wouldn't want to let her out of his life.

Hannah took another tray of baked challah out. It let off the most fragrant steam.

"Is this why you write, to nourish the community spiritually?" Arnold asked.

"In a way, yes. There are many poor members in our community. Their spirits are broken."

Arnold nodded and faced a set of four strands. "Let me

try to braid one." He set out to knot two strands together like a rope. "Is this right?"

"That's not even close." She laughed, bewitching him with her smile. Her ever so slightly crooked canines stood out from her impeccable teeth and kissable mouth, giving her the right amount of edge. She was so earnest and uninhibited.

She gave him the hard part, forming the strands.

"It doesn't seem too difficult for you." He shot her a glance, then took off his coat and pulled up the sleeves of his white linen shirt. "Quite difficult and quite out of the ordinary, I have to admit." He gave her his best rakish smile but it didn't work.

Something else came through, something stronger, sweeter. She was staring at him, ogling him, if he didn't know any better. And he didn't. He enjoyed being the subject of her admiration and flexed his arm muscles as he kneaded the dough.

"My arms get tired after the fourth or fifth challah, and that's when I'm in good shape," she admitted, sweat glistening on her hairline. But her gaze still clung to his arms as if she were trying to come to a decision.

CHAPTER 15

t nearly three in the afternoon, they had one more set of challah to deliver. This one to an elderly lady. Then he could go home and take a bath. Arnold dreamed of his hot steaming tub and the freshly pressed clothes his valet would lay out for him. The heat from the oven hadn't helped either. They'd been up since six in the morning, and Arnold was exhausted, hungry, and he smelled like dough. Tired, he flopped into his carriage.

They'd dropped Lenny off with Lizzie in the morning, but he'd not even mustered the energy to go inside after rolling all these strands of dough for Hannah to braid. He'd given Lenny a note for Lizzie when they switched from the hired hack to one of his family's carriages. The fresh challot were wrapped in cloth and carefully piled in the crates, giving off the most delicious steam. Arnold's stomach growled.

"*Channi, Maidale*, you have outdone yourself today."

The toothless old lady beamed; two frayed shawls layered over her hunched back.

She opened the door to a stuffy little abode, with few windows, faded furniture, and many, many portraits on every table, cupboard, and all the wall space. It appeared like a well-loved place, full of sentimentality and … dust. Arnold leaned against a flimsy dining table with a table-cloth on one end only, set for just one person. This old lady evidently knew loneliness in this bustling town as if she lived in a dark cave of memories.

"And who is your dashing friend here?" The old lady took Arnold's hand and patted it, moving up his arm to hook her own in for support. In his presence, she seemed womanly, eager to stand up straighter.

"Arnold. At your service." He bowed and placed a gentle kiss on her knuckles.

Hannah beamed.

"And what is your family name, my boy?"

"Ehrlich, Madam."

The old lady's eyes darted to Hanna. "*Er iz eyner fun aundz.*" He is one of us.

Hanna nodded, acknowledging that Arnold was Jewish, too.

"How come I've never heard of your father?" the old lady pressed on, protective of Hanna and genuinely curious.

"He died when I was a little boy. My uncle, Gustav Pearler, and Aunt Eve took my mother and me in. I've lived with them ever since. Gustav has been like a father to me."

The woman seemed dissatisfied with his response. He

realized that she needed to place him. "We are the Pearlers, Jewelers."

She looked at him as if he'd emptied a bucket of water over her head. Then she gave Hannah a pained nod and turned as if she were taking her leave from a sick child.

"Thank you for the visit, Mr. Ehrlich," the woman said with all the grace she could muster. "And to you my child, a *git Shabbes*." A good Shabbat. She didn't make eye contact with Hannah and shut the door.

Arnold felt as if he'd just been kicked out. Had the woman said goodbye to Hannah for good?

* * *

HANNAH SAW that Arnold had noticed. She knew the members of her community were close-minded. They narrowly fit everyone into a tight little role for which they had a preconceived opinion that was usually not based on their own deductions. In times like these, she wasn't sure that her father's preaching, her circular, and all her efforts could ever correct such short-sightedness. Arnold had proven himself to her today. There was more to him than a rakish traitor and businessman of the ton. He'd been kind, generous, industrious, and … he'd lit something within her, a ball of light that glowed large and warm.

The lightness from her step had left. All the morning's work dissipated into that moment. He'd been unjustly dismissed by their last delivery. He didn't deserve that.

Back in the hack, Arnold broke the silence. "Do you do this every Friday?"

She nodded.

"I understand now," he said.

She didn't respond, but fixed her eyes on her hands.

He wanted to make it ok somehow. "It's a *mitzvah*," he said, calling Hannah's Friday activities a good deed.

Her eyes met his. "I'm sorry," she said.

"You shouldn't be after all you've done. You brought the warmth of Shabbat to twelve other households, all in need..." his voice trailed off and frustration brewed. "Who has the right to make you sad after all that..." He waved his hand.

She smiled. "A *mitzvah's* purpose is not to make *me* feel good."

Arnold enjoyed her metaphysics of morals. "How very philosophical of you." But he couldn't keep his bewilderment at bay. This was the most well-read girl he'd ever met. She flaunted grand concepts of Western philosophy alongside the ancient teachings of the Torah.

"She insulted you. For that, I am terribly sorry," she said.

Arnold raked his hands through his hair, a trait he shared with his cousin, their telltale gesture of frustration. "She didn't say anything but niceties." He decided to wash over it. He didn't want the old lady's bitterness to ruin his day with Hannah.

"She implied..." Hannah seemed to second guess whether she should continue.

"She might have, but it's not true," Arnold said frankly.

Hannah waited. Did she need an explanation?

"Do you think it is?" He knew this was a turning point. Her answer would make or break him in her eyes.

"I don't know what to think anymore," she said.

He knew she had an inner compass of fairness, but she'd been indoctrinated by the community.

"Maybe I don't know you well enough to form an opinion yet."

Her qualified response disappointed Arnold. She must have felt the heat between them and yet, she resisted. Would he rise beyond his reputation in her eyes?

CHAPTER 16

᪥

$\mathcal{A}$s Hannah walked up the steps to Arnold's home, she tugged on her old dress. She couldn't help but feel inadequate, not merely dressed in old clothes, but unworthy of the attention this prince paid her. Arnold took her hand, and she looked for an escape route. Before she could find a way out, an elegantly dressed man with white hair and a side-part opened the door. The butler.

"Hannah, oh Hannah, you won't believe it!" Lenny rushed toward her and fell into her arms. "Lizzie taught me gammon!" He beamed.

"*Du zehst aoys freylikh vi a furim kalatsh!* You are as happy as a *Purim challah!*" Rachel mocked his enthusiasm with a Yiddish endearment and smiled thankfully at a young woman with golden ringlets piled high on her beautiful head. She was a vision in a pale pink tulle frock with white and golden embroidery. A princess in a castle, Hannah thought while she ironed out imaginary wrinkles of her woolen dress. The princess didn't seem to notice—

or at least she had the sense not to make Hannah even more self-conscious.

"Hannah, please meet my cousin, Elizabeth," Arnold said.

Hannah was unsure whether she should bow, but the princess reached out for a welcoming hug.

"Call me Lizzie, I'm only Elizabeth when I get into mischief."

Hannah was oddly uncomfortable in the fancy entrance among such friendly hosts. "Y-you look like a princess," she mumbled.

Lizzie curtsied and gave Arnold a glance that showed how close they were. They understood each other without words, like Hannah with her siblings.

"So, what's this gammon about?" Hannah asked, turning her attention to her comfort zone, mothering Lenny.

"It's a game of wins, with dice and a board with triangles on it. I was red and Lizzie was black!"

Hannah stared at Lenny as if he'd misspoken.

Lizzie understood and whispered to Hannah, "The winner is just that, the winner here. I didn't tell him that people gamble in gammon."

Hannah seemed appeased.

"So, where have you been?" Lizzie asked Arnold. "You look tired."

"We delivered challot to the community," he told her.

"Your cousin helped me bake them in the morning."

"Ah." Lizzie gave Arnold a top-to-bottom stare. "Where are they?"

"Where are what?" Arnold asked.

"The challahs," Lizzie said.

"Challot," Arnold corrected her and Lizzie grimaced.

"I … ehm … we gave them all away," Hannah responded.

Arnold stood up straighter and gave Hannah a sincerely perplexed look. "You mean, I woke up at six o'clock in the morning to bake twenty-four challahs with you and I don't get any for Shabbat dinner?"

"Challot," Hannah corrected him.

"When I don't get any, I may as well say challahs," Arnold snarled.

"We had ours delivered already. They're set up for dinner," Lizzie said, seemingly familiar with the mood swings of hungry men.

* * *

"YOU HAVE *SHABBES* DINNER?" Hannah asked.

"Of course, we do. You do know we're Jewish?" Lizzie asked. "Arnold sent note that you're Rabbi Solomon's daughter?" She looked at Arnold for guidance, but he gave none.

Arnold knew Hannah was testing the water, ever smart and careful. He couldn't quite explain how she'd been impulsive enough to return his kiss, but he couldn't dwell on that question right now.

Lizzie picked up an envelope on the side table with a *kuf*, the Hebrew letter K, as in Pavel Klonimus. "Pavel was here and left this for you. I told him you weren't home."

Arnold grabbed the note and opened it.

None of the ships carry any gemstones or pearls. The last

shipment of gold was months ago, and I gave you and Fave all I had left. My contact at the docks refuses to speak to my son, Caleb. It appears all these shipments depend on one fleet. If we are to stand a chance at the competition, we must find a way to procure the materials. I am afraid we will run out of time.

Arnold crumpled the paper in his hand. He hated nothing more than depending on others, and right now, he depended on Pavel's supply for Fave's designs. Without raw gems and pearls, they couldn't create the pieces Fave had drawn so intricately. Their chance to earn their place as crown jewelers was in jeopardy. And Arnold feared there were greater forces creating obstacles than Pavel's suppliers.

CHAPTER 17

*H*annah's doubt about her humble dress turned into outright shame as she took in the majestic home. She felt out-of-place in the foyer lined with white marble pillars topped with intricately painted *Ming* vases. Hannah recognized the vases from similar pieces she'd seen at the British Museum. Some were paneled, while others had little porcelain vines and flowers wrapped around them. They were so thin the light shone through them, making them look like enchanted elf homes, frozen during the day but alive at night.

She shook her head; she was always on the prowl for fairy tales for her siblings, but today she needed to be an adult. But this was no faire tale. She'd ruined her reputation with a single kiss. Yet, her bad conscience was more because of her lack of remorse. She didn't regret knowing Arnold. She wanted to know more about him and his family. But she dared not ask because she felt small, meager compared to Arnold and his home. The synagogue could fit into their entrance hall four times over—with room to spare.

She noticed Arnold's mien darken as he read a letter. Likely, some bad news had angered him. His eyes shimmered with a mix of sadness and fury. It was uncanny how his emotions played out in his gorgeous bright eyes.

"You are staying," Arnold said as he tucked the crumpled letter into his pocket.

Lizzie frowned and folded her hands. "The competition?" she asked quietly.

"Yes," Arnold snarled.

"Lenny would surely love to stay but I ... er..." Nobody was waiting for her at home except a leaky roof, drafty windows, and a rat somewhere in the walls. It had been terribly cold in the carriage on the way to the Pearler's stately home. Hannah rubbed her freezing hands together. She could think of no compelling reason to go back to the cold so soon and remained silent.

"It's decided then. I'll add two settings to the table." Lizzie clapped her manicured hands, then she took Hannah's rough hand and pulled her into the foyer of Pearler's palatial four-story home. "We don't usually entertain on Friday evenings. Most of our guests ... er ... need not know of our Shabbat dinners. We had the table set in the small dining room."

Hannah was surprised how domestic Lizzie was, she'd thought of her as a haughty brat considering the opulence of her house dress. But maybe Hannah had been wrong all along about Arnold and his family. Their reputation among the orthodox community was at best incomplete but probably outright false.

Hannah scurried after Lizzie, careful not to knock over any of the precious vases. She walked rather graceless compared to Lizzie. She floated elegantly along the carpets lining the *parquet* floors as if the bottom rim of her frock were repelled by the carpets. Arnold followed with his hands folded behind his back like a prince.

The hall connected several rooms, each with ornate double doors and golden handles. Hannah's eyes trailed along the stucco to the coffered ceiling and stopped on the images of the *Gobelins*. These busy embroidered Baroque tapestries, framed by decorative pillars on the walls depicted fascinating images. Hannah guessed the carpet must be made of silk for the white petals in the oriental design to shimmer in the light.

Arnold smiled proudly, a most irritating kind of glower, unlike any expression she'd seen on him before. He opened a set of double doors and inclined his head. Hannah stepped behind Lizzie into what must have been a large version of a dollhouse. Every part of the room was decorated with minute attention to detail. Tall wooden panels soared to the ceiling in little squares, each adorned with leaves, vines, and figurines. The rugs mirrored the same shades of reds and browns, a warm foil to the white-painted wood panels that had leaf carvings on them. At the center stood a long table, with a damask tablecloth and several crystal vases holding lush bouquets of white amaryllis, pink-orange alstroemeria, and hellebores. Hannah walked to the flowers and leaned over to inhale their fresh spring smell. Two large challot —much shinier than hers and not at all lopsided— peeked out from under the covers embroidered with shiny silk thread, reading *Shabbat v'Yom Tov*. Shabbat and Holidays.

She knew Arnold and Lizzie were watching her, but she couldn't stop her curious dancing around the elegant room, where Jewish elements lived in harmony with the finest art from around the world. Never had she seen such beauty concentrated in one place. One of the wall tapestries caught her eye. Arnold and Lizzie walked toward her, stopping on either side.

* * *

ARNOLD FOLLOWED Hannah's reaction to his home with great interest.

"Where are they?" Hannah stared at the people pushing carts of flowers and exotic fruits. There were palm trees on either side of them and monkeys hanging from fan-like branches.

"In the West Indies. Grandfather brought this back from one of his travels," Lizzie explained.

"Long before we were born," Arnold added.

"This is a coconut tree. Grandfather said you punch a hole in them and drink the juice before you eat the hollow fruit," Lizzie said.

Hannah smiled and gazed up along the tall palm tree. "That's what the monkey is reaching for?"

"I suppose he is. I've never noticed before," Lizzie replied warmly.

"This is so … different." Hannah stood before another piece of art, a framed picture showing roses and birds on flowering branches along with lily pads and blossoms along the bottom. "Is it painted?"

"No, it's carved mother of pearl," Arnold said. This was his domain. "It's a tiny mosaic."

"Where did it come from?"

"Probably from China. It's made of shells of oysters and mussels, they can be quite thick and ground or shaved down into little pieces," Arnold explained, but his eyes weren't on the picture. He couldn't stop admiring Hannah's innocent expression.

"And people put them together to form a picture?"

"Yes, basically." He smiled at Hannah's explanation. She was in awe, admiring the art wholeheartedly. He couldn't detect a shred of jealousy or disdain. So much sweeter than any of the noblesse, she must have a big heart.

Hannah appeared to be still in a trance. "I had no idea…"

"No idea about what?" Arnold asked.

"That such beauty existed on Earth."

Arnold wanted to hold her. Even a day with him had brought nothing but tumult to Hannah's world, yet she was gracious and open-hearted. Through her eyes and by her side, he'd no longer be bored. How many times had he walked past the Gobelin from the fifteenth century, a sign of the wealth that had catapulted his family into the ranks of the British aristocracy? Instead of enjoying their afflu-ence, they'd become embroiled in the competition, gossip, and pressure to maximize every luxury. Their riches had brought on a cold-hearted war to outdo others, without taking time to slow down and enjoy the spectrum of flavors the world had to offer. Arnold tasted acid as he thought that Hannah wouldn't fit into the ton's uniformity, their catering to gossip.

Hannah would add the warmth of cinnamon, the spice of ginger, and the pungency of cloves to his life just as she did to her kitchen. She'd made the modest, outdated kitchen a magical place of sweet scents and titillating tastes. She'd do the same if he let her into his life. If he were to consider her as his bride, she would have to fit in —not vice versa.

For now, he appreciated her astonishment at his family's wealth. As he'd expected, she didn't take it for granted as any debutante of the ton would have, but she also surprised him with her astute observations about the artwork. She wasn't a simple mind. Maybe she'd rise from her humble upbringing like a phoenix from ashes. And just maybe, he would help her spread her wings.

CHAPTER 18

~

Hannah pulled her shrug over her shoulders. It was not yet sundown even though this winter weather called for a shorter day. It was April, and the Shabbat candles should be lit just after seven o'clock, signaling the start of the Jewish Friday evening meal. Arnold had excused himself and thus, Lizzie continued Hannah's tour. They chatted merrily as if they were old friends. Hannah took in the beauty of the house while she decided she'd have to find a way to let Arnold out of their betrothal. What a silly idea her father had had, almost as if he'd reached for the stars.

Just before dinner, Lizzie brought Hannah to the library, and Arnold returned. He'd changed into a navy velvet coat and cream-colored breeches. His dark brown boots were the same color as his hair. All in all, he looked exactly like the prince she'd seen in the sanctuary yesterday. Freshly bathed, he smelled of the intoxicating lemon and rosemary concoction she'd fallen prey to the day before. Hannah couldn't quite understand what it was about his scent that drew her in. She hoped he'd not notice that she kept trying to come closer to find out.

"I'll see if Lenny would like any of our old stuffed animals. There's a toy lion he might fancy," Lizzie said. She pivoted and glided out of the room, pulling the door shut behind her, giving them privacy that would compromise a girl, but somehow it no longer mattered.

"There are more books here than I've ever seen." Hannah beamed as she trailed her fingers along the leather spines. There wasn't even a speck of dust on the mahogany shelves.

"This is Adam Smith's first book." Arnold handed her a thick leather-bound volume with embossed lilies along the edges. "You cited him last night, so I thought you'd read his work."

"I have read some of it." Hannah stood on her toes to see the higher shelves and read the spines of the extensive collection. "There's a whole section on political science and society."

"Those are mine. Everybody else in the family thinks this is too dry, but I read about people and how they work before I go to bed," Arnold admitted. "There are certain universal principles, and I find Adam Smith's observations—"

"Where's your bedroom?" Hannah asked. She couldn't help but picture Arnold, shirtless, in bed, studying dense readings in candlelight.

Arnold laughed. "It's most unseemly to ask me that, don't you think? It begs for an invitation."

"Oh!" Hannah clutched both hands over her mouth.

"Or is that what you intended?"

Hannah blushed, but her embarrassment only lasted a moment, for Arnold closed the distance between them. Her heart pounded in her chest.

He kissed her lightly on her cheek and lingered close for longer than the chaste kiss demanded. "I promise I'll show you, but not today." He inhaled deeply, and Hannah hoped there'd be more than just a peck on the cheek soon.

* * *

ARNOLD COULD STILL TASTE the memory of their kiss from last night. And he longed for another. He tore himself away from her like a starfish from a rock and tried to stay away from her soft lips. But she eyed at him as if she were expecting more. And he wanted to give her all.

She flashed her sweet, toothy smile. The moment he saw her lips, he dropped his mouth onto hers. There was no controlling it, for he was falling with a velocity of a waterfall, unable to swim upstream, against the current of attraction he felt for her. He kissed her even though he knew what it would mean to do so at home. He'd make her stay—not out of obligation but because there was truly no other way now that she was in his life—and he couldn't keep his hands off her.

"Is kissing me in the library allowed?" she whispered sheepishly.

"Hmmmm-hmmm." Arnold nuzzled her neck.

CHAPTER 19

*rnold's entire family had gathered for dinner. His Uncle Gustav and Aunt Eve were seated at the heads of the table, overseeing the close gathering. Hannah was seated next to Lizzie and Lenny, across from Arnold and his cousin Fave. She noticed Fave's hand did something to his wife Rachel under the table. It made Hannah chuckle and blush.

"Oy, a lebn af dayn kop!" Life on your head! Eve gave the Yiddish blessing when Arnold told her they'd baked and delivered two dozen challot to the poorest and loneliest in the Jewish quarter.

Hannah felt a pang of guilt, as if her pleasure in hearing this blessing from someone other than her mother were a betrayal.

Arnold's aunt said the prayer when they lit the candles and his uncle Gustav blessed the wine and the challah with a traditional *kiddush*. According to kosher traditions, there was no pork or shellfish. Lizzie had told her tonight's dinner was fish anyway because the dessert had milk.

Hannah appreciated the warm and traditional Shabbat dinner, but it irked her that she felt so comfortable. She was taken by how much sense the Jewish traditions made among the international artwork and opulence. The Pearlers had an established routine, firmly grounded in the same traditions as Hannah's. They took Judaism out of context, without orthodox restrictions. She suddenly cared little whether the meat would or wouldn't be kosher, it *was* a Shabbat dinner even without the strictest rules. And it didn't matter for tonight anyway; no meat was served. She had a great time, and maybe that was the point of *Shabbat*.

"You're not going back into this dreadful cold, my dears," Eve declared when Lenny asked if he could play in the nursery a bit longer before they went home. "I'll have two guest rooms made up for you."

After Fave and Rachel retreated for the evening and Lizzie took Lenny to the nursey to show him the volumes of fairy tales and adventure stories, Arnold invited Hannah to stay for an *ocrep mit milkh,* hot milk diluted with water and sweetened with honey.

She was silent and fiddled with her hands, unable to decide what she thought of Arnold and his family.

"What's on your mind?" Arnold asked.

Maybe it was the expensive wine at dinner or the warm milk afterward, but Hannah blurted out, "How can wealth and poverty coexist in such a limited geographical area?"

Arnold pondered the question for a minute, then said,

"They don't merely coexist, Hannah, they're dependent on one another."

Arnold's reply startled her. She expected the ton to be shallow, happy-go-lucky aristocrats without much backbone, but Arnold was at the margin, as a Jew he was neither here nor there. And he had depth! She'd seen it during their chess game, in his response to her father, and now again. This wasn't good. He passed every test, and she had few remaining arguments in her arsenal to oppose her feelings for him.

He explained, "The rich run the country and drive the economy. If they didn't, then we'd lose the framework of societal order."

"They?" She asked incredulously.

Arnold chuckled, "Oh trust me, you haven't seen wealth." He waved at all the opulence in his home. "We're simple people, we work for our money."

"And the truly wealthy, as you call them, don't work for it?"

"Of course not. They just spend it. The money works for itself, growing wealth from wealth," he said matter-of-factly, seeming to enjoy her confusion. "Maybe I'll show you. The season just started."

It was only April and Hannah knew the ton were gathering for the season. Arnold would be welcome anywhere among adventurous women. He *was* a sight to behold. His invitation lingered in the air, mixing with his earlier explanation, causing Hannah indigestion—or whatever this stomach condition was that she suffered around him. But if she were to join his world, she'd be transplanted like a tree with clipped roots, forced to adapt to a new surrounding or perish. Like a tree, she'd be set into a new hole, a different, albeit comparable, set of problems. She didn't fit into the orthodox community because of her wit, but she didn't fit into the ton either. Arnold's world may have respect for their Jewish roots, but it was a far cry from orthodox living. What did it mean exactly to be Jewish among the ton? How high would the price be if she fell in love?

CHAPTER 20

*fter Arnold had shared the hot milk with Hannah, he gave her a chaste kiss good night— on her knuckles. Granted, he'd lingered, taking in her scent, but Arnold longed for more, so much more. He raked his hands through his hair in frustration. She was taboo. Hannah was not another pastime he could tup recreationally. She was real, witty, and innocent. He delighted in her blushing at his kisses.

The grandfather clock in the hall chimed ten o'clock. Arnold sighed. He had to meet with Gregory. It could only mean more bad news, just like Pavel's letter. He'd burned it earlier, watching the bad news crinkle in the fireplace and blow away as flakes of ashes.

He straightened his back and knocked on the door to his uncle's study. Uncle Gustav, Cousin Fave, and Gregory were already taking a drink.

"Ah there you are." Fave smiled wolfishly. "Did you let her get to rest after all?"

"Stop it," Arnold hissed. Hannah wouldn't be the subject of masculine ridicule as an after-dinner sport.

"Good to see you, Greg. How's your mother these days?" Gustav asked warmly as he poured Arnold a drink of the dark amber whiskey.

Gregory's mother had gone blind over the course of a few years.

"We take it one day at a time," Gregory said sadly. "The doctors gave up all hope for her to regain her vision, and she's retreated into darkness."

"I'm so sorry, my friend, I hope she allows you to bring some light to her life," Fave said.

Gregory smiled and took the glass Gustav had refilled for him. "Fave, you've got to cease reading all this mythology, you sound like a poet."

"He's gone soft since his bride joined our family," Gustav said, simultaneously proud and mocking.

"*Mazal tov*, my friend, a toast to the luckiest match of the season." Gregory congratulated Fave in Hebrew and raised his glass.

Arnold smiled and took a sip, the whiskey burning his throat. Alcohol assaulted his senses that were already overloaded with desire for Hannah. He needed to dull that ache and get his mind back to business. Usually, he didn't like the passive heat swelling his head after too much indulgence. He preferred to exhaust his body with exercise, his muscles burning with strain. But this was a business meeting, so a certain flair and expensive liquor were *de rigeur*.

"Thank you all. I hope you'll have the pleasure of meeting Rachel at the ball tomorrow. My mother's hosting a grand affair," Fave said. "What can we do for you?"

Gregory placed his glass on a coaster on the side table and rubbed his hands uneasily along his upper thighs. "There's a little situation with the candidate who I outran for my appointment." Gregory had recently been appointed after his father got a small barony.

"What happened, Greg?" Gustav asked.

"The Prime Minister and the Chancellor came to dinner a few days ago, the eve of the day I found you, Arnold."

Arnold nodded.

"An imposter claimed to be the heir of the Earldom of Sutton, whose title reverted to the crown years ago. He wants my spot in parliament."

"What's his name?" Gustav asked.

"Marvin Thompson."

Gregory's declaration ricocheted like a bullet around the study, hitting all three Pearlers, including Arnold, on its path.

Silence washed over the men as Gregory emptied his glass.

Arnold knew Marvin all too well. He'd been Fave's best friend at Eaton until Fave told him they were Jewish—against Arnold's advice—and then he'd crossed them. Since their school days, Marvin and his father had blackmailed Arnold and his family and capitalized on the Pearlers' secret.

Later, Marvin Thompson had been at Oxford with Arnold, Fave, and Gregory. And most recently, he'd married Allison Bustle-Smith, the blackmailing dowager's only daughter, who nearly prevented Fave from marrying his beloved Rachel. Allison and Marvin were indeed a match made in hell.

Gustav rose and refilled Gregory's glass.

"What does he have on you?" Arnold asked.

"He's sabotaging my fleets in America. He knows I depend on the contract to finance"—Gregory waved both hands in the air, the liquor in his glass nearly tumbling out with a splash—"everything, including my seat."

"How so? I thought peace terms have been reached with the colonies," Fave asked as he shot Arnold a glance. Arnold understood his cousin's reservation about meddling with a nation at war. In the American War of Independence, the Jews were either not allowed to fight for their countries or used as cannon fodder.

"It's not ratified by Congress, the parliament they formed in Washington," Gregory explained. "I'm not certain that the problem lies in the customs or tariffs with the United States of America."

"What then," Arnold asked, "Thompson?"

"How would he do that?" Fave interjected. "He's not that sly!"

"One moment," Gustav, as the eldest, took the steering wheel. "How does this affect your new position as a member of parliament?"

"That's just it, Gustav, and that's where I need your help." Gregory was now pacing the room. "This other candidate, Thompson, is threatening my *entire* fleet. He has some pull. I can't figure out exactly what he's done, but if I don't bring in the financial lubricant"—he rubbed his fingers together as if it were self-explanatory that money dulled the sharp edges of politics—"then the Chancellor won't vote for my ratification and Thompson can take my place."

"Ah!" Gustav leaned back and folded his hands over his belly. Arnold felt a pang of fear—his uncle was clearly aging. He'd been working himself beyond exhaustion for this competition, and Arnold feared it would threaten his uncle's health. If Arnold could help them to win the competition, Gustav could step back and look after himself. It would solve so many problems. He and Fave would step up. But doing so when Marvin Thompson and his devilish wife, Allison, had a say would be an awful world in which to take the reins.

"I remember Thompson from university. We crossed paths more recently, and he's as slick and slimy as ever," Fave said, "but he's also careless and not terribly bright."

"I was hoping to have your support, at least until my position is a bit more secure," Gregory said.

"Understood," Arnold said. "Tell me, what do you need?"

"I'm not sure. I haven't done anything wrong, but I keep losing contracts. Without my fleet, I can't hold my seat in parliament."

"And without your fleet, which pays for your seat, our suppliers can't bring our materials for the competition for the crown jewels." Arnold wished he could wash his mouth after summarizing the facts.

Gustav raised his brows, and Arnold realized there was more to the story than Gregory let on.

"He's turning one after the other of my suppliers away.

He's a barrister, you know, and he offers them contracts with other fleets."

"And those suppliers don't engage in the trade of gemstones, pearls, and gold, I assume," Fave added.

"Right," Gregory nodded.

"So, without suppliers, your ships would travel empty?" Fave asked.

"Yes, but no. Under the current laws, ships cannot make empty passages, so if I don't bring anything to England, I can't export, the ships would be stranded at the harbor—"

"And your crews would be out of work," Arnold added.

"Exactly." Gregory nodded again as he sank into the chair behind Gustav's desk.

"So, you need to find something to bring to England. But what?" Arnold asked.

"I don't know." Gregory dropped his head. "He's ruined my contracts for tea. I can't import it from India nor export it to America these days, so I can't bring the gems from South America nor the pearls from China." Gregory took a breath. He seemed to want to say something but couldn't get it out.

"What else are you not telling us, son?" Gustav asked with a stern tone. He knew Gregory's family, even his grandfather. Despite the Stones' deviation from Judaism, they were an upstanding family with honest businesses. Gustav had told Arnold many times that he admired how well the Stones' treated their crews.

"Well, I'm on the Charter Act committee, you know." Gregory should have been proud of this, but his eyes held a twinkle of pain.

"What is this committee for exactly?" Fave asked.

Arnold shook his head. If his cousin had his head in the newspaper instead of the Greek myths he collected and apparently memorized with his new bride, he'd know the committee's agenda was a bill of the United Kingdom Parliament to renew the charter issued to the British East India Company to continue its rule in Asia.

"Since the Company's monopoly in India has ended, the crown's been losing money," Gregory explained.

Fave frowned, evidently still puzzled. Arnold growled. How could he be so ignorant of developments in the empire? "Cous, the British can only trade tea and a few other raw materials—"

"And we can trade with China," Gregory added.

"You mean, this bill reflects upon the growth of British power in India?" Fave asked.

"Yes!" Arnold said. Finally! He wanted to get to the bottom of Gregory's issue, not tutor Fave in current affairs.

Gregory blinked at Fave impatiently, who seemed to mull this over.

Arnold lost his patience. "So Prinny's splendor is hanging upon a thread."

"And with the greatest jewels, he'll showcase his success as an imperialist," Gustav said as he sank into his desk chair.

"I still don't understand your involvement, Greg," Fave said.

Arnold had to give him credit now. Fave always honed in on the essence of a matter.

"Well," Greg began as he rubbed his chin with the base

of his palm, "my fleet was key in the trade routes. Without the contracts, my fleet is stranded here. And without my fleet—"

"Prinny's glory fades," Fave said.

Gregory pressed his lips together and nodded.

Gustav buried his face in his hands. This, Arnold knew, was a terrible sign. The stakes were higher than ever. The winning jewelers wouldn't only be commissioned by the regent, but they would help the crown restore some of its glory, a tremendous opportunity wrought with impossible obstacles.

"The Nabobs," Gustav grumbled.

"Yes, that's one of the concerns I heard in the house of Lords," Gregory said.

It was well known that parliamentarians were worried about the eccentricities of the Company's officials in India. They'd exploited natural resources and were reckless with British funds and the crown's reputation.

"Prinny's concerned that he can't curtail the Nabobs and that perceived injustice toward the Indians' welfare and education could … er … reflect badly upon the crown," Gregory explained, obviously playing down how the British misbehaved overseas. "If my fleet comes back empty-handed, the situation will only get worse."

"So, unless your fleet brings riches back to England, you'll jeopardize the bill and lose your seat in parliament," Arnold said.

"And unless Prinny gets to show off his jewels and secure the imperial reach of the crown, you'll lose supplies," Gregory said.

"Which could be the end of our business," Gustav grumbled behind his hands.

"Pavel already told us his suppliers can't deliver," Arnold whispered to Fave, who nodded.

"And Marvin Thompson is throwing every possible obstacle our way," Fave said.

"We need to fix this pretty soon, Greg." Arnold turned to his friend, but Gregory seemed beaten and didn't return his glance. Thompson had put him in quite a pickle.

"The competition could make or break us," Gustav said.

Arnold, Fave, and Gustav's eyes met in assent: they needed to help Gregory to help themselves.

CHAPTER 21

*G*regory left, but Arnold and Fave remained in Uncle Gustav's study a while longer. The road to their success had split with Gregory's news: one path led to doom, the other to the king's palace. But they didn't seem to know which way to go to lead their business and, thereby, their family to glory.

"I'm telling you boys, I'm too old for this," Gustav said.

"Father, you're not old." Fave gave a fake chuckle.

Gustav shook his head, patted Arnold on the back, and gently touched Fave's cheek. "I'll always support you, son, but it seems the two of you need to step up this time. I don't think I can carry our business through the competition and this crisis alone."

GUSTAV DROPPED his head and left the room like an abdicating king.

Arnold felt as if Gregory's news had laid chains around his lungs, restricting his breathing. His malaise could only be lifted by the Pearlers' victory in the competition for the crown jewels. If he could help them win, he'd have repaid them for their years of kindness, for taking him in, and—he felt it in his bones—he could satisfy his need to earn their love. And now their success had become contingent upon an international trade war for Gregory's fleet. What a disaster!

Arnold and Fave sat in silence. The glasses of expensive liquor remained on the table, spreading a pungent smell in the room. Suddenly everything smelled bad to Arnold, and he had a bitter taste—or was that just apprehension?

"How exactly did we get from a friendly competition for the crown jewels into a trade triangle between India, America, and England?" Fave asked.

Arnold forced himself to breathe. "I don't know, Cous, but we need to fix this."

Fave drew a deep breath and closed his eyes. He did this before he fenced, his telltale sign of readying himself for a fight.

"Alright, here's what we know." Fave got up and began to enumerate the facts on his fingers. "Marvin wants Greg's spot as an MP, so he's sabotaging his fleet—"

"By hijacking his contracts," Arnold added.

"Right," Fave continued. "And without his contracts, Gregory's fleet can't ship tea from India to America, so they can't come back with the gold and gems we need for our business. So, we have my designs, but no material to make them with."

"I spoke to Pavel already, Fave. Consider the continental European dealers dried up until the trade routes are open again," Arnold said.

"I know. And my designs are useless if we have no material to produce the pieces." Fave stared Arnold squarely in the eyes. This was the first time they'd leveled as adults, as business partners, as equal heirs to Gustav's hard-earned jewelry empire. The weight of their family's fortune rested upon their shoulders.

"What I don't understand is how Marvin can single-handedly sabotage Greg's contracts," Arnold said.

"He must have his claws all over the ports," Fave said.

"Who do we know at the port authority?" Arnold desperately searched for a clue.

"Louis Cox?"

"No, he moved to Liverpool a few months ago."

"Hm…" Fave bit his lower lip.

Arnold joined him and they paced the room together. It had grown dark; the sun would come up soon.

"Ah, I know! Sir Stuart Murphy!" Fave said.

"The admiral?"

"It's worth a try," Fave shrugged.

They agreed to see him first thing in the morning.

EVE AND GUSTAV treated Arnold like a son, but he had none of the restrictions of a Cohen. Gustav was a Cohen, so Fave was, too. He had to remain celibate until marriage and find a bride of impeccable virtue to carry on the Jewish privileges associated with his bloodline.

Arnold had always covered Fave's tracks to keep face

among the ton, tupping every merry widow and willing spinster of the aristocracy. Fave had kissed a few, but Arnold had bedded them. It had been fun for a while but had grown tedious since Allison Bustle-Smith had shoved some of her friends on him. The devil's spawn, she was called behind her back, and she knew she could thrust anything at Arnold or else carry on her mother's blackmail of the Jewish family. She'd gotten away with it until recently, when Eve and Gustav essentially exiled Carol Bustle-Smith to the countryside. Allison had been on a vendetta against Arnold and his family since that day.

It was the peak of the London season. London's haute bourgeoisie and aristocracy mingled at the weekly balls at Almack's marriage mart and the many balls in town. Just last week at a ball at the Parker's house, a prominent ton family, Arnold had turned a titled spinster down. She was one of Allison's entourage of snappish wolverines, Evelyn Fraser. Her crooked brown teeth and wiry hair were testament to how spoiled she was. Allison had sent Evelyn into a side room when she must have known Arnold would be there alone. It had been a vain attempt to compromise Evelyn, and Arnold hadn't taken the bait. That had set Allison into a fit of anger and gossip. Arnold hadn't told Fave about it—no need to worry him while he was on his honeymoon—but it was time to face reality and put a halt to Allison's fury.

Of course, she'd try to avenge her mother, the Pearlers had expertly sent her off into the countryside and taken her house in partial repayment of her decades of debts and blackmail. Arnold was still riding the high from the pride he'd felt when Eve and Gustav had finally evicted Carol Bustle-Smith, Allison's daughter. But he also had a pit in his stomach, fearing that Allison's groundless methods to avenge her mother would be unscrupulous compared to her mother's. She'd stop short of nothing.

CHAPTER 22

$\mathcal{O}$n Saturday morning, Hannah walked through the pale green hallway and descended the stairs on the way to breakfast. Her hands trailed along the sleek wooden rail, and she examined the marble steps. The white wooded balusters contrasted against the light grey marble steps. A long thin carpet followed the steps, affixed to the back of each one with a wide metal bar. Her footsteps were dampened but there was a slight echo to her counting. "Twenty-eight, twenty-nine, thirty, thirty-one—"

"What are you counting?" A voice came from below—Fave Pearler, Arnold's cousin.

"Oh, pardon me, Mr. Pearler."

"Please call me Fave. Mr. Pearler is my father."

Hannah nodded and blushed. She saw the resemblance between him and Arnold. They were about the same age, although Arnold was a bit taller and darker. Fave's hair shimmered golden in the sunlight that streamed through the large windows on the stair landing.

"I trust your stay here is pleasant?" Fave asked with one hand on his chest and the other behind his back. His manners were impeccable. Hannah felt like a lame goose compared to the charming men in this palace.

"I... er... your family is most generous. I hope not to overburden your hospitality," she said, clutching her book.

"You do know you could never, don't you?" Fave grinned.

"I don't understand."

"We're like family. I think your grandfather, my grandfather, and Pavel, came to England together many years ago. They were like brothers."

Was that why her father trusted the Pearlers? Is this what her father had meant by the apple tree from which Arnold stemmed?

"I know you think our life is a betrayal of traditions or customs, but I assure you we have our own ways of keeping the faith." Fave's earnest tone hung gravely in the air. Hannah wasn't sure what to say. How could she insult a man in his own house?

Fave tilted his head and waited for her to speak.

"I read about a baron, he was baptized and is most ... er ... adjusted to the nobility—"

"His name is Greg, Gregory Stone. He's an old friend of mine, we went to school together."

Hannah nodded and mumbled, "Traitor."

She didn't expect Fave to hear, but he arched his amber brow. "Why do you think so, Ms. Solomon?"

"Because he chose the easy path. He's assimilated or

whatever people call his conversion to Christianity." She was finding her second wind, her spirits less intimidated by the luxuries around her. "How dare he betray his ancestors' sacrifices just so he can engage in politics?"

Fave kept his hands behind his back and stood still, attentive. "So, you consider our faith a burden then?"

"Not exactly," Hannah added a bit quieter.

"But it's an onus for you?" Fave probed.

"A responsibility," Hannah corrected him, unsure whether she was overstepping.

"I happen to agree with you, Ms. Solomon. And I appreciate a conversationalist who pays careful attention to word choice. Well done!" He inclined his head and turned to walk away.

Hannah was perplexed. "Mr. Pearler—"

"Please, call me Fave. I'd hope to call you among my friends." He turned back to her but didn't come closer.

"Fave, why don't you condemn Mr. Stone's betrayal?"

Fave took a deep breath. "Because, Hannah, the world isn't black and white."

"I think it is."

"Very well, that's admirable. It certainly makes *your* life easier, but it also shows that you haven't seen much of the world yet."

"Have you?"

"I'm afraid not."

"Then why are you his friend?"

Fave walked back toward her and put one hand on the stair railing. He seemed more relaxed, deep in thought now. "Greg didn't convert. It was his father. His mother followed suit and was baptized before Greg was born."

"*A batoyfter id*, a baptized Jew," Hannah whispered.

"Exactly. And he's a friend of mine because I have no reason to fault his character. It's better to keep people close than to alienate them. We have enough enemies in the world, especially outside of England, don't you think?"

Hannah processed this and didn't respond.

"My wife was persecuted in Switzerland. Her baby sister froze to death in Lake Geneva. She and her family fled to England three years ago."

"That's terrible, I'm so sorry."

"Thank you, but that's not why I am telling you this."

Hannah eyed him questioningly.

"She says that all people deserve a chance to make their own choices. Even though she was a victim of some excruciating acts of violence against Jews, she finds it in her heart to see the good in people. I hope you do, too."

That stung. Was she so prejudiced as to not give those a chance who didn't share her burden? Or who weren't privileged to carry on the responsibilities of the chosen people, as the Jews called themselves?

Hannah frowned and clutched the book close to her chest.

"I see Arnold gave you an Adam Smith. It's one of his favorites. I prefer the Greek philosophers, but it's all the same."

"How is it the same?" Hannah couldn't help but admire Fave. All the Pearlers. They wore such accomplished thinkers, and they had goodness within them that Hannah had never seen before. Why were the less fortunate Jews so much more limited in their world views? What had she missed in her seclusion?

"It doesn't matter what you read—the Torah, the Talmud, Plato, Socrates, Adam Smith, Machiavelli, or Montesquieu—when it comes to morals and ethics, the rules level off. Even the church condemns crimes, doesn't it?"

"You mean everything converges toward the peak, with the ten commandments?"

"In a way, yes. But there are derivative virtues that all people share. If more people honored these virtues, the world would be a better place." Fave bowed to take his leave.

"Thank you, Fave." Hannah said as he took the first step to ascend.

"For what?"

"For opening my eyes."

He bowed to her and went upstairs.

CHAPTER 23

⊂⧓⊃

*A*rnold hadn't slept. He'd sweated through his bedsheets just thinking of Hannah. His mind had been tired, but his body was tense, so he came to exercise.

A few years ago, Gustav had let Fave and Arnold convert one of the two bedrooms in the attic to a fencing room. They'd removed all the furniture and painted lines on the parquet. Since then, whenever they didn't want to go to their club, they met in this room at the crack of dawn. Arnold's triple knock on Fave's bedroom door had been a signal for him to join him. Since Rachel had moved in, Arnold could no longer just barge into Fave's room. The newlyweds were doing whatever it was that aggravated Arnold's frustration.

He pulled his sword and swung loudly. There was an empty bedroom below this room, so none of his thrusting, parrying, and riposting woke anyone else up. Arnold had also built a set of wall bars and a horizontal bar for his exercise. Sometimes, he just needed to push his muscles to the pain of complete exhaustion. It was his way of coping with the bad conscience of being an imposter. And with the dilemma of the competition freshly in his mind, no amount of athletic vigor could calm his mind.

"Where have you been?" Arnold snarled as Fave entered their attic fencing room. "I've been here for almost an hour."

Fave smirked. "As a matter of fact, I had a little chat with our house guest."

Arnold dropped from the wall bar and stood before Fave. "This early? What did you do?"

"Nothing really. She's carrying around an Adam Smith from your collection." Fave grinned mischievously.

Arnold was stunned. He'd not expected that she'd read his book. It was a dense text and most people merely flattered themselves by owning it.

"She thinks Greg's treason of our faith is inexcusable," Fave told Arnold.

"I know. I agree," Arnold said, "but what can we do? He's our friend."

"I'm afraid she condemns our lifestyle, too," Fave added.

Arnold nodded and again he felt that pit in his stomach. "She won't fit in, will she?"

"No," Fave said.

"She's from a different world," Arnold said sadly.

"More like a different era. Rabbi Solomon kept her in quite the dark ages."

Arnold raked his hands through his hair. He'd been sweating, but his body felt removed from his mind. His thoughts kept returning to Hannah. He was physically exhausted, but his mind tirelessly attempted to grind down the coarseness of his desire, as if he could pulverize his affection for Hannah and blow it away like dust.

"You look awful. Come on, get your blood pumping," Fave said, ever the eager athlete. "En garde." He charged at Arnold.

Arnold stood still and scratched his head. He was a more forceful fencer, while Fave was the speedy and jumpy kind. "Where do you get the positive energy, Cous?" Arnold eyed him head to feet while Fave pranced around him.

"From my sweet and oh so lovely wife," Fave beamed.

It was sickening. He only ever came out to eat and fence. Arnold knew all too well what Rachel was letting him do to her or did to him ... his body ached at the tension. He'd spent the night with an agonizing flagpole, unable to turn and sleep, thinking of Hannah in her little white apron making blintzes. He felt impaled by the forbidden fruit that was Hannah, but she was so deliciously juicy, like a cool orange on a hot beach day. Every time he closed his eyes, he twitched at the image of Hannah and her strands of hair that he had tucked behind her sweet little ear when they had been baking in her kitchen.

"Are you going to fight or not?" Fave bounced around Arnold waving his sword.

"Not."

Fave froze. "What's the matter with you?"

Fave's brotherly tone always made Arnold weak. He trusted nobody in the world as much as his cousin, but he didn't want to tell him what he'd gotten himself into.

"Does this have anything to do with ... say ... our house guests?"

Argh, Fave knew. He'd probably figured it out.

"The little one is sweet. We should arrange for Sammy to show him around. Are we buying Lenny his own fencing gear, too?" Fave was already making a match between Rachel's brother Sammy and Hannah's brother Lenny, as if they were soon to be in-laws.

"I know what you're doing, Cous."

"And what's that?"

"Probing."

"Ah..." at that, Fave pressed the point of the sword at Arnold's heart.

Arnold inclined his head as a threat, but Fave caught his gaze and held still.

"You like her."

"Who?"

"Arnold!"

"Pfff," Arnold hissed. "Alright, a little bit."

"Ah, a little bit. Nah, come on." Fave dropped the sword and slid it into the holster. "You've never liked a pretty girl a *little bit*."

Arnold sighed. "I may have gotten myself into a bit of a pickle."

"Is she pregnant?"

Arnold pulled his sword and held the horizontal of the blade against Fave's throat. "Take that back!"

Fave hit the sword with his flat palm, and it flew through the air. The metallic crash when the blade hit the ground made Arnold flinch. It was an impulsive brotherly attack, but he'd gone too far.

"Get a grip of yourself. I only asked!"

"I'm trying. But I can't get a grip. I try and I try! She's just not like other girls. She's not ... and then she asks me a witty question and my bones ... I'm telling you; I feel her smile in my bones! Do you know what I mean? I'm sick," Arnold said.

Fave raised his brows and smiled. "I do know, actually. But you're not sick. So, what's the problem then?"

"She's Hannah Solomon."

"The Rabbi's daughter. I know. The emancipated gossip columnist. She and Lizzie get on marvelously."

Fave's interest was piqued. If Arnold told him the whole story, he suspected Fave might even let Rachel wait in bed for an extra minute or two. This was more than just a pickle; it was a barrel full of pickles. He had to marry her; it was the custom. And the worst was that deep down, he had no objections.

"I kissed her."

"You what?" Fave threw both arms in the air. "That's even stupider than what I've done!"

"How so?"

"I thought I was kissing a *goy*"— a gentile—"but you kissed the Rabbi's daughter. Soon I'll be giving you a wedding band as a gift. She's an opinionated wench and you're in for a lifetime of lectures on chastity and virtue."

Arnold couldn't hold Fave's gaze. "She's not like that. There's a purpose behind her diatribes."

He closed his eyes. This was agony. He'd been so happy to make wedding bands for Fave and Rachel; they were perfect for each other. But this was a disaster and a match between an orthodox girl and him would alarm the ton.

141

His liaison could even jeopardize their chance in the competition—the last thing he intended. The minx had him all tangled up, and not just with her sweet-smelling challah braids.

"Her aunt caught us. The Rabbi expects…"

"Oh no!"

"Oh yes." They both sank to the floor.

"I think I need a drink," Fave said. "I thought you were just helping her with the roofers. That's what Lizzie said."

Arnold lifted his chin in direction of the clock, the only item on the walls beside the exercise equipment and some hooks. "It's half nine!"

"I'm going back to bed, then." Fave smiled, and Arnold knew his blushing bride was there, waiting for him. But for Arnold, Hannah's room was off-limits, like castle gates forged in fire. He just had to pretend there was a moat around the bedroom door like he and Fave had done when they were little and he wasn't allowed into his mother's sick room.

"Tell Rachel, I say hello."

"Will do." Fave rose and walked away. Then he turned back. "Arnold?"

"Hmm?" He was still on the floor, with his back to the wall.

"I'll stand by you wherever your heart takes you," Fave said.

Arnold let his head drop onto his knees. He knew the Pearlers would all stand by him. And that was the problem. He wanted to earn his place in their family.

CHAPTER 24

Meanwhile, Hannah took a cup of tea from the buffet in the breakfast room. A footman brought her some scrambled eggs and she buttered a piece of toast to eat while she was reading. The house was still quiet. She turned the page in the book Arnold had given her.

Chap. IV Of the Nature of Self-deceit, and of the Origin and Use of general Rules

Is that what she had done, deceived herself?

There are two different occasions upon which we examine our own conduct, and endeavour to view it in the light in which the impartial spectator would view it: first, when we are about to act; and secondly, after we have acted. Our views are apt to be very partial in both cases; but they are apt to be most partial when it is of most importance that they should be otherwise.

PAIN POUNDED in Hannah's skull. She was unable to evaluate her actions objectively. Was *Tate* right, was she obligated to marry Arnold after she'd kissed him? Or was she obligated to set him free? After all, she didn't fit in his world. Her clumsiness would compromise his secret Jewishness. She tried to justify why she might have a chance with Arnold. At the same time, her heart ached with the realization that she should remain impartial to her desires because she should let the gorgeous man she loved live his life.

Loved.

Hannah closed her eyes. Oh no. She'd set herself up for heartbreak. She leaned back in her chair and closed her eyes. This was agony. She was an inexperienced, uncultivated girl, swimming in deep waters outside her community. Here, she was just a little fish in a big sea, unable to latch onto anyone helpful.

"Did Adam Smith put you to sleep?" Arnold asked, startling Hannah back into reality.

The statuesque man leaned over her. Had she drooled as she slumped sleepily into the chair?

"Not at all," Hannah said with as much dignity as she could muster.

Arnold chuckled. "So, you were deep in thought then? My apologies for disturbing you. I'll just have a bite and take my leave."

"Don't leave on my account." She put her hand on his upper arm.

He sat beside her. Why couldn't she keep her hands off him? He must think her a veritable idiot.

She forced her gaze away from Arnold's chiseled face, his creamy skin, and the slight scruffiness lining his chin and jawbone. She swallowed and tried to focus on a painting on the wall.

"It's a 1783 by Thomas Whitcombe, a British painter," Arnold said, nodding at the painting, clearly thinking she'd been staring at the precious artwork in his home. "This shows the Battle of the Saintes on April twelfth in 1782. The Ville de Paris surrendered."

"Oh." Hannah didn't know how to respond. He was so knowledgeable. So, accomplished. And she was … smitten. She'd have to surrender, too, when he glowered at her with those gorgeous dark eyes. His bangs curved perfectly over his forehead, and she wanted to touch them as she'd done at home over a friendly game of chess. But now, the battle strategy applied to the real world, and Hannah didn't know the chessboard Arnold navigated. The contrasting squares of Judaism and the ton never mingled, yet formed a pattern that he and his family were maneuvering with an elegance Hannah could never muster.

"Have you ever traveled by ship?" she finally asked, unable to come up with anything more intelligent.

"Small rowboats only, I'm afraid. I've never been outside England." He sounded somewhat melancholic.

"Would you like to?"

"Travel? Maybe. I've never really considered it."

"Is this what Mr. Stone's fleet is like?" Hannah asked.

Arnold locked his gaze onto the painting. "I don't think his are warships, but essentially yes. How do you know about that?"

She shrugged. "I read between the lines."

"Lizzie?" Arnold asked, and Hannah gave him a sideways smirk.

"I think I'd feel quite safe on a fleet with so many sails," Hannah mused. "The more sails, the faster the ships travel, isn't that right?"

Arnold turned his chest toward Hannah but didn't say anything.

Hannah began to rock on her chair, uncomfortable under his scrutiny.

"You're a most unusual girl, Hannah Solomon. Do you know that?"

She frowned. "I'm afraid so, it has dawned on me that I don't fit in."

He smiled.

And with the widening of his mouth, his cheeks moved up, his eye ablaze with his lovely boyish glow, and Hannah knew she could never be objective again. He'd changed something within her, and she never wanted to look back.

CHAPTER 25

*A*rnold and Fave arrived at 37-38 St. James Street, the notorious White's Gentleman's club at noon sharp. It was an inconspicuous four-story building from the outside, but the shakers and doers of London frequented the establishment. Arnold detested what usually went on here, from the harlotry to the gambling, and he knew Fave shared his disgust. The occasional fencing matches were the only events he tolerated, especially because he or Fave usually won.

They asked the maître d' for the admiral's whereabouts, and soon, they found him in the arms of two voluptuous women who didn't speak English. It appeared the admiral cared little for the ladies' conversational skills. The stench of alcohol, sweat, smoke, and semen permeated the air. Arnold felt instantly dirty and longed to swim in the cool ocean to rid himself of the images of this middle-of-the-day debauchery.

"Ah, Mr. Pearler and Mr. Ehrlich, long time no see!" The admiral waved to them from the corner of his red velvet settee in a semi-private area curtained-off in the back room. He had an air of normalcy as if this hell hole were an office and he was about to engage in the most proper business.

Arnold turned to Fave, who seemed to be holding his breath, tensing his lips at the stench. Arnold was smoother with these sorts of men, so he gave Fave a blink to indicate he'd take the lead.

"Admiral, what a pleasure to see you tonight!" Arnold sat next to him and waved for a glass of scotch to share with the knighted navy official.

"Admiral Sir Stuart Murphy," Fave added, "you chose the best scotch. I compliment your impeccable taste, as usual." Arnold stifled a laugh as Fave sang the lie through his teeth.

The admiral, however, gave one of the women sitting on his lap a slap on the bottom and shooed her away. The other woman remained but slid to his side. The admiral kept his hands in her hair as if to control her head. Arnold tasted acid at the vulgar show of the old man's dominant intimacy with a stranger.

"Gentlemen, aren't you the athletic types? I rarely see you here at this hour. I say, you're a few hours too late for a fencing match." The admiral laughed, tilting his head, giving Arnold a glimpse of his rotten teeth. Arnold noted his slurred speech, a good chance to get information out of him.

"Isn't this one a gem, Mr. Pearler. I say, you know how to tell a true diamond in the rough." The admiral pushed the woman toward Fave, inviting him to feel her. Fave's eyes shot to Arnold in alarm. He'd never lay hands on a loose woman, much less now that he had the love of his life safely at home in their chambers. Arnold swallowed acid as he realized he'd have to save his cousin.

"Darling, come here, I need to ask you for a favor." Arnold stood and whispered something in the woman's ear. She giggled and scuttled off, feathers shaking on the back of her ... what was this undergarment called if it served as her "work clothes"?

Fave gave Arnold a thankful nod, and Arnold turned back to the inebriated navy officer, who said, "Your loss, young fella', she's mah favorite!"

"Thank you for your willingness to share her ... um ... graces with us, Sir, but I'm recently married and—"

"What he's trying to say is that it's been slim pickings this season," Arnold added to stop Fave before he could irritate the admiral further.

The man's mien sank, and he asked Fave, "Isn't your sister making her debut this year?"

"Yes, she is."

"Ye better keep'n eye on the lass. A pretty one, she is."

Fave's cheeks flushed. Arnold sympathized. This had to end before this slimy bag of corruption could further soil Lizzie's image.

"Sir, we came to ask you about Mr. Stone's fleet. Do you know—"

The admiral waved his thick greasy fingers, revealing a large signet ring in his little finger. "Everyone knows, gentlemen."

The feather-adorned woman returned with three

glasses of scotch and set them on the table. Then she dutifully resumed her post on the admiral's lap.

"What is it everyone knows?" Fave asked.

"The bills of lading, of course, they're—" The admiral coughed, a productive hacking befitting his demeanor. His face turned bright red and he looked like a slaughtered rabbit on the butcher's table with his head hanging over a cutting board. He coughed all over the glasses.

Arnold and Fave jerked their heads backward in synchrony.

"May I order you a cup of tea?" Fave asked.

"Well, that's just the thing—er," the admiral said through his cough, "'twas no tea!"

"What do you mean?" Arnold asked.

"I saw it myself, Stone's bills of lading. Someone had signed off on the shipments of tea, but the crates were empty. Ain't nothin' to sell the lad. Darjeeling and Ceylon were supposed to be sold at a premium this year. Pity that." He sipped of his whiskey.

Arnold was about to say something when the admiral burped in his face. "This is why you sought me out, lads?"

Fave laughed as Arnold wiped his face. Arnold would get him for his *schadenfreude* later.

"So, you're saying that the shipments were lost?" Fave asked. He must have seen that Arnold was holding on to his dinner with all his willpower.

"Nah," the admiral said, "someone emptied the crates and forged the bill of lading. Happens all the time. Simple sleight of hand, like in a friendly card game."

"And who paid for the shipments?" Arnold asked, since this was not "friendly" to him at all.

The admiral pushed the woman off his lap and leaned toward him. "*You!*" He spat.

Arnold felt Fave's eyes on his, but he didn't break eye contact with the drunkard before him. "I beg your pardon?"

"Well, you both, y'all paid for the shipments. Odd question that!" the admiral said.

"I don't understand, Sir, we never bought any ship-ments of tea and we never—"

"I signed off on the bill of ladings of a least four ships with your seal on them: Pearler with a big curly P and a little E." He made a swirly motion with his hand in the air.

Arnold turned to Fave and swallowed. It was their seal. He usually hated seeing his first initial, the E for Ehrlich, tucked under the larger P for the Pearlers, but all he could think of right now was to bring his family to the safe side of business. "Do you still have those bills of lading?"

"Certainly, mah boy. Have a drink and come to the docks on Monday. I'll let you review my books, but y'know ... my wife can't find out about my lady friends here."

"Maybe a pearl bracelet will set her mind at ease?" Arnold suggested, all too aware of the bribery required to round corners among the gentlemen at White's. How much longer could he keep this up without supplies? Lubricating the influential in London was an expensive part of his business.

The admiral nodded and raised his scotch.

Arnold was trapped in a transaction he'd never entered into. He'd never put his seal on those bills of lading. He had to see them—whoever gave his seal of approval was more fiend than friend.

CHAPTER 26

❦

*A*rnold was glad the poison patrol had agreed to go to the synagogue and resolve the rodent problem. This way, Hannah and Lenny could stay a few more days, and he could keep his promise to the Rabbi of looking after them. What was more, he could keep Hannah close and consider whether she'd make a suitable bride for him. Arnold was glad they were safe at his home, but he also enjoyed having Hannah here for more selfish reasons. If only he could focus more time on her instead of being distracted by the competition. If only he could get the supplies to make cousin Fave's designs. If only…

HE'D GONE to every wholesaler he knew, but none of them had enough pearls for Fave's tiara designs. And he knew not to change Fave's designs, they gave them an edge over the other jewelers. Fave applied rules of architecture and ancient mathematical formulas of harmony to the designs, and they needed a Fibonacci number 377 of pearls for the tiara alone, another 1597 for the imperial orb, 233 for the pearl strands, and 4181 small diamonds for the pavé work. Fave had started to calculate the best angles for cutting a rough emerald Pavel had given him, but he didn't dare make the first dent yet.

Arnold was at an impasse about how to get supplies and the day had been taxing. He really just wanted to say hello to Hannah and think of something other than work.

LATER THAT EVENING, Arnold came to give Lenny a book. When he arrived at Lenny's door, dim light flooded the room and he saw Hannah's back.

"I promised, so here's a story," she said softly.

Arnold tucked himself against the wall to listen.

"Is it about the knight?"

"Yes, the girl knight. Do you remember her colorful helmet?"

"With the peacock feathers?" Lenny's voice was enthusiastic.

"Exactly. She came to the castle. The prince kissed her in the last scene."

"Ugh! Blah!"

Arnold stifled his chuckle. He leaned toward the door now, not even a little sorry to be eavesdropping.

"Well, her time with the prince is over. He left for the coronation ceremony. She stood alone on the balcony, trailing her fingers along the marble balusters. A shooting star burned a trail of light through the clear night sky and disappeared."

"Was she hit by a comet?" Lenny asked.

Arnold tucked his mouth into his collar to stifle his laugh.

"No, *kleyner sholtic*. Little rascal."

"She realized that her fire had burned up like the star's. It was time to go home to her land."

"Why couldn't she stay with the prince?" Lenny asked.

"You know why! Her mission was complete. She retrieved the elixir and had to bring it back to the fairy king."

"But if she kept it, the fairies would become visible. Then maybe the prince could see them and help!"

"That's not how the world works." Hannah's voice was sad. Arnold realized she wasn't talking about fairies. "The fairies have their own kingdom."

"But if they're invisible, the prince can never protect them! They're right under his nose, but he has no idea." Lenny's sweet innocence brimmed with hope.

A moment of silence passed, and Arnold heard the rustling of the covers. She must have been tucking Lenny in.

"Do we really have to go home tomorrow?" Lenny's voice was sad.

There was no answer.

Lenny sniffled. "We're fairy people, aren't we? We stay underground."

Hannah sighed.

Arnold's heart fell so forcefully, it was a miracle the thud wasn't audible.

"I'm sorry, I made a mess, didn't I?" Hannah's voice was low with sorrow.

"Ikh hub di lieb." I love you. More rustling of the covers. Probably a hug.

Tears pricked Arnold's eyes and he blinked a few times.

"Me too," Hannah said.

Arnold heard her blow out the candle, and she emerged from the room. He couldn't muster a word and let her catch him eavesdropping.

Her eyes met his as she pulled Lenny's door shut.

"Why won't you have me?" Arnold asked, hurt evident in his voice.

"I would make you visible."

It was true. Her community ties would compromise his camouflage among the ton. Theirs were two realms colliding, stacked together in London, and yet worlds apart.

Arnold whispered, "We need to talk."

CHAPTER 27

❧

*A*rnold had surprised Hannah when she'd tucked her little brother in and now he ushered her into the adjacent room, her bedroom.

"You shouldn't be here," she said when he shut the door.

She was wearing a sheer robe, but didn't seem as ashamed of her nudity as others might be. She took a book laid flat on the covers, closed it and placed it on her nightstand. It didn't matter how insignificant her movements, Arnold was mesmerized. Was this the Adam Smith she'd been reading? She made no effort to cover herself. Most girls were more prudish when a man entered their bedrooms.

He gestured at the nightgown. "Is this Lizzie's?"

She nodded. It bothered Arnold that Lizzie even owned such revealing and beautiful nightgowns. He still thought of her as his little cousin.

Hannah's legs were bare from her knees down. They

seemed smooth and probably felt like the finest satin. Her feet were adorably small. Arnold would willingly enjoy the privilege of kissing her feet.

She crossed her arms. "You wanted to talk?"

The silky nightgown was buttoned up over her breasts, but the thin fabric draped over her nipples. They hardened and poked out as he stood there—she must have felt his gaze. Her lace sleeves gave him a clear view of her upper arms and shoulders. Before him stood the most gorgeous siren of allure. Her curves rose and fell in all the right places.

Arnold approached her, drawn by her beauty but careful not to scare her away. He'd suddenly forgotten why he wanted to speak to her. Her eyes pierced his, dark and intelligent. Her lashes were so beautifully long, they jutted from her profile as if she were painted with the courageous strokes of a master artist. She fixed her gaze on him. But he was afraid she'd jump away like a young deer if he came closer.

"I noticed you didn't mention the wedding to Aunt Evie." Arnold had to start somewhere, but he felt like he'd fallen into the house with the entire front wall.

"I didn't think you'd go through with it. I still don't."

"Your father seems to consider it settled. He even left you in my care," Arnold said.

"He knows I can care for myself."

"Were you always going to care for yourself? Like the girl knight in your story?" Arnold asked. He'd caught on, she expected to be a spinster.

"Yes." Her admission hung in the air.

Arnold chuckled. It was absurd that such a beauty

wasn't the subject of scandal. If Hannah had been a debutante at Almack's, she'd been ravished and married off
within the first week.

"Well, that's a shame," he said.

"Why?" she asked earnestly. This erotic goddess
wrapped in a touch of silk had no idea of her effect
on him.

"There are certain pleasures that a man and a woman
can share. It would be a shame for you to miss out on
them entirely. If I were your husband, I'd care for you and
keep you safe."

Hannah wrinkled her nose as if considering his state-
ment. "As you're keeping me safe now?" She wrung her
hands and dropped her gaze to her flexing toes.

Arnold came one step closer. He could touch her now,
but his hands were anvils, weighed down by his scruples
about taking the Rabbi's daughter. Whatever he did, it
wouldn't be inconsequential. This was Hannah, she'd
become his friend. She seemed to understand him. *She'd
been of quite some importance in his mind and her opinion
mattered.*

"What are those pleasures?" she whispered.

Arnold's mouth fell open. Then he noticed a slight
smile growing on her face; she was toying with him. He
liked it. This he knew. She'd joined him in his comfort
zone of flirting.

"Were you never to find out?"

She shook her head.

His heart sank. "Why not?" Arnold waited for to her
continue. Someone had scared her.

"After Aunt Rivkah caught us, she, um, told me it'll be

my duty to lie under my husband and let him have his … er…"

"She told you that?"

Hannah nodded.

"And what else did she tell you?"

Arnold didn't know how he got there, but he found himself holding Hannah's hand. Suddenly, he understood what Fave had told him. It was just as Fave had described: love would sweep through the gates of friendship. But it was different for Arnold. He knew carnal pleasures. He'd had the best and most beautiful ladies of the ton. It should have meant something, but in this moment, his experience paled in comparison to the beauty by his side. A floodgate of emotion washed over him, and he felt it not only in his breeches. His heart had opened. He was terrified but mesmerized.

"You could never have lived the life of a spinster," he said.

"And why is that?" Hannah asked.

"You're too beautiful." He took a strand of her hair between his fingers. It still smelled faintly like rising dough, baking crispy and soft in the ovens. But there was something else, a sweetness that wasn't a perfume. It was her.

His pulse was racing now. "You know, what Rivkah told you was wrong."

"Oh, I can't imagine. She has five grown children!"

"It's not just about procreation." Arnold laughed more than was becoming, hoping he could cover up his nerves. He noticed she was ogling his open mouth.

"What are we going to tell my father when he returns?" she asked, cutting his laughter short.

"What do *you* want to tell him?" Arnold had to let her choose. He'd compromised her, maybe, but he didn't want to trap her.

"The decision is hardly mine," she said, lowering her glance.

"I don't even pretend to know what you're talking about, Hannah."

"I'm a girl. I don't have a say. The question will be whether you take me or whether—"

"Whether you're doomed to spinsterhood?"

She nodded.

"And would you want that?"

She inclined her head and thought about this. "I have many duties in the community. A husband would distract me, or maybe forbid me from writing. He'd take me from my brothers and sisters. My children."

And when her eyes met his, he knew she'd never abandon her role as the replacement mother for her siblings.

His eyes opened wide. "That would be cruel!"

She looked at him curiously.

"You're the most independent, capable, and spirited girl I've ever met. A man who'd even try to forbid you anything would clip your wings." He shook his head at the preposterous thought. "Cruel."

She turned to him, visibly pleased by his speech. He realized this hypothetical husband would be him, could only be him, for she was ruined for all others. And he'd barely touched her. Oh, but he wanted to. "The question should be whether you'd rather have your freedom?"

"Are you giving me the chance to refuse the match?" she asked, emotion betraying the steadiness of her voice.

He felt a pang in his heart. He wanted her. But not by forcing her into marriage.

So, he nodded but he held her glance. "Aunt Evie is your chaperone, Lizzie and Rachel are here. You could emerge from your stay with us unscathed. Nobody needs to know about the kiss in the temple, we could ask your aunt to forget it."

She seemed to consider that for a moment. "But it was unforgettable," she said, rubbing his hand with her fingers.

CHAPTER 28

*A*rnold admired her little hand in his, her delicate fingers strained by the duties to her family. "I might not suit you," he said.

She laughed and hopped off the bed, where they'd been sitting side-by-side now.

"Why are you laughing at me?" He was irked. This girl never ceased to irritate and surprise.

"Can you see yourself?" She stepped back pointing at his head, his chest and looking down.

He stayed seated even though his gentlemanly inclinations were to rise when a lady rose. The stretching of his breeches was most unbecoming, and he had to maintain the last shred of dignity the fabric was hiding. He couldn't lay his attraction to her bare.

"I'm sure I don't know what you mean." Arnold felt tightness in his crotch and embarrassment in his chest. Perhaps he should grab a pillow and hug it over his lap. No, that would be too obvious.

She turned, her long honey hair trailing after her. "Let me see. You're the picture of a gentleman. A successful jeweler, you have impeccable workmanship and take pride in your work. You clearly make the world a better place." She enumerated his traits on her fingers as if counting his faults. "Your family is … is … Nice. Beyond measure! They're … how do I say it… Magnificent!" She slouched. "And you, you … You're…. You're capable, handy, brilliant … Your smile … and your hair, and your eyes, and your chest, and your shoulders … I think all of you is absolutely perfect."

"You think?" He cut her off, unable to curb a smile. But he couldn't get up, she'd see his glorious cock sticking out at a right angle from his body.

"Well, I don't know for sure but I imagine." She seemed miserable and Arnold enjoyed himself tremendously.

"You do?" He nudged her on.

"Of course, I do! Even if you call me a girl, I'm actually quite grown up and capable of the thoughts of a woman." She put her arms on her hips.

Surely, she was unaware that her gesture lifted the hem of the gown enough for him to see her knees. Her legs were gorgeous, slender, soft and … he grabbed the pillow after all. He leaned on it, trying to play down his amusement with an air of indignation.

"I'm a writer and look what you do to me!" Her rapprochement was earnest, but she was too cute for Arnold to care. "You're so handsome, I have no words!"

"If I understand correctly, you listed all my beneficial features and you're unsure whether I'd suit you as a husband." His heart was pounding, but it had to be said. He couldn't imagine himself as a husband but for this girl … oh dear.

"Er…" She wasn't sure how to respond.

He loved her discombobulated. It was adorable. "Thus, you have two choices. Me or spinsterhood?"

With a puff, more of a hmpf, she turned around. "I … It's not true. I could go to stay with my cousins in France and find a husband there and stay or bring one back to London. But either way, I'd lose my newspaper." She was resigned now.

"I'd never make you give it up," Arnold said simply.

She looked up at him. "You wouldn't?" Incredulity speared her tone.

"Why should I do such a cruel thing?"

She blinked in bewilderment.

"But it doesn't matter because you seem to have it all figured out. Except if I suit you," he added.

His heart was aching for her, but he wasn't ready to admit it to her.

Then her tears welled up and he had to stand. The pillow fell to the floor. He kissed her eyes. The tears tasted salty, and he loved every bit he got to taste of her.

"I … you wouldn't … you say I am a girl," she said, her eyes still closed in the aftermath of his kisses.

"I know you're untouched. Nobody has made you a woman before," Arnold said. "That's what makes you a girl."

"Oh." She opened her eyes now. "Would you want to?"

His heart hit the floor. How could he be so lucky as to

have this gorgeous girl allow him … No, he couldn't do it. He felt dirty. Suddenly, he wished he could wash not only his body but his memory of all the women in his past.

"Hannah, if I touch you thus"—his hands came to her upper arms, holding her gently as he would a precious jewel—"I'd have to marry you."

She waited.

"I won't force you to marry me, even though most girls of the ton would swoon at the thought."

She was speechless, her mouth opened but no words came out.

"You may not have noticed, but I cut an acceptable figure in coattails … some might even say that I'd be a handsome groom." He gave a wolfish grin.

"I've never thought about it."

"About a wedding?"

She nodded.

"I don't understand. Everyone has treated you like my bride."

"Yes, I know, it's true. But still…"

"I don't understand. You strike me as a person who thinks of everything."

She nodded. "Oh, I've thought about the marriage, not the wedding. I'm selfish, I'm sorry."

He had to process this for an instant. Most of his acquaintances were so absorbed by the glitz of a wedding that the resulting marriage faded into oblivion. And yet, most ton marriages were tragically loveless, dull, or even heartless. The marriage he'd been the closest to was Eve and Gustav's, and they were loving, kind, and supportive of each other. Their union had nourished Fave and Lizzie, and himself for nearly two decades. They set an example, although it was shrouded in secrecy from the ton, tucked safely away from the toxic gossips.

"You're telling me that you're unsure whether we'd suit in a marriage, and you find this selfish?" Arnold summarized.

She blushed. She was truly magnificent. The most intelligent and far-sighted person he'd ever met. He didn't just see her as a girl or a woman, he saw her as a scholar of life. She was smart in a practical way, not bookish.

"I am afraid to disturb the order in your life, Arnold."

"And I yours?"

They could say nothing else, for it was true. They'd uproot each other. Their worlds would be shaken into an emulsion, but the mix would never be homogenous. They were too different. At some point, oil and water repelled each other just like their worlds would. And they'd be left in limbo.

And yet, Arnold looked at her smart and dark lashes rimming the apples of her eyes as if they were pavé diamonds framing a precious center stone in a ring.

She seemed strong but her heart was made of butter vanilla. Arnold wanted nothing more than to take in its sweetness and get stuck in it forever.

"What are you thinking?" Hannah withdrew her head slightly.

He took her other hand, interlacing his fingers with hers. He brushed her cheek with his. Then he stared at her deeply. "Your eyes are like black opals."

She seemed puzzled.

"Black opals are the rarest black gems in the world. They only occur in Australia."

"I ... no, I didn't know that."

* * *

"YOUR EYES, if they were gems, would have the highest carat price."

"Why?" She wasn't sure whether to take this as a compliment.

"I've never seen such an iridescent, glittering pattern." He tilted his head and nudged her gently to raise her head to the window. "Depending on the angle of the light, your iris shows depths of gold flakes, swishes of blue and the edges glisten in turquoise."

He was close and she could feel his breath.

"There are specks of carmine and ... I'd say glitters of stars being born. They're only half as hard as diamonds, but their depth and intensity make them even more precious. Hannah, you're so precious. If only you could see what I see."

His gaze was so focused on her eyes that she didn't dare move. She felt a bit like that time when *Tate* took her and all the siblings to an eye exam and the doctor used a lens to find the optic nerve. But Arnold wasn't a physician, and he was seeing deeper. It wasn't just flesh and blood with him, he felt deeply, ardently. His spirit was fiery, and his mind was even more beautiful than his face.

Hannah's eyes fell to his mouth as he was speaking.

"Your eyes are phenomenal, Hannah. I know I should doubt whether we suit each other, but I don't."

She gasped at his declaration. Could he share her feelings?

He lowered his mouth onto hers and she closed her eyes, giving in to the sensation of their lips touching.

"I can never live up to being your equal. The decision is yours." He rested his forehead against hers. He'd laid his heart out to her, baring his insecurity.

Her fingers traced up to his head, and she placed a hand on either side of his face, looking into his eyes.

He stepped back slightly and unbuttoned her chemise. She allowed him, trance-like despite her better judgment. The silk pooled at her bare feet, and Arnold's eyes burned up her body.

And just like that, the girl was gone, and the woman emerged from a silk cocoon.

"You make me feel…"

"How do I make you feel, Hannah?"

"Scared."

He stood back and took his hands off her. "I'm scaring you?" He raked his hands through his hair, keeping his eye on her face, not trailing to her nudity.

"Yes, I'm scared, but I have the urge to show you everything. I have … I don't know what to call it, an emptiness and an ache in my stomach whenever I'm close to you."

"What kind of ache?"

"It's odd because it started when I first saw you and counted the pearls."

"Hmm…" Arnold said, stepping a bit closer, but still not touching her. "Tell me more."

"Well … I haven't told anyone. Maybe it's a sign of faintness. But I twitch when you … like right now, when you look at me like this." She frowned, unsure whether she was talking him out of marrying her if she was feeble and sickly.

He came closer, undeterred, and ... was he amused?

He was close now; she could touch the tip of his nose with her tongue if she dared. Why did she even think to measure distance in this way?

"Hannah, where do I make you twitch?" he rasped, barely audible. His hand reached for her center. "Here?"

She didn't just twitch, she shuddered at his intimate touch, but she allowed the pleasure to flood her body. He was right in front of her now, one hand there and the other reaching behind her head. He kissed her mouth but nothing more. And his hand was doing something that made her lose her footing. He held her and played her like a maestro an instrument. She gave up any lingering resistance, for she trusted he knew what to do. And yet, she longed for him to touch her more, to lay on her, but he didn't. His mouth was on hers and his hand...

She was in a daze, confused and absorbed in a dreamy trance of something that felt so right and so necessary, as if she'd taken a bite of a freshly baked challah dunked in milk on a cold day. Arnold caught her when she melted into an ocean of pleasure and carried her to the bed. He lay her down without a word, without breaking the kiss. Suddenly Hannah realized why she hadn't been embarrassed. She wasn't wicked either. She was curious! Arnold had lit a flame within her that only he seemed able to control. She was on a path of discovery that only he could illuminate. Ever since she'd touched his lips, every turn of events had led her to this moment. She felt as though she belonged right here, right now, in his arms. So, she allowed herself to discover the highs of passion. She let him control her until she flickered into bliss, brightly embracing the light he shone all over her body, from her scalp to her fingertips and the toes on her feet.

CHAPTER 29

*O*n Sunday morning, April truly wore its proverbial white hat. Hannah lay in her bed, blissfully satisfied and sore at the same time. It was a cathartic experience: disgrace, and pleasure combined with a heady concoction of Arnold's touch. She touched her lips against the soft pillow cover, licking her lips in memory of Arnold's tender but strong mouth on hers. She closed her eyes and dug her face into the pillow. She'd fallen. She hadn't just tasted the forbidden apple, she'd quintessentially felled the tree and burned it. And yet, a new world was sprouting in her mind, a world full of possibilities, full of Arnold.

"*Channi!*" After a brief knock on her door, Lenny stormed in.

Hannah sat up, trying to fix her tousled hair.

"Did you see? It snowed." Her little brother jumped onto her bed and started bouncing. The shock on the mattress threw Hannah into the air and she bumped all over the bed, noticing the soreness between her legs more acutely. Without Arnold, she felt hollow and dry. She didn't like that. Hannah hated girls whose every mood depended on a man.

She shook her head and got off the bed. "Look at all this snow!" She smiled at Lenny who stood by the window overlooking Green Park.

Somewhere in the hallway, she heard Eve screaming, "My flowers, my pretty, pretty flowers."

And in swept Rachel with Lizzie in tow.

Rachel froze as soon as she saw Hannah in a state of … whatever her state was called. "Well, you are glowing." Rachel tilted her head sideways and gave Hannah a darting glance.

Hannah blushed and rushed to the hairbrush on the little vanity table by the wall mirror.

"Did she give you permission?" Lizzie asked Lenny. They were quite the pair, two mischievous imps.

Hannah smiled. "Permission for what?"

"Ice skating!" Lenny beamed. He smiled a lot here. More than at home.

Hannah gave Rachel a questioning blink.

"Oh, I have no reservations," Rachel said. "He'll be in good hands. I've skated in Switzerland every winter."

"Fave and I will be there too, we'll watch him," Lizzie added.

"Come with us, pleeeeaaase." Lenny tugged at her nightgown.

Hannah looked down at him and shook her head.

"Don't be a coward, *Channi!*"

"A coward is full of precaution," Lizzie said.

"I'm not a coward," Hannah said. "I'll be careful."

"Yay!" Lenny leaped at her and hugged her tightly.

A pang of remorse shot through her, she'd shamed the family and this could have a ripple effect on him as the eldest son. She was brazen and independent but also a bit stupid. Or a lot. Had she given the milk without offering the cow for purchase? Rivkah would say so, but Hannah knew the act had not actually been done. She'd been raised *shomer negiah*, abiding by the Jewish laws of the *halakha*getting away on a technicality was not an option.

Pfft! She wasn't a cow for sale, and Arnold was irresistibly handsome. So be it if she enjoyed herself this once in her life … except she was already contemplating how to repeat last night's encounter.

"I promise I'll be careful," Lenny said into her belly as he gave her a hug.

"If you can't be good, be careful." Lizzie was on fire, a veritable encyclopedia of platitudes.

Hannah chuckled. "I've never skated. I don't have anything to wear." She looked helplessly at Rachel and Lizzie.

"You can borrow my skates, I have a few pairs," Lizzie said.

"I'll lend you my coat," Rachel added. "If there's one thing us Swiss Jews have on you Brits, it's warm winter clothes."

An hour later, Hannah, Rachel, Lizzie, Lenny Fave and —to Hannah's delight—Arnold went ice skating. The gentlemen donned fur hats and cashmere scarves. Arnold lent his arm to Hannah for the short walk to the frozen pond in St. James square. Through the cold, Hannah could not smell his tantalizing scent but she felt his bulking arms under the tight winter coat. She chastized herself for enjoying his strength so, but she could swoon at his feet when he made eye contact.

At the pond, quite a few skaters were already on the ice. Many more people gathered on the pond's snowy shore, variously donned in mink mufflers, or white shrugs with small black dots. A woman in a red coat glided by on the ice and lifted a leg into the air as she spiraled into a pirouette. Hannah's eyes widened.

"You seem a bit scared, dear." Rachel slid her arms under Hannah's elbow. "Relax, it's really quite easy once you find your balance."

"Why balance?" This was getting worse and worse.

"Because we're strapping these on." Lizzie handed her a pair of what looked like sword edges with leather straps. "Blades."

Hannah searched for Arnold, but he was bending down on one knee, fixing blades onto Lenny's boots. Fave was by his side, already standing on his skates. Hannah watched Arnold tighten the straps with a forceful pull.

"Is this too tight?" he asked Lenny.

"Tighter, tighter, let's go!" Lenny jumped onto his wobbly bladed boots, and Fave took his hand.

Lizzie rushed to them, "Wait for me! I don't want to miss it." The four darted off without as much as a glance back at Hannah and Rachel.

Rachel sat on a nearby bench and showed Hannah how to put the blades on. Lizzie had given her a pair of mutton-lined boots with a groove in the sole that fit the blade.

"Are you nervous?" Rachel asked when she reached her hand out to Hannah the moment they stepped onto the ice.

"Terrified," Hannah admitted. An understatement. "What if I fall?"

"Then you get up. Take my hand." Rachel pulled her slightly to help her glide. Hannah's legs were stiff. She managed to balance but not move. "Keep your knees slightly bent and push the whole edge of the blade off … like so…" Rachel let go of Hannah's hand and slithered elegantly across the ice.

Hannah watched Rachel slide away and felt her knees weaken. She was slipping, her footing unsteady, and swoop … Arnold caught her just in time. His sensual lemon rosemary and mystery scent had reached her before he did. She immediately felt safe enveloped in his embrace.

He smiled at her. Had he been behind her all this time? "I got you, love," he whispered as he put her back on the blades. She grasped his strong biceps, and he held his arms out to steady her. She was clearly out of her depth, but with Arnold, she'd learn to swim. She couldn't take her eyes off him. He moved his muscular legs gracefully along the ice, never letting go of her. Was this what it would be like? Would she have friends now and Arnold to catch her if she fell?

CHAPTER 30

*rnold looked around at his family, the other skaters, uncountable familiar faces from the ton. The rich and wealthy of London had gathered on the ice at St. James Park to enjoy one of the last winter activities before the spring. He'd never been one for a public display of their affection, but Hannah had already changed so much in his life in the past days, and this was no exception. Thus, he reached out one hand to receive hers, and placed his other hand on the small of her back. She faced forward, and he steadied her from behind. With a rhythmic swish-swosh, they scraped a four-lane trail onto the ice under their blades. Hannah was teetering at best and relied on Arnold to hold her. Having her trust gave him a heady feeling, as if her future was in his hands as much as his in hers. The moment felt greater than the maintenance of balance, it was about how they could connect their lives and complement each other.

Hannah leaned further toward him, her back still facing him. The air was crisp and fresh, the sky white with clouds. A few buds on the trees peeked out from under tufts of snow. And in his arms was the warmth and coziness of the girl he loved. In just a few days, he'd fallen in love with her and the realization made him woozy. He lowered his head and pulled Hannah closer, wrapping both his arms around her belly. She stiffened until her back touched his chest, then she relaxed into his embrace. Arnold knew this was a scandalous declaration of their betrothal, but he didn't care. He cherished the chance to hold his precious girl in his arms and be her stronghold on the ice.

She leaned her head slightly back toward his chest and closed her eyes. He was about to place a gentle kiss on her forehead when

"Arnold!" a familiar shriek cut through the beautiful morning. Allison Bustle-Smith, now Thompson. "What have we here?

He flinched and grasped Hannah more tightly. She assumed an upright position on his side, holding his left hand with her right. Arnold loathed Allison for interrupting their moment of intimacy, he couldn't get enough of them. At the same time, he didn't want to make a scene among prying ton eyes—the gossip would spread like poison in veins.

"Arnold Ehrlich, what a funny coincidence." Allison came to a halt, expertly pivoting on her skates, a little too close, invading their personal space. "By the looks of it, you'll be wed soon?"

Hannah gave her a cold stare from top to bottom—
when had she learned that? Arnold considered it a declaration of war among ton debutantes; Lizzie was accomplished at the stare-downs.

He pulled Hannah closer knowing Allison's sharp
tongue would threaten the bliss he'd only just found with
his girl. "If you'll excuse us, I believe my cousins are
waiting for—"

"Oh, but I'm certain a Rabbi's daughter will be a most
interesting diversion for the ton this season, getting
hitched to one of our most notorious rakes." She sounded
exactly like her evil dragon lady mother.

"Allison," Arnold said menacingly. She knew she
mustn't divulge their secret.

He hadn't figured out how to manage the ton, for he
couldn't hide his pious bride from them for long. But he
wasn't willing to renounce the chance of a lifetime. Love
with Hannah was unlike anything he'd imagined even in
his wildest dreams. And oh, were his dreams wild!

"So, you'll soon leave Marvin's bachelor lodgings and
find a house for your young family?" he asked, feigning
innocence. This was a low blow since his family had
evicted Allison and her mother from their house.
Deservedly, she was stuck with her new husband in a
small apartment far from her usual entourage of ton
witches. It wasn't really their house anyway, seeing how
Uncle Gustav had paid for it *and* both mortgages levied
upon the residence over the course of twenty years in
response to Allison's mother's ongoing blackmail.

Allison gave him one of her nefarious smiles. All her

teeth ended in a straight line; he was sure she'd ground them to powder in her clenching bitterness. She behaved more and more like her mother, with a frown line over her nose and eyebrows that were far too thin.

After Allison skated away with her hands tucked in a muff before her tummy, Hannah faced Arnold. "I'll never fit into your world, will I?" Hurt brimmed in her eyes.

"Don't say that." He tenderly tucked a stray strand of her hair behind her ear, feeling the heat inside her fluffy fur hat.

"But she's threatening you. I am not that naïve. I know she can hurt your business."

Hannah was clearly ignorant of the threats Allison truly wielded. If Allison betrayed their secret and the ton found out they were Jewish, they couldn't sustain their business. And if he didn't soon figure out a way to get supplies, there wouldn't be a business to protect. And then there was the competition. Uncle Gustav longed to win, and Cousin Fave had created the designs of a lifetime— masterpieces that would secure their place as the crown jewelers. And somehow, Arnold suspected, this could all depend on him.

A screech rang through the air. A child. *Lenny.*

* * *

"*She pushed me and ... ouch!*" Lenny sat on the ice, clutching his hand.

Hannah bent over him and nearly lost her footing. Arnold held her with one hand but let go to pick up

Lenny. He carried him to the bench on the snow-covered grass on the side of the pond. Rachel and Lizzie each offered Hannah a hand to bring her ashore and help her out of her skates. Fave darted away, and Hannah followed him through the corner of her eyes. He stopped Allison on the ice and threw his arms in the air. Hannah couldn't hear them.

She inspected Lenny's tear-stained face. "How did you fall? You were doing so well, *Lennikush!*" Hannah mumbled his Yiddish last name softly for fear they could be heard.

"Someone came and pushed me on the hip. I fell and then..." He held out his hand to show her a cut. It was superficial but right in the flesh. Blood dripped and stained the snow.

When Hannah saw the red stains, she knew Allison had pushed him and somehow managed to get him to cut his hand on the blade as he tumbled down. Hannah had been warned, but she'd ignored the signs. The ton was another world, a force to be reckoned with. The nobles were floating in the government, the people in charge of the country. She had no place here. No chance.

Suddenly she felt more out of place than ever. She wasn't in her own clothes, not in her own home.

Fave skated back to them, came elegantly to a stop, and hopped off the ice. He came to Lenny and bent down before him. "Are you alright, little one? Let me see..." He took Lenny's hand in his.

Arnold took off his scarf and offered it as a bandage.

"This is cashmere," Hannah exclaimed.

Arnold shrugged and took his blades off. "Time to go home," he said as he wrapped Lenny's hand in his scarf. Surely it would be ruined, but he didn't seem to flinch. He treated the elegant scarf as nothing but a bandage.

And Hannah agreed it was time to go home indeed.

CHAPTER 31

*H*annah seemed rather upset by the incident on the pond and had asked Arnold to take her home. She'd told him she needed to retrieve a few things before the roofers would come the next day, but he knew it was a ruse to get away from Allison. He'd seen Hannah's look when they'd brought Lenny back home. She was pained and seemed trapped. Not even Aunt Evie's hot chocolate could appease Hannah's melancholy.

Half an hour later, Arnold and Hannah got into his phaeton, and he drove to the synagogue. It was a slow ride, but they remained silent throughout. Hannah averted her gaze and seemed lost in thought, picking at her gloves, so Arnold stared out the window at the snow dusting along the London streets. The trees lining Pall Mall had green buds topped with snow. All the street lanterns were lit, and it was altogether a gloomy morning. The crocuses in front of the buildings were overstuffed with snow. Their delicate orange and purple petals spread too wide to recover. Next to them, the droopy little daffodils let their heads hang low under the weight of snow. It was late April and there were no tulips in sight. The flora mimicked what was in Arnold's heart—spring was struggling to emerge with so much at stake, the competition, his career, and his family's livelihood.

As the phaeton pulled toward the synagogue, a small crowd of onlookers caught Arnold's eye. A fireman waved the crows away, a few others carried axes and jackhammers. A tall ladder was leaning against the facade of the temple but the roof ... was gone.

"What happened?" Arnold asked the fire chief through the window. He wore a polished badge on his chest and a medal ribbon. Arnold had recognized him immediately as the man in charge.

"T'was the snow, milord. The old roof couldn't take the weight of it."

Hannah jumped out of the phaeton and ran toward the ruin.

A tall fireman clutched her arms but she screamed, "This is my home! I live here!"

Arnold leaped out of the carriage and rushed to her side. "Touch the lady again, and I'll show you what pain is!"

He didn't recognize himself, shouting at an official from the fire department. And yet, the man had showed the audacity to touch his Hannah. *His girl.* She stood before the fireman. Her chest rose and fell rapidly, and she let out a pained cry and scrunched, kneeling and hugging herself.

"T'was empty, if that's any consolation. There wasn't anyone inside. Found no bodies, my men."

She snorted and gulped air, but her cries damped into quiet grief.

Arnold put his hands under her arms and pulled her up. He wrapped himself around her, damn what the people on the street thought. They stood there like a couple and so be it. She needed him and there was nowhere else he'd rather stand than by her side.

"It wasn't empty," she said between quiet sobs.

"I know, it contained your life."

She looked at him, eyes red-rimmed and swollen, tears staining her red cheeks in the cold. Shivering, she held his gaze.

"Do you know if the main sanctuary...?" Arnold asked.

"All gone, milord," the fireman said.

"The Torah," Hannah cried.

"I'm going in. Wait in the carriage, Hannah."

* * *

Hannah promised to stay in Arnold's carriage, and the fire chief guarded the cabin door. Arnold borrowed a helmet from one of the firemen and traded his hat for an ax. Hannah watched him through the window, trembling. She felt empty and damaged, but that was nothing compared to the synagogue building. Shingles were sliding off the collapsed roof, crashing mutedly into the snow. No sound emerged—as if the demise of the cornerstone of the Jewish community had to make as little disturbance as possible. How symbolic that the fall of the

Great Synagogue waited for Hannah to leave the orthodox quarter to collapse.

She took a deep breath and felt the weight that the overburdened support columns of the fallen temple would understand if they had souls. Oh, but they did to her. The whole building had soul and character, as well as the memories of her childhood and her mother. Without it, she would face a new era. Hannah shivered and searched through the carriage window for Arnold. He'd come into her life and stirred it up, but he'd also given her hope.

Fabric from the sanctuary blew in the wind, attached to broken wooden beams. Arnold was somewhere in the ruin, out of sight. She held her breath. Suddenly, she realized his wellbeing mattered more to her than the building that had contained her entire life, her family's sanctuary.

Was it all her fault? She knew she wasn't the pillar holding up the roof, but in a way, she bore the weight of the community. It was a bad omen. She'd turned her back on her home and betrayed her community. She'd let go. And it all came crumbling down.

Where was Arnold? What was taking so long?

She heard a crack. The building shifted, and something made a loud thud. Firemen ran toward the ruin.

"He's still in there!" the fire chief yelled.

Hannah froze. She was a walking, talking mascot of bad fortune. First the synagogue and now … no, Arnold was a prince, brimming with health and masculine perfection. He was so beautiful. Hannah hoped that the immense material loss would not claim the life of her prince to make matters worse. Her eyes fixed on the devastating scene outside the window.

A piece of wood fell. On the side facade. A noise followed by more cracking. And then Hannah heard nothing, only the ringing in her inner ear. She would have closed her eyes if she had been able to look away but it was too terrifying. The long front wall with the arched doorways and heavy wooden frames folded inward like a paper doll house. If it had not been for the painful noise and cloud of dust that replaced the spot where the wall used to be an instant ago, Hannah would think this was a dream.

* * *

ARNOLD KNOCKED on the helmet he'd borrowed and thought it was rather flimsy. Nonetheless, he fastened the leather strap but did not bother to pull the buckle too tight. He'd be in and out of this ruin, there was not much to salvage. As he looked around, he could barely believe that he'd spent a night in this building. It seemed run down but he would have never expected such disaster to strike.

How could a synagogue collapse on itself? Wasn't it protected by all the goodness that people brought here? He'd seen the rows of seats and imagined dozens of pious Jews chanting ancient prayers in harmony of belief. What a magical place this had been, where people came together and freely shared the love for their tradition.

What was that?

He stood between a fallen stained-glass window and pieces of furniture, maybe one of the benches. A few pieces of fabric caught his eye, velvet covered in dust and gold embroidery. Then he saw the reflection of something metallic. He made his way over the fallen bricks and benches. The old tile floor had burst open from the weight of the crash.

Something moved and cracked but Arnold was too focused on avoiding the sharp shards of glass everywhere.

There it was. The Torah crown and the finials mounted on the Torah case or on the staves of the Torah scroll were jammed under the pieces of the cabinet. He tugged on the chain from which the breastplate that adorned the Torah hung and it moved. Almost. One more pull.

And then he heard a crack and felt the wind pushing toward him as if someone were closing a large book and he was nothing but an ant getting crushed inside. His hands came to his neck and he bent over, folding his head toward his stomach. Something heavy and blunt was falling and he dared not look up.

* * *

HANNAH RATTLED THE CARRIAGE DOOR.

"Let me out! I have to help him!"

The fire chief called out to the brigade, "Stay back!"

She tore the door open and just as she wanted to escape from the cabin, the firemen froze. A figure emerged from the cloud of dust.

And there he was, appearing from what used to be a door but was now open to the skies. He held something in his arms.

As Arnold came closer, she saw him clutching the

Torah, the sacred Jewish scroll. It was wrapped in the *paroketh*, the Torah arc curtain. The dark brown velvet and extensive appliqués embroidered with silk and metallic threads were unmistakable.

His helmet was gone. He came closer, holding the ancient scrolls as if carrying them into the future. When he was close enough, he stepped into the carriage and Hannah's mind went blank with fear.

"You're bleeding." She reached out to touch his forehead but didn't dare. She didn't even own as much as a tissue anymore to clean his wound. It didn't run deep, but there was blood, nonetheless. It had to be cleaned.

He sat down and attempted to hand the Torah to her.

She jerked away. "I can't."

"Can't what?"

"Touch the Torah. I'm *tumed*, ritually impure."

Arnold snorted. "Nothing in this world is purer and more perfect than you." He placed the Torah on her lap.

She sucked in the air, frozen by the gravity of the moment. The scrolls contained the Old Testament, the pillars of Judaism, the law of her upbringing. She'd never seen a woman touch the precious scrolls, much less hold them on her lap. Heat flowed through her body, the greatness of tradition radiated from the package in her lap and warm love for it filled her as if she were holding her baby sister Ruthie.

Arnold retrieved a white cloth with white lace from his coat and wiped his wound.

"Let me." Hannah set the Torah carefully on her seat and took the handkerchief. She moved to the small bit of the bench on Arnold's side that his strong body didn't occupy. After a brief hesitation, she placed a small amount of her saliva on the handkerchief and tapped it on his wound.

Arnold flinched, clenching his teeth.

"I'm sorry," she said. Her other hand impulsively grabbed his cheek to steady him—muscle memory, for she'd cleaned her siblings' wounds uncountable times.

Arnold's eyes darted to hers and burned into her soul. The air grew thick and heavy. Arnold tapped on the roof of the cabin and the coachman whistled. The horse stomped into the dirty downtown snow.

The carriage slipped on the slush and Hannah tumbled forward.

Arnold caught her with one arm and the Torah with the other.

"We wouldn't want that to fall, could you imagine the—"

"Catastrophe," Hannah said, only half-joking, considering the synagogue lay in ruins behind them.

Arnold threw his head back and roared with laughter. His mouth opened wide, showing snow-white teeth in pink gums, arranged in a perfect row, his molars solid and big, slightly pointier than the front. For a split second, Hannah saw straight down to his pink throat. He was masculine perfection. If this is anything like what Eve was faced with when she fell from Eden's graces, then Hannah also wanted to bite the dust. He was delicious. Her appetite was overpowering. The sudden movement of the carriage had dislodged the knot within her.

For the first time, Hannah was glad to be a girl—and to have her hands on this boy.

* * *

HE SUDDENLY FELT her hand on his neck. She grabbed and pulled his head up to her … Then her tongue was in his mouth. All of it. Oh, this girl…

Arnold returned the kiss, aflame with unprecedented passion. Their mouths devoured one another but their hunger spiraled to starvation. He felt as if he was high in the mountains and the air grew thin, he could only breathe her freshness, like pure oxygen. The restraint he'd shown in her room last night was gone, burned up somewhere between the wall that almost fell on him and her touch. His hands found her back, then her bottom, and he pulled her onto his lap. She mewled and broke the kiss for a breath. He let his mouth trail down her jaw, to her neck. She dropped her head to the other side, giving him access. Giving him permission. He had taught her how to kiss.

His body knew what to do, but it all felt new in his mind. He was an explorer of unfamiliar territory for he'd never seen such beauty, felt such supple firmness … her breast was in one of his hands and her taut bottom in the other. He held her tightly, but she still seemed too far away. He needed more. All of her. His breath caught in his throat. He wanted her so badly. She couldn't possibly know what he wanted, and he was so desperate to show her.

"Hannah…" Her name was a benediction on his lips. She was wild. Her enthusiasm made up for her clumsy attempts to pull him closer, but she was innocent, clueless as to what he could give her.

He picked her up by her bottom and lay her on the bench.

"Hannah, I cannot take you in the carriage," Arnold said, unconvinced himself. "I won't."

"I … I…" she rasped, crazed, arching her back to close the space between them.

Her mouth was reaching for his. His erection twitched, ready to burst out of his body and explode in hers. They heated the air around them. He pushed himself slightly away from her petite frame. Elevated by passion, like two thunderclouds charged to a breakpoint, bound to spark a flash of lightning.

And then the carriage came to a halt. He was home. If only he could rein in his energy and halt like the horses. Instead, he wrapped his hands around her head and took her mouth for one more searing kiss, sucking her beauty up like the air before a deep-water dive. Any second spent detached from her would resemble holding his breath.

The moment came to an end, and Arnold stepped out of the carriage. Reality assaulted his senses, his trance ousted by the busy goings-on of the street. He saw her blinking through the carriage door. She reached out, and he lifted her down, holding her closely and certainly longer than was proper. But she fit into his arms like a cup on its saucer. She belonged there. He brought her home, to his home. And he hoped it would become hers, too.

CHAPTER 32

⌘

*A*s soon as Arnold and Hannah came through the front door, James, the butler, showed them to Gustav's study. Arnold had known James since he was a little boy, and the butler had a special talent to usher people to where they needed to be. He knew about everything in the Pearler household.

"Could you bring this to my uncle, I'll be there soon, I need to change—" Arnold wanted to hand him the Torah.

"I'm afraid you may wish to proceed to the study immediately." James gave him a knowing nod.

Arnold complied, with Hannah huddled quietly behind him, holding his hand. He carried the Torah in the other arm. So, everyone saw them holding hands when they appeared at Gustav's study—a large group that took Arnold by surprise. Uncle Gustav and Pavel were leaning over Gustav's mahogany desk studying Fave's drawings. Fave stood by the window; his arms crossed. Rachel, Lizzie, and Aunt Evie were seated around a side table

193

covered in more of Fave's drawings. They were in what seemed a heated discussion, but when they saw him with Hannah, clutching the Torah, they fell silent.

Arnold felt all their eyes on his hand, which was still interlaced with Hannah's. His clothes were dirty from the ruin, and he was getting a once-over from everyone who mattered in his life. Instinctively, he tightened his grasp of Hannah's hand.

"What's this?" To Arnold's relief, Fave broke the silence.

Hannah bowed to the group, and Lizzie rushed to her side, pulling her along to warm her with a cup of Rachel's jasmine tea. Its characteristic scent filled his uncle's study, a flowery lightness that clashed with the tense atmosphere.

Pavel closed the door and addressed Arnold. "You and Hannah?"

Uncle Gustav gave Arnold a puzzled look and put his hand on his shoulder. Arnold looked into his uncle's eyes, then he glanced over to Hannah, who stood beside Lizzie, watching him, waiting for his answer. He hoped for a signal from her, but none came, so he dropped his gaze and nodded, placing the Torah on a nearby chair.

Another moment of silence wobbled in the room like a planet out of its orbit. Then, Aunt Eve rose from her seat and rushed to Arnold, embracing him in a tight motherly hug. At first, he hesitated, dirty from his Torah-saving mission in the snow and dirt. But then, he returned the hug and put his cheek on her shoulder. It had all been a bit much, a wall nearly collapsing on him, and then there was the matter with the girl who had cracked his heart open like a walnut shell over the past few days. The motherly hug was a welcome gift of love.

Love. It really all came down to that. And to the price he'd have pay for it.

Aunt Evie broke the embrace and brushed his hair from his forehead, focusing on the bloody bruise on his forehead. *"Vus iz geshen?"* What happened?

Arnold and Hannah told them everything. From the collapse of the roof to the information the admiral had given Arnold and Fave at White's. They filled Hannah in on the details of the competition, and Fave picked out the designs they'd chosen for the crown jewels. He handed the sheets to Arnold, but Arnold's head wasn't in business.

"What will happen to Hannah's family when they return?" he asked Uncle Gustav, realizing that a single father would return with a horde of children to no home.

"Zol ich azoy vissen fun tsores!" I haven't got the faintest idea, Uncle Gustav said, "But we'll find a solution together."

"Ziskeit." Sweet thing. Pavel waved Hannah over. *"Red' ofn, tachles afn tish."* Spill the beans.

She approached, her head low and her gaze on the floor.

Lizzie came up behind her. Then Rachel on her other side. Arnold felt a pang of happiness that Hannah had found friends in his little cousin and new sister-in-law. The three would be a force to be reckoned with. Hannah wrung her hands, her eyes searching for Arnold.

"Ver volt dos geglaibt?" Who would have believed it? Pavel gently touched Hannah's arm and she lifted her gaze. Her eyes darted to Arnold, then back to Pavel.

Arnold thought he saw a tear on the rim of her eye, but she blinked it away.

"*Ir gefelt mir zaier,*" You please me greatly. Pavel broke the tension between them.

"*Azoy?*" Really? Hannah gasped.

"*Dayn mame volt geven freylekh aykh tsu zen farlibt,*" Pavel added. Your mother would be happy to see you in love.

Uncle Gustav stepped up to Arnold and said, "*Zolst leben un zein gezunt!*" You should live and be well!

Arnold's chest swelled with hope, pride, and fear for what the future would hold.

Lizzie and Rachel gave Hannah a group hug, and Fave patted Arnold on the shoulder to congratulate him. Arnold wasn't sure why being in love was a matter for celebration; he was numb. It had all happened too fast, and nothing had been resolved.

"What do we do about the gems?" Arnold asked.

"We don't have remotely enough," Fave replied.

"And now you just want to give up?" Arnold stomped angrily around the room. "I'm not giving up! We need to earn our place!"

"If we haven't earned it by now, maybe it's time to retreat," Uncle Gustav said. "Especially if the secret comes out with your *chasseneh*"—wedding—"to the Rabbi's daughter. He appeared old and frail, less energetic than even Pavel, who was his elder by several decades.

"I'm not giving up! It's a merit-based competition. We're the best in town and need to show the ton that we belong. I am so sick of their rules and conventions and unspoken—"

"I agree! Let's give it all," Fave said.

"There's no all, boys. Even if Pavel and I pool all our resources, we don't have the materials to make three sets of jewels," Gustav said.

Pavel sighed. "I can't get any new shipments."

"Arnold, I'll do as you said. Consider my visit here perfectly chaperoned. The ton never needs to know that I—"

"That you what, Hannah?" Arnold snapped.

She jerked back.

"Stop!" Rachel leapt toward Arnold. "I'll make arrangements with my friends in Bordeaux. You and Hannah will go on a honeymoon in France and when you come back, we'll present your new wife. No questions asked." Rachel crossed her arms, pleased with her idea.

"The ton won't bite," Aunt Eve said. "That's what we're doing tonight."

"Tonight?" Uncle Gustav growled. "About one hundred and fifty of the ton's worst will be here"—he checked the wall clock, it was almost noon—"In about eight hours!"

Arnold looked at Fave in alarm and raked his hands through his air. The wound on his forehead was still raw and sore. "I'm so sorry! It's your night to present Rachel, and I'm making a mess of it."

"Thank you, Rachel," Hannah said solemnly, "but I have to care for my siblings. I couldn't possibly go to Bordeaux."

"But you deserve a chance at love!" Lizzie cried before Eve gave her a chastising stare.

"Please, don't worry about me. I'll be gone as soon as my father returns," Hannah said.

Arnold couldn't decide what he was more irritated with—her readiness to give up on him at the first obstacle or that Uncle Gustav and Pavel were ready to withdraw from the competition. Suddenly, it wasn't merely about proving his worth to the Pearlers, it was about saving their business and his future with Hannah.

"What if we sell all we have left tonight and show the ton how beautiful the pieces are?" Lizzie asked.

"How is that different from what we have been doing since"—Gustav waved—"always?"

"We have no other choice," Fave said. "We need to do something we've never done before!"

Gustav seemed alarmed. Eve sat down and steadied herself holding on to Lizzie's arm.

And Lizzie clapped her hands together in glee. "I love a good putsch!"

"We'll infiltrate the ton," Fave announced.

CHAPTER 33

*H*annah withdrew to her room after the family discussion and spent the morning lying awake, thinking about her dilemma. What a mess. In only four days, she'd brought shame on her family, given her heart to a man whose life had no room for her, and their home had collapsed. Her world was crashing down on her in a way that she could barely understand.

She'd be a fallen girl in the community if she didn't comply with her father's request to marry Arnold. But she'd be fallen in her own self-respect if she threw herself into his arms too easily. And if she truly loved him, she should get out of his life as quickly as possible—or she'd jeopardize his jewelry competition.

Someone knocked on her door. Then again. She jumped off the canopy bed and pulled her shawls over her shoulders. It was already afternoon.

"Hannah?"

Was that Lizzie's voice?

"Maybe she's sleeping."

Rachel.

"Knock again, oh—"

Hannah opened the door, and the two young women toppled into her room. Well, it was their room more than hers, but she was the guest occupying this lavish gem of a room. She'd admired the beautiful layers of the dusty-mauve curtains while she'd lain on the bed mulling over her sorrows. The shades of purple shimmered in the gold and orange of the afternoon sun that came through the windows. It was the loveliest room she'd ever seen, and she felt undeserving of it.

"Oh good, you're awake." Lizzie swept into the room holding two large linen bags. Did she hide a body in there?

"You should tell her why we're here," Rachel said with a mischievous smile to Hannah that flashed her perfect teeth.

"Did you kill whoever's in this bag?" Hannah pointed at the biggest one as Lizzie laid it on her bad. "Oh, pardon me, I was just..." Hannah started pulling the sheets straight to make her bed when she spotted layers of lacy ruffles peeking out from the linen bag. Her heart sank.

"I'm afraid, I... er ... can't repay you for the hospitality with ... I—"

"Quit that, Hannah," Lizzie said.

Rachel came closer and plowed her fingers through Hannah's hair, twisting it behind her neck. "You have a ball to attend this evening. We're here to help you ready yourself."

Hannah eyed her incredulously. Were the ruffles for her? She'd never had any ruffles on her frocks, and she wasn't sure she wanted any. It all seemed a bit like baby Ruthie's frilly dresses for Shabbat services.

"Now, my dear," Lizzie said, "Arnold told me about the misfortune of the leaky roof. I'm certain your evening gowns are ... shall we say... too wet to dry in time for the ball?"

Oh no, she'd become their charity case. "I can't possibly accept—"

"Our friendship?" Lizzie asked.

"My mother never let us, I mean, my sisters and I ... she said, 'Beauty is the sister of idleness and the mother of luxury.'"

"Hah, that's rich." Lizzie clasped her hands. "A new one for my proverb collection!"

"Hannah," Rachel said, "I know exactly how you feel. It's overwhelming to be thrust into a ball of the ton, I know firsthand it's not a fairy tale affair." Her low and beautiful voice was precocious and dignified. Hannah liked Rachel, even though she seemed much wiser than her age.

"You're dressing for battle, it's plain and simple." Lizzie clapped her hands together, eager to begin whatever she was about to do. "You'd never go to war without armor. And you don't go to a ton ball without a dazzling gown."

"Let us provide some armor, dear," Rachel added as she took Hannah and positioned her before the tall mirror in the corner of her room. "Look at you, you're beautiful," Rachel said.

"You need refinement"—Lizzie blinked at Hannah—"but we'll get there."

"By tonight?" Hannah asked like a scruffy mole

peeking out from a hill at the first rays of spring's sun. She decided to allow them to transform her appearance, for she felt quite transformed already since Arnold had awoken her with his kisses. She longed to change on the outside as much as she felt different on the inside. Although surely, she couldn't be overhauled and readied to sparkle beside the two princesses fussing over her. "I think I'll read." Hannah resigned herself to her comfort zone. "Arnold gave me a book, and I'd like to study it."

"What book?" Rachel asked, her eyes alight.

Lizzie put her hand in the air, signaling halt. She rang the bell on the side of the door twice, paused, then again. What was she signaling?

"Mother already said you're our guest this evening. No buts." Lizzie stepped over to Hannah and took one hand, then the other. She inspected her nails, her skin, her hair.

"Lizzie, I am certain you have the best of intentions, but I am not like you, I'm not…"

"I'm afraid you're right, Hannah." Lizzie sounded rather grim now. She nodded at Rachel, and said, "I see you're reading Adam Smith, a smart man. But he'll wait for you till tomorrow. Today, you're going to a ball." She clapped as she twirled in her blush dress.

"You're far more beautiful than you know, and you'll be breathtaking when we're through with you." Lizzie said with an air of finality. "I'm from a family of jewelers, I know when I see a precious sparkle. And you, my dear, are a gem rough…"

Lizzie tilted her chin toward her index finger and blinked. Then she snapped her fingers and rang another bell. Hannah was not sure what the many bell functions were but, within minutes, two lady's maids came in.

"This is Emilia," Rachel said, "my lady's maid."

"And this is Connie, mine," Lizzie said.

Both young women bowed to Hannah. Nobody had ever done that before, and she turned crimson. She'd never had servants fuss over her.

"You do the hair, you the nails." Lizzie signaled to Connie first, then to Emilia.

CHAPTER 34

An hour later, Hannah had taken a hot bath in rose water. Her hair had been wrapped in egg yolks and washed with chamomile tea. Connie swore it did wonders for the shine and softness. Now, Hannah stood in a towel on a stool with Connie circling her with a narrow-toothed comb and sharp skinny scissors. She was combing Hannah's hair in every direction, snipping away. Hannah had flinched the first few times she saw her hair fall to the ground, but she felt increasingly liberated and transformed as Connie worked.

"May I speak freely?" Connie asked.

"I think every woman should," Hannah said.

Connie laughed. "Your hair will look longer when the ends are trimmed."

"That sounds illogical. You cut hair to make it appear longer?"

"Oh yes, the hair frames the face and flows better." She

reached her hand to Hannah and brought her to the large mirror in the bedroom.

Hannah nearly dropped her towel.

Connie handed her a brush with a silver rose carved into its back. Hannah took the brush to her hair and marveled at the silkiness. She had no idea her hair could be so smooth. It poured around her like dark honey and clung to her shoulders. "You did that?"

"No, this is you. I'm just peeling you like a fresh apple, you have the beauty in your flesh."

Hannah's mother had called her an egg. Maybe she wasn't only hatching and stuck in the nest. Maybe she could roll off into the world like an apple?

Without knocking, Lizzie stepped in and strutted over to Hannah. "You're beautiful, Hannah. You just don't know how to flaunt it." She took the brush and pulled her hair together, twisted it and piled it on top of her head.

"I ... er ... was raised to be efficient." Hannah couldn't, however, take her eyes off her image in the mirror.

"Beauty, unaccompanied by virtue, is a flower without perfume," Lizzie said.

Rachel returned and handed a smaller brush with stiff bristles to Emilia. "You have cultivated your virtues," she said to Hannah, "and now you get to cultivate your beauty."

Rachel nodded and Emilia brought the chair and a little table over to Hannah. She sat across from her and spread a dishcloth over the table. Then she retrieved a bowl from Connie and guided Hannah's hand into it.

"Ouch!" Hannah pulled her hand back, but Emilia held

it in what Hannah recognized as hot wax. "Why are you burning me?"

"We're not burning you. She's sealing your nails and cuticles," Lizzie said, her back to Hannah. She unwrapped the pile of cloth-covered frills. Evening gowns.

"Tonight, you'll meet many new people. And should you choose to, shall we say, remain on my cousin's arm, you need to make a good first impression. Beauty is a good letter of introduction." Lizzie Held up a blue dress, no it started out blue at the bodice and paled to white at the hem. Several layers of sheer fabric were cinched at the top but formed a huge pile at the bottom. Intricate embroideries adorned the neckline.

Hannah marvelled at the enormous amount of fabric and the delicate layers. "I'm afraid I'd tear it," she whispered.

"Oh, sweet dear," Lizzie said, "it doesn't matter if you only wear it once."

"W-why only once?" Hannah already felt the loss of what she hadn't fully taken possession of.

Lizzie shot Rachel a glance.

"Let me see." Rachel circled Hannah, patting her chin thoughtfully with her index finger. "Either you won't come to another ball, so you'll have no use for this dress again, or—"

"You'll stay with us and have a new dress for every ball." Lizzie said.

Hannah took a sharp breath.

"There, my lady." Emilia removed Hannah's hands from the hot bowl and started to file her nails, push her cuticles, and polish her tips with the hard bristled brush.

When Emilia had finished fussing over Hannah's hands, Hannah could barely recognize them. If they hadn't been attached to the ends of her arms, she wouldn't identify these long slender fingers and grown-up lady-like nails as hers. Gone were the cracks at her fingertips, the white flaky skin around her nails. Her knuckles blended evenly in color into the rest, the redness from the heavy house-work had vanished.

"H-how did you get my nails so shiny?" Hannah asked Emilia.

"I brushed them and buffed them a bit. But not to worry, milady, they're sealed with the wax."

"I'm not worried, I'm... I'm..."

"Glad you approve, my dear. On we go." Lizzie laid out the gown on Hannah's bed and hung some others over the armoire's open doors while Hannah got a pedicure.

Connie plucked her eyebrows and wrapped her hair around tiny rolls of fabric while Lizzie held several ribbons against Hannah's hair, seemingly deciding which complimented her complexion.

When the four women had finished fussing over her, Hannah looked terrifying—dozens of white pieces of linen sticking out from her head like a cauliflower. But she was told to sit still for an hour so her hair could dry into curls. Rachel promised that someone would return to help her into the gowns in the evening.

At about three in the afternoon, Emilia brought Hannah a day dress and a robe with a cloak. The tiny white bits had come out of her hair and Connie had set her hair in a thin mesh that she called a hair net to keep the spring in the curls, whatever that meant.

"Lady Pearler is expecting you for tea, we shall help Lady Rachel and Lady Elizabeth ready themselves now," Connie said before she left Hannah to admire herself in the mirror.

A soft and delicious version of herself had come to life. She felt wistful at the idea that it wouldn't last and that it was only because Arnold was so hospitable. None of this belonged to her. She didn't belong. Oh, but she enjoyed it. And for once in her life, she wanted to feel young and light, like Lizzie and Rachel. She wasn't a mother of seven now. She just wanted to be Hannah, one-and-twenty. And she longed for Arnold to see her like this.

CHAPTER 35

⚮

When Hannah walked into the lady's drawing-room, Eve Pearler, Arnold's aunt, was staring at the door, perhaps lost in thought. Eve sat on an embroidered high-back chair that had nailheads aligned to hold the tufted cushions in place. It seemed like a throne. A cup of tea had been poured and steam coiled into the air. Hannah felt herself to be a puff of steam, transient and pale in comparison to this woman of substance. Although she looked transformed, she was still self-conscious—and confused about her affection for Arnold and the wedding that everyone else assumed would happen but her. Maybe Hannah would soon return home, leaving behind nothing more than her fingerprint on the nailheads and an imprint on the cushions.

"Darling girl, come sit with me," Eve said and pointed her open palm to the empty chair and the full cup at a right angle from her. The precision of the seating arrangement wasn't lost on Hannah; she'd spent her entire life moving chairs to ensure her siblings could sit exactly where they'd wanted, which was usually as far away from another sibling who the first one had been fighting with.

Hannah sat.

"I'm afraid we don't serve this tea with milk and sugar," Eve said.

Hannah brought the fragrant cup to her mouth and took a deep sip. Exhausted from the probing, rubbing, trimming, and filing of her hair and nails, she welcomed the hot beverage. "It smells marvelous. I've had the pleasure of tasting it a few times during my visit. Thank you so much for hosting Lenny and me. We're most grateful for your hospitality."

Eve paid no attention. She seemed to have a precise agenda for this summons and Hannah swallowed uncomfortably.

"It's jasmine tea. My new daughter-in-law, Rachel, introduced us to it. I refuse to return to black tea now. Do you know that I'm introducing her to the ton at this evening's ball?" Eve took a sip and closed her eyes, apparently relishing the aroma of the flowery concoction.

Her question begged no answer. The matter had been discussed in Pavel's presence earlier. Hannah saw Eve taking her tea like a queen and sipping dignified from her cup. A pleasantly bitter aroma unfolded in her mouth, the warm liquid caressing her senses. After she swallowed, the essential oils of the jasmine lingered in her mouth, sending the most titillating scent to her nose. She closed her eyes for a moment to savor it—a bouquet for the senses, not merely tea.

"I'm glad you like it," Eve said. She didn't wait for

Hannah to set her cup down, but retrieved a piece of paper and handed it to Hannah. "This arrived for you today."

The thin envelope was folded in the middle. Hannah broke the seal immediately. *Tate's* handwriting. Hannah read it eagerly.

MAIDALE,

I am afraid I am needed here for another fortnight. Joshua was born at four this morning, the brit milah is set for eight days from now. But the baby has not had anything to drink yet, he needs to learn how to suckle. We shall not return until we know the baby is safely gaining weight.

HANNAH'S EYES darted to Eve's attentive stare. "My sister had a baby boy, but they must remain in Birmingham for another week." Hannah handed her the letter and Eve skimmed it.

"As I had hoped," Eve said as she set the letter on the table and folded her hands in her lap. "Not that the baby isn't eating, for that I'm sorry, but I'm glad you can remain with us."

Hannah bit her cheek nervously.

"My darling girl, you've led a deprived life. You're like a candle in a glass jar, with wind hustling about to blow you out. A shame, a true shame." Eve took her cup with the saucer as if to take a sip but then her other hand lifted Hannah's chin with a curled index finger.

"I don't understand," Hannah said in a low voice.

"Oh, but you do, my dear." Eve gave her a warm smile. "Arnold has ... how can I put it ... discovered you."

Eve got up and walked to a small secretary desk, opened the drawer and returned to Hannah with a pile of her newspapers.

"Lizzie has been reading your column for as long as I can remember. Your writing is cunning, sincere, and ... you're an intelligent young lady, Hannah. I'd be honored to take you under my wing and sponsor you for a season if the circumstances were different."

"I don't understand the circumstances. I'm not a debutante."

"Of course not. But you may find yourself with a husband by the end of the season regardless."

Hannah felt her eyes wide, unable to blink. Had Arnold told his family about her father's decree to marry them?

"Hannah dear, my nephew, Arnold, is not how you think. He's earned himself a certain reputation, but his mind and his heart were never aligned until now. I saw it in his eyes at *Shabbes* dinner and again this morning. You've sparked a flame within him."

Hannah remembered how Arnold had set her aflame with his sultry eyes and soft kisses, but she hoped her demeanor wouldn't betray her thoughts.

"Yes, I think I've caught his eye somehow..." Hannah said modestly, considering honesty was the only way forward with the matriarch.

"I think you caught more than his eye; I know what he's like when a girl catches his eye." Eve paused and gave Hannah a significant look.

Hannah focused her gaze on her hands. She'd realized what a wonderful miracle the lady's maids had performed on her, but now she missed the chance to pick at her cuticles.

"Hannah, darling, you've caught his heart."

Hannah's heart somersaulted and flopped to her knees. She felt frozen to the chair, her arms heavy with the real-ization—the hope—that Eve's words could be true. Considering Eve's tone, it seemed a matter of great importance to be the object of the golden prince Arnold's affection. Even though she was only his aunt, Eve was protective of him like a mother. That was something Hannah understood well, for she was like a mother to her siblings and would never do anything to betray their trust or luck. Oh, how she missed them all, especially little Ruthie. It had been three odd nights without Ruthie's crib by her bed—without the steady attention she was used to paying to the baby. Maybe Ruthie could distract her from Arnold once she returned home. In her mind, the betrothal was absurd, like an impossible dream.

Hannah was thoroughly uncomfortable and felt like an imposter. Plus, she didn't recognize her hands now she considered the matter again. They didn't look like her reliable hands, they were the hands of a grown-up lady, with clean white tips and brilliantly smooth nails and an uncertain future. Her rough hands kept her steady. She knew how every day unfolded back home, but that was no longer … Hannah felt like a hermit crab in the wrong shell.

Eve placed her hand on Hannah's lower arm. "I see that Arnold held out for a truly special girl." She pursed her lips and then made eye contact with Hannah. "I'd like to smooth the path for you to find happiness together."

"You would?" Hannah's eyes grew wide. "You mean, you approve?"

Eve smiled warmly and said something else, too, but Hannah could only hear her doubts and chastised herself for her affection for Arnold, the Jewish prince. Was he still unattainable for her? She was unable to process this. Were they cleaning her up to ensure she was suited for Arnold, prince charming on a white horse? No. Her Jewish prince in a white castle searching for ... what exactly could he be missing that *she* could give him?

Hannah wanted to excuse herself and crawl into bed.

But it wasn't her bed, this was Arnold's bed, it belonged to his family. Everything did, he was so rich, he could probably buy England if he didn't already own it. And she was nothing but the Rabbi's daughter. Yes, she had her siblings, the circular, the community... and was that enough? She shouldn't be greedy; Arnold was Jewish royalty.

And then it happened. Like a bubble that burst, Hannah realized that she wanted to be his princess.

CHAPTER 36

$\mathcal{H}$annah noticed Arnold poke his head through the door, and it only took Eve a second to realize he was sneaking around outside the drawing-room.

"Arnold, dear, sit down here. How good of you to join us," Eve said.

Hannah was still flushed, and her fingers had turned white from how tightly she'd interlaced them.

Arnold gave his aunt a peck on the cheek and stood in front of Hannah, seemingly unsure how to greet her. Hannah felt herself break into an uncomfortable sweat. Luckily, the moment was broken by James, the butler, who knocked on the door to the drawing-room.

"Mrs. Allison Thompson," the butler announced.

The young blonde shoved the butler aside and entered with an attitude of grandeur. "I don't need an introduction. Ah, Evie dear..."

Eve's eyes tightened. Arnold had told Hannah he was

the only one who called her Evie.

The elegant hostess gave Hannah a look of horror and then blinked. As soon as she opened her eyes, her face was placid, almost serenely friendly. How did she switch mien so quickly?

"Allison, dear, you are radiant this afternoon." Eve stood and held out her arms, taking the woman's hands, holding her at a distance. She was good. Like a siren of etiquette and poise. Hannah watched in awe.

The young woman wore a green dress the color of Ruthie's poop when she ate spinach. It reminded Hannah more of curtains than a gown, cut to flatter her plunging neckline as if she tried to distract from the essence of evil underneath. She had a shearling hat, but her curly hair peeked out, so stiff they must have been dipped in wax. All in all, Hannah thought the woman looked like a swamp snake.

"Would you care for a cup of tea?" Eve asked graciously.

The woman's eyes fell to the tray of biscuits, and she pulled a face of distaste. "No, thank you."

If Hannah didn't know any better, she'd think that the woman convulsed at the sight of food—a sign of pregnancy.

"Let me introduce you. Allison Thompson, née Bustle-Smith, this is our guest, Ms. Hannah Solomon." Eve resumed her seat on the high-backed chair, like a queen giving an audience.

"Solomon, you said?"

Eve tensed at Allison's question. Odd.

"How long have you been Mrs. Thompson?" Hannah

tried to be polite.

"A week," Allison gave a snappish retort.

Oh my, she was most certainly at least two months along if her condition had already begun to give her nausea. Hannah knew all too well from her mother's many pregnancies. She couldn't only pick the signs; she could also pinpoint the progression.

"I'm only here to pick up my invitation," Allison said.

"Which invitation?" Eve asked as she brought her teacup to her mouth. Hannah could have sworn she was smiling secretly behind the cup.

"For tonight's festivities, Evie. Surely you were holding it until I returned from my honeymoon."

"And how was your honeymoon, dear?" Eve set her teacup back on the saucer ever so controlled. She wouldn't overlook any guests. If she hadn't sent one to Allison, it wasn't an accident.

"We went to Brockton House, as you know," Allison snapped.

Lizzie had told Hannah, so she knew that Allison's mother had blackmailed the Pearlers, and now Bustle-Smith was stored away in a secluded country home as the Pearlers' tenant.

"I know, I know. And how is your mother, dear?"

"Befitting the circumstances," Allison growled.

"Alli, watch your tone with me." Eve gave her an icy stare.

"What do you expect? You ousted her from society! You had her kicked out of Almack's." Flushed red, Allison appeared ready to toot like the engine of a train.

Hannah stifled a grin. She didn't like this woman

much. Clearly, neither did Eve.

"Oh, don't be melodramatic. It's not like I cut off her air. I simply stopped sponsoring her after decades of her blackmail—"

Allison stepped close to Eve, leaned forward and propped herself on the armrests of Eve's throne. "She'd been sponsoring your kind for dozens of years and you repaid her with exile."

Eve remained unimpressed, maintaining her perfectly placid mien. But she made eye contact. "As far as I know, Somerset is in England. One can hardly speak of exile." She leaned forward for a biscuit, forcing Allison to retreat.

Allison straightened her back and held her pointy chin up high. Her eyes were too big for her face, and she looked like a creepy doll. "My invitation," Allison demanded, her hand stretched out as if she were holding an invisible tray.

Eve got up and stepped to the escritoire in the corner. She opened a drawer and rustled the papers. "I don't have any here. I had only as many made as I intended to extend, you must understand. The gathering for my daughter-in-law is an exclusive event. Go to the study and ask James for the sample print. It'll do for entrance."

Eve turned back to Hannah and poured her another cup of tea as Allison stomped off indignantly.

"Allison"—Eve stifled her tirade before she was beyond the threshold of the drawing-room—"if you as much as sidestep or cross any of us—"

Allison didn't let Eve finish and puffed away like an affronted steam engine.

"May I be excused for a moment, please?" Hannah

asked. She wasn't done with this one.

"Certainly, dear."

As she walked into the hallway, Allison came out of the study. She turned right and left and took something from her sleeve, a small metal object. Hannah was too far away to see what it was.

Allison walked right toward her, holding a small cream-colored card. "I'll see you this evening, Ms ... er..."

"Solomon. Hannah Solomon," she said.

"Ah, of course. Jews are all over this city—rats."

Hannah didn't let the insult sit. This woman trailed a rodent's ringed tail like a shadow of malice behind her. "You pushed my brother."

"Who?" The blonde witch snarled, her chin pointing high.

"My little brother. He's only seven, you should know."

"I decide what I should and shouldn't know," Allison snapped back.

Hannah grimaced. A rare sort of anger swept through her; one she knew her father wouldn't condone. But then again—"How far along are you? Two months? Three?"

Allison's eyes grew wide. "What did you say?"

"You're with child, aren't you? A few months along but you just returned from your honeymoon?" Hannah allowed a smirk to surface; it was her time to deliver a punch now.

"Who. Are. You?" Allison enunciated every syllable.

"Hannah." She smiled. She had plenty of sisters and knew how to handle herself with a wrench like Allison.

"Hannah. Hm..." Allison eyed her from top to bottom. And Hannah knew she'd been stamped an enemy.

CHAPTER 37

*A*rnold was in a terrible mood. It was half-past eight and most of the guests had arrived. He stood in the great hall with Fave and Gustav. They were welcoming the scheming, conniving, lying members of the ton, the reasons he needed to win the competition so desperately—which seemed impossible right now. If their guests were tolerant of other world views, the Pearlers would have a firm place among the British noblesse, not one they had to hold onto by hiding their true identities. And worse, it was a society Hannah could never blend into. He wasn't sure if she wanted him. Well, she wanted him, but did she want to be with him forever?

Then the air caught in his throat, and he lost his train of thought.

Lizzie would have found the right words, something along the lines of "beauty doesn't travel in a pack," but Arnold had no words for this. For her. When Arnold laid eyes on the girl entering alongside his beloved little cousin and his new cousin-in-law, he didn't recognize Hannah at first. The air in the room changed, crackling with something that had always been missing from his life. She seemed different. He'd noticed her hair styling when they had tea with Aunt Eve in the afternoon. Such a beauty, this girl. She glowed in her finery and his cock tried to escape the prison of his tight evening breeches.

She looked like an upside-down delphinium blossom, with the stem soaring into the laced-up bodice that was wrapped around Hannah's body. He'd never begrudged anyone anything before, but right here, right now, he couldn't imagine sharing her beauty with the hundred people in the room.

Her hair had been piled in curls atop her head, like a crown of shiny silk rolls, then it draped over her right shoulder, framing her face in a swirl of softness. Arnold couldn't blink for he didn't want to miss even a fraction of a second of the sight of sheer beauty.

Her eyes skimmed the room. Was she searching for him?

Her hands were folded elegantly into a triangle, Lizzie had probably taught her. Her dress was every shade of blue, from aquamarines to lapis lazuli. Rachel whispered something into Hannah's ear and she smiled. Then her eyes found his and his heart lashed into its pouch like a turtle would withdraw into its shell.

The music started, and Fave bowed before Rachel. This was their grand night. He took her to the parquet.

Arnold was thrilled for Fave to have his bride. Rachel was Jewish, but her family also hid it so they could integrate to society. If only Arnold could so easily introduce

Hannah to the ton. He looked for Lizzie. She was nowhere to be seen, and Arnold imagined she must have dissipated into the crowd in her golden yellow dress, chatting with her friends. But Hannah was still framed by the thick white door. She rocked back and forth; her hands clasped together behind her back.

Arnold walked toward her, although he had no recollection of moving his muscles, so enamoured was he at the mere sight of the vision in fading midnight hues.

"Good evening, Hannah. You are breathtaking tonight." He bowed, relying on flattery like on muscle memory for the platitudes. She was taller than usual, probably because of her slippers, which were hidden under the soft layers of tulle cascading around her. From his vantage point, she appeared like the center of a snowflake with the depth of the universe radiating from her. Her shoulders were covered, but he could see her clavicle. His mouth went dry at the sight. He was parched for … for her.

She moved with the music, but her legs were stuck to the floor.

"Would you like to dance?" He offered the flat of his hand, and she placed hers on it.

"I can't," she said, with an honest smile that gave off such a refreshing breeze that another smile would turn into a raging tornado and blow him off his feet.

"Have you ever learned to waltz?" His voice came out darker than he anticipated. Honestly, he was surprised he wasn't laid flat from the tension bursting through him. He felt green like he did at Oxford, naive and unable to speak to women. He'd practiced, like a muscle, building strength, force, and resilience. But Hannah was no athletic endeavor, she was his ultimate challenge. Somehow, this delicate flower had disarmed him, stripping him of the memories of his experience with women, his skill of seduction. At the receiving end of her charms, all he could do was follow her cues as if he were the lingering whiff of her enthralling scent. She smelled like appletree blossoms, chamomile, and honeysuckle.

She was so crisp and clear, he felt as though he would muddy the clear stream of mountain water that was Hannah if he took a sip, but he was suddenly so thirsty that only she could keep him alive.

"Come with me," he held out his hand. "Please."

CHAPTER 38

*H*annah wore a costume, she wasn't herself tonight, she was a peacock fairy in a wishful story. Soon enough, she would awake. But not yet. Not now. Her heart would break. So, she decided to float in Arnold's world for as long as he'd let her. She placed her hand in Arnold's and followed him along the hallways, through a door, down some steps, and into a smaller dark corridor. Better judgment told her she shouldn't be there, not with him, alone, but she took a chance.

"Where are you taking me?"

"The courtyard," Arnold said.

"But the gardens are in the other direction? It's too cold for—"

"A dance lesson. Just come." He opened a narrow wooden door. It looked old and scratched, like their back door at the synagogue that was held open with crates and tools during daily errand runs.

He put his hands around her waist from behind her

and hugged her. Her dress bounced forward, and she thought the petticoat would stick out from her at nearly a right angle. She tensed at his intimate touch. His hands came to her eyes and covered them gently.

"I can't see!" she said with a smile. Excitement prickled inside her chest, ready to burst out as soon as he gave her a signal. She was giddy near him, mollified by his touch and flattered by his attention.

"Just a few steps forward, and I'll release you."

Hannah did as she was told, and something cold cracked under her feet. Snow. The slush melted against her feet, but she wasn't cold.

"Where are we?"

"One more step … now turn." Arnold kissed her shoulder, then her neck.

Then he pushed her shoulders lightly with his elbows, his hands still on her eyes.

And he let go.

Hannah blinked a few times in the semi-darkness. As her vision focused, she saw effervescent glimmers everywhere. A blur of pinks and whites in the background with glittering dots of light flickering ever so slowly. "W-what is this place?" she asked as she turned to face Arnold.

His eyes glowed in the candlelight.

"This is Aunt Evie's peony garden."

"But the snow … and the candles?" Hannah admired the magical place. Wall sconces held hundreds of candles. The snow lightly dusted the ground. She could still sense the gravel under her thin soles.

"Aunt Evie grows her own peonies for Lizzie's room. It's an old superstition," Arnold explained.

"Peonies are a superstition?"

"Yes, they're said to have mystical powers that can attract eligible suitors for a daughter. They stand for a blessed marriage."

"Ah!"

Snow glittered on the blossoms; the candles flickered gently. "There's no roof, but it's so warm here." They were essentially in a large cylinder, surrounded by the house and the roof, but open to the sky above.

"That's because of the candles. She keeps the servants on their toes giving the flowers as much light and warmth as possible, so Lizzie won't be without peonies," Arnold explained. "But let's not talk about them now, please. I brought you here—"

"Oh, I shouldn't be here."

"Why not?" He sounded a bit hurt. "I happen to think that this is exactly where you should be."

"I … er … I…"

"At a loss for words? The journalist?" Arnold gave her the most boyish smirk. It tingled her skin, even though she disliked his sarcasm.

"I promised to teach you to dance." Arnold held out his hand, palm up. He wrapped his other arm around Hannah's back. "Did I tell you how absolutely breathtaking you are tonight?" His voice was so dark and lovely, it vibrated in her bones.

She placed her hand in his and nestled into his embrace.

"Now, in a waltz"—he held her gaze—"I step forward with my left foot, so you step backward with the right, then we move to my right, your left, then you bring your left foot close to your right as I do the exact opposite."

"Oh my!" Hannah looked down at the complicated patterns trailed by Arnold's black boots. Shiny thin leather boots with brown rims that slid swiftly on the snow.

Arnold gently pulled Hannah toward him, and she stumbled.

"I got you." He smiled. "Let me lead. It's a waltz." His breath was so close that she could almost taste him. "You step forward, I step backward. Feel me."

Hannah tried to give in, but it was against everything in her mind.

"One, two, three. One, two, three…"

"I can't," she protested.

"Of course, you can. You made me braid challah, with one up, two in the middle—"

"You did listen!"

He smiled, "Just feel me."

She did. And she let him pull and nudge her in a rounded square. He stepped forward, she back, then to the side. And slowly, her feet understood the pattern. She followed.

Arnold stopped counting. He held her, closer and closer, until her belly touched his. "Use your knees, feather them…"

She instinctively lowered herself into a more dynamic stance. His knee came forward, between her legs. Only the layers of the tulle gown separated them. She felt him close and then he was gone.

He stepped back, pulled her along, holding her gaze. "Just look at me, not your feet."

She did.

The peonies and candles rushed past her, her peripheral vision taking in the glittering snow. Only Arnold's face remained in focus, narrow slits with dark brown lashes rimming the top, accented by the perfect amount of brow. His chiseled face was perfection and Hannah couldn't believe her luck. He was more than a prince to her in this moment, he was all she never thought she could have, all the luck and happiness she believed possible. His soft shaved cheeks were contoured by the shadow on his wide neck, crowned by a short wave of brunette hair. He was so beautiful, she had to close her eyes.

She glided in his arms, held upright by the circle of their arms and chests.

Arnold held her down for a dip, and she dropped her head backward. Her hair slid out of its coiffure, but she didn't care. A few curls had fallen out on the sides, and they brushed over her neck when she came up. She opened her eyes. Arnold grinned boyishly, proudly, and swirled her around herself twice. She had no idea how he did it, but he was still holding her and she returned safely into his arms.

He steadied her exactly in front of him.

She blinked. He swallowed and she noticed his Adam's apple jumped in his throat. Then his eyes fell to her mouth. Her lips swelled with anticipation.

"And you said you couldn't waltz," Arnold rasped.

"I can't." Her voice was merely a whisper, damped by

the snow and illuminated by glimmers from the candles' reflections on the snow-capped peonies.

"You see, you let me lead."

Her heart thumped so hard it was almost painful. But he kept her in his arms, still in the dancing position, arms held sideways. She was so close to him that his heartbeat vibrated into her stomach.

Then he pulled her again, and they waltzed around the small cylinder of the courtyard, twirling, swirling. She laughed, heady with joy.

His hands moved to the small of her back, holding her, pulling her in. But he no longer needed to pull, her middle found his naturally, magnetically, as if she'd found the other pole of her center, inevitably leading to him.

"You lead. I promise I'll follow." She couldn't believe the words that came out of her mouth.

"No, *you* lead now. *I* promise to follow," Arnold said.

Hannah's heart raced so quickly and she was so aroused, she did not know where to start. Her chest rose and fell with gasps of passion, and she couldn't channel it.

Arnold let his eyes fell to her cleavage. The bodice of her dress had dropped lower from their dancing. He looked down, asking for permission. Hannah remained silent. Thus, he placed a gentle and lingering kiss on her collarbone. In response, she dropped her head sideways, giving him access.

CHAPTER 39

*rnold held Hannah firmly in his arms and brought her to a cold stone bench. It was wide, long, and hard under her body. She tried to manage the layers of her gown but clumsily wrinkled the fabric. When she turned around, he was nude. She'd bathed her younger brothers and wasn't ignorant of the independent mind of a ... but this was a surprise.

"It's ... oh no..."

"What is it now?" Arnold was busy nuzzling her neck now, fumbling with a part of her dress that he hoped would grant him better access. She felt the pressure of his erection against her stomach.

"I'll disappoint you, I'm afraid."

He stepped back. "What are you talking about?"

She eyed his erection, drooping into a friendly hug and letting her shoulders hang.

Arnold burst out laughing so hard he had to let go of

her. His entire body was shaking, and she frowned. Naked.

* * *

WHEN SHE LOWERED her head and emerged from the blue tulle and white silk pooling on the snow-dusted gravel, he reached for her, steadying her on the tiny slippers. She wore nothing but her high-heeled shoes. Arnold had never seen anything more erotic. But then he saw her face, flushed, aroused, confused, expecting something, and Arnold sobered from his daze.

"I'm sorry. Let me do this right when we're clothed. I promise you a proper proposal, I do, but you're so sweet…" He swept her up, pressed a deep kiss on her mouth and lay her down on his velvet coat, which he'd spread on the stone bench. Everything sparkled: Hannah's eyes in the flickering candlelight, the tiny star-shaped bits of snow all around the lush pink peonies. He knew this was a spot secret enough for their encounter, but she felt so special to him that even floating in clouds on rays of sunshine wouldn't suffice. He wanted to lay his world at her feet and give her every fiber of his being.

He touched her gently, worshipping her body. Every bit of contact intensified the effervescent tingle that shot through him. If this was love, the passion he might reveal with Hannah would take even him off guard. He wanted to slow his onslaught and tune in to the signals of her body, but her every move fired him on further.

"You're the most beautiful woman I've ever…" He couldn't break the kiss long enough to speak. Arnold had to drink from her as if she gave him all the nourishment to make his soul whole.

Her hands brushed all over him, touching, stroking, exploring.

He realized that she was trying to get to his cock, so he sat up and pulled her up onto him. Had his legs not been bent under his bottom, she'd have sat on his lap, facing him.

"Here." He offered himself to her, hoping she'd accept him as the hand-me-down he was, previously used and what he now thought—soiled—by past encounters. The blinding beauty on his lap eclipsed his experiences with others and he couldn't recall specifics any longer. He knew what to do, but with her it was different. She was unchartered—liquid lava, engulfing him in her heat and rustling like an earthquake in his heart with every kiss.

Her hands came down and touched him. He twitched under her exploration. She was tender with him but curious, proving that she was as he'd hoped, innocent and brazen. This brilliant mind of hers was taking him in, all of him. It was a grandiose pleasure and humbled him to his core.

He tried to control himself, for he wanted nothing more than to plunge right into her and rip through her virginity, making her his. And he wanted to thrust, hard and fast. But not now. Something told him this would be an exquisite experience and he tried to cool himself.

"You can do to me whatever you want, Hannah." He adored her name on his lips almost as much as he liked her lips on his. "Please, Hannah," he leaned backward, leaning his upper body on his elbows, "I'm all yours."

"I don't know what to do," she said, smiling. She was like a child that couldn't tear the toy out of its packaging, unable to uncover what was underneath.

"Then you do to me as I do to you," he said.

"But Aunt Rifkah said—"

"Pffff." Arnold marveled at his loss of words. "You are my equal, and everything I may do to you, you may do to me."

Her eyes grew wide, and he was afraid he'd scared her off. "I mean, whatever I may do to pleasure you, you may try … argh…" He raked his hands through his hair and when he opened his eyes, she'd climbed higher onto him.

Hannah rode him astride, leaning down toward his face. Her hair had fallen around her head like their own private curtain and she smiled. "Am I too heavy?"

He laughed and noticed that she focused on his mouth.

"Equal?" she asked.

"Of course, or … er…" He saw his cock in her hand and her thighs spread in his lap. "You're probably my superior," Arnold finally said, considering she was sitting on him.

But he knew what his words meant to her. It was more than just her position; it was her place in their relationship. Somehow, inexplicably, it made him happy. He wanted to serve her, make her happy. But he wanted an equal, a partner, not a girl toy. She was everything he'd ever wanted and more.

His heart skipped a beat, or several, while the floodgate took it in a storm. He adored her face, her undone hair, her eyes wide and dark. Frozen by the power of the moment, Arnold lowered his head to kiss her mouth and took her head in his hands to deepen their connection.

They explored each other's mouths with a vigor that came from deep inside as their bodies rubbed against each other. Arnold trailed a few kisses along her chin, her jawline, and then down her neck.

She pushed him slightly and returned the gesture. Nobody had kissed him like this before. She was mirroring him, copying, learning. His chest filled with awe at the pleasure of being her tutor. Well, honestly, he was so well-versed, he was more like a professor of the field—none of which mattered any more.

He kissed her shoulder, moving toward her clavicle and then up her neck back to her mouth. Every time he paused, she copied him, returning every scintillating favor.

When he reached her mouth, she opened up willingly, shyly, but she'd grown hot under his tenderness. Then she kissed his shoulder. But she stopped at his clavicle and didn't come to his face. She was no longer copying him now and trailed her own path of kisses along his body. Instead, she moved down. She dropped a path of kisses along his middle, past his chest, along his abdomen. There, she dwelled for a long time and then ... did she just lick? His muscles flexed under her lips. He was beyond control and let out a groan of agony. His restraint started to hurt, and his breath grew ragged. She was so good, too good to bear. He surely couldn't hold on much longer.

She sat up, her hair wildly framing her face as if she were Aphrodite aflame. She was an image of soft skin and silky hair. But Arnold was so excited, his vision blurred.

"Why is it like this?" she asked.

"Like what?" He could barely speak.

"Your stomach is ... you can see the muscles underneath your skin."

His arousal was breaking through his body in waves of sweat. It was harder to hold on now.

"Exercise, I guess. Energy to burn." He shrugged. "Do you like it?"

She studied him like an artist admiring the work of another. Then she looked at her own narrow waist, her flat stomach, and her smooth skin. Arnold watched her comparison of their bodies. Hers was the same color as his, but it had a different shape and texture altogether. The ideal female complement to his masculinity.

His hands came to the narrow of her waist and he lifted her up ever so slightly to position her above his member.

She looked at him, she understood. "No."

He froze. If she withdrew consent now, he'd perish on the spot.

"I don't just like it. I enjoy it." She smiled wistfully and leaned over his stomach to kiss—and lick a little.

That was his undoing. He leaned forward to kiss her and at that she lifted her center onto his. He felt the wet warm cradle of her legs around him. He dared to poke at her a little bit, as if to ask for permission to step inside. And then she did the unspeakable. She reached for his cock and put it directly at her opening. She leaned on him and moved, enveloping him. This was new and hot and oh so erotic. He pushed a bit in, carefully for he felt her stretching insides. Her first time. Then there was her barrier. He knew it would hurt her, for it was fully intact. She was perfect. Just for him.

"Hannah!" Her name a rasp in the cold air, steamed by the heat of their unity.

Then *she* did it. She *used* him to pierce her hymen. She took her own virginity with his body. And there was nothing more exciting and flattering than this moment. She sat up, fully facing him.

He was buried to the hilt and struggling to maintain control. He waited.

"Please show me what comes next. Make love to me?" She smiled. Her immaculate white smile drew him in. But he felt a pang in his heart for he felt so unclean compared to her.

"I don't make love," he whispered sadly, an admission of guilt like a green boy.

"Then what do you do? Make babies?"

He laughed at that. "Absolutely not!" His stomach shook with mirth. Hannah held on to him and furrowed her brows.

How sweet. He allowed his member to twinge inside her. She responded with a clench.

"Are there ways to avoid it?"

He was growing tired of talking and eager to move on. "Indeed. Don't you know?" Then he remembered she was one of eight children.

She shook her head.

"Do you want to make love to *me*?" She asked innocently and invitingly at the same time while sitting on his cock, hard as an oak trunk.

His eyes darted to hers, then down to her lips, past her

chin to her collarbone, and then lower to her beautiful firm breasts.

He raised his upper body to kiss her chest and felt her nipple with his tongue. "Yes," he said with her breast in his mouth, "but I've never tried that."

"Try it now," she whispered and pushed her body closer to his.

Then his hands landed on her crisp little bottom. He pulled her in and began to grind. She understood quickly and moved her hips. And in what seemed a short moment but must have been longer for their sweat beaded down their skin, she lost control. She was flushed, hot, and crazed. She ground against him until the point just before pain, but Arnold didn't stop.

They moved in an ancient dance together. Arnold had finally found a worthy partner.

When she tilted her head back and her hair cascaded along her back, a bit of it tickled Arnold's leg. He couldn't hold on anymore and pushed her gently on her back, holding her head in his hand and laying her on his crumbled-up shirt. Then he thrust into her with all his force. Somewhere in the back of his mind he was still afraid to hurt her, but he felt her nails on his back, clutching him and holding on. He knew she was near.

She moaned and let out a high-pitched noise, a sound of undefinable beauty that pushed him over the edge. She gave him pause, a welcome break. He looked at her again, admiring her beauty. She was flushed and glistening with sweat. He adored it and tasted a drop of the salty essence of her skin. He felt as if he were diving into a mist, a fog of warmth descended upon him like a cloud that had fallen from the sky and shrouded the hard British landscape in a softness that … maybe this was more than the act. Maybe he was making love to her indeed.

"Oh, Hannah!" He groaned and thrust himself one more time, deeper and stronger than ever.

She held her breath, surprised. Overcome. She tensed around him as he poured himself into her. He held her bottom in place, pulling her closer for there was no air between them and even their skin touching was too far. They were one and yet striving to come closer.

They were both out of breath and Arnold reveled in her beautiful face, thoroughly kissed, her lips swollen, her breasts pushed against his chest. They were still joined in their middles. All barriers between them had been shattered.

She opened her eyes when she came down, and he hugged her tight to his sweaty body.

"What happened?" Hannah finally asked.

"I thought it was quite obvious. But if not, I'll have to do it again." His smile widened. "At your service." He brushed a kiss on her forehead. And he sank his face into her hair.

"Nobody told me *this* could happen," she said.

"I would hope not." He was joking now, reveling in the flattery of his manhood. He had quite literally made her lose her mind. It was glorious.

"Does this happen to all women?" she asked.

"You're asking the wrong person."

"Do you think Rachel would speak to me?"

Now he was alarmed. Was she doing research to consider how he measured up? "Are you trying to decide whether I suit you?" He wasn't sure he was still joking now, and fear crept into his chest.

"I think we both know that you do." She lay her head on his shoulder, but he had to see her.

He began to get up but the drying fluids had glued him in place.

"Ah!" she complained. "Don't come out."

"Did I hurt you?" Arnold's face wrinkled with concern.

"No. But stay."

So, he did. And he swelled up again down there and filled her completely. He held her as long as he could without being found out, kissing, marveling in her beauty, worshipping her body. He felt like he'd arrived at the tip of a mountain and the whole world was unfolding underneath him. It was time to bid goodnight to the guests at the ball and to take charge of his future. His perspective was redefined, solitary Arnold had become a "we."

CHAPTER 40

*A*rnold must have carried her upstairs because when Hannah awoke, she was in her bed and the clock on the vanity table chimed six times. She was still naked, covered in the soft sheets of her guest bed. She blinked, barely able to focus on the clock face in the back of the room. Her gown hung on the armoire. Her head felt groggy, as it only did after the four cups of wine on a Passover Seder. What had come over her that she let Arnold … she had no words for what had happened. But still, she felt no remorse. She couldn't recognize herself. Had she been corrupted by the riches and his good looks?

Hannah sat at the edge of her bed in the Pearlers' palatial home and realized that she was still herself. No, it wasn't that. Arnold's rakish smile came to her mind, the sweet dimples that formed when he smiled—oh how she wanted to kiss them. And his entire face. She wanted to drive her hands through his hair every time he smiled and those boyish dimples surfaced. Last night, she'd tasted the most delicious cake that was Arnold. She had her fill but knew she'd want more every day of her life. Without this cake, without Arnold, her life was bland. She loved being part of his world despite its dangers. She'd somehow find a way to carry her own world over. She loved … oh that was it!

Her heart raced at her epiphany! It was just like in the books she'd read. Except that the authors usually skipped the insightful parts, the points where the heroine's life changes profoundly, and she understands why. Hannah smiled to herself. She was *in love*. It was the only explanation for her cerebral quiescence. She trusted Arnold—not with her mind but with her heart. And she'd allowed her body to follow suit. Intrigued, she decided to make the most of it.

* * *

MEANWHILE, Arnold was his usual energetic self again. But the attic was freezing. It had snowed a little more, and their exercise room wasn't heated.

"Why are you so ruffled?" Fave asked.

"I er … had to leave the ball early to teach Hannah a few dance steps." Arnold stood in a wide stance with a wide grin on his face.

Fave removed the sword from his holster and polished the tip. He hadn't caught on.

"Cous, I said, I left early. With Hannah."

Fave looked at him, squarely in the eyes this time. "Oh no."

"Oh yes," Arnold couldn't help but smile.

"You and the Rabbi's daughter?" Fave rubbed his chin, a smirk and confusion taking turns in his expression.

"I really wasn't thinking of the Rabbi last night."

Fave raked his hands through his hair. It was his way of taking a moment to think of what to say next—Arnold knew, he did the same.

"You had a virgin?" Fave asked.

Arnold stopped smiling and deepened his stare at Fave. "She. Had. Me."

Fave closed his eyes as if he were in pain. "She's Rabbi Solomon's daughter. He married Rachel and me *two weeks* ago." Fave sounded exasperated.

But he was exhausting Arnold. "You're not listening to me, Cous." Arnold put a hand on Fave's shoulder and inclined his head, speaking down to his cousin. "I said, *she* had *me.*"

"What are you talking about? You surely had each other..."

Arnold shook his head. "At first, she used me."

"Oh, how terrible, it must have been pure agony."

"You're not listening, and no, it wasn't *agony.*"

"Alright, explain." Fave put the point of his sword on the parquet and leaned on it like a walking stick. The thin metal bent, but Arnold wasn't impressed by Fave's ill-treatment of his custom-made sword. Nothing mattered, his heart was filled with joy, and he'd burst if he couldn't share it with his cousin.

"It was like this..." He told Fave everything. Every last detail.

Fave's mouth opened at some point, and it never

closed, nor did he form any audible words. He may not even have been breathing, Arnold couldn't be sure, for Fave turned positively white.

"Are you done now?" Fave finally asked.

"Oh no, I think I'm just getting started," Arnold grinned with the smile of a tamed rake.

Fave let out a haughty laugh.

"I'll set the Melo Melo—"

"What?" Fave asked. "That's the most expensive … the rarest pearl. You've had this pearl since grandfather—"

"Exactly. It's perfect."

"What are you thinking?"

"Definitely white gold for the bands, Cous." Arnold beamed.

"I meant what you were thinking of telling her father … wait, what?"

Arnold loved seeing Fave's surprise. He wished he could frame a miniature of his expression in this very moment. He could barely say the words, but he had to share the joy in his heart with Fave. He wanted to propose to Hannah. "Didn't you promise to make the wedding bands for me?"

Fave's mouth dropped open. "What about the crown jewels?" he asked.

Arnold's heart sank. This was the crux of the matter, not the heady sweeping romance that would be his nuptials. If they didn't win the competition for the king's jewels, if their place in society went without the crown's backing, then he'd be outed as a Jew with the Rabbi's daughter by his side. He and the Pearlers would lose

England's richest as clients, and the circles of Jews wouldn't accept them back. His future with Hannah depended on the competition. He'd win it all or lose more than he dared to gamble for.

CHAPTER 41

*ater that morning, Arnold had to return his mind to business. The competition was even more important now for his love was at stake. He needed to win for the past to honor the Pearlers *and* the future he wished to have with Hannah.

"He wants a what?" Arnold's voice thundered through the house, but he didn't care. He wasn't going to pay for shipments he'd never received. Especially not now, when he needed the gold, gems and pearls more desperately than ever before.

Arnold, Fave and Gregory were standing in Gustav's office as if his uncle had abdicated. And Arnold tasted acid. He wanted—needed—to restore honor to their family business.

"Hannah," Fave said when she peeked her head through the door.

Arnold rushed to her side. "Good morning," he whispered and placed a gentle kiss on her forehead. She blushed and Arnold immediately took a step back. Fave and Gregory were so close to him that he didn't hesitate to greet her, but he realized they were strangers to her.

"What's the matter?" she asked, "I heard you shouting."

Fave stepped forward. "Ms. Hannah Solomon, please meet Gregory Stone, Member of Parliament."

Hannah gasped and Arnold knew that she'd written about him, the baptized Jew, the traitor.

"Is this the Rabbi's daughter?" Gregory gave her the once-down and arched a brow.

Arnold predicted that this meeting would go from bad to worse. Hannah's eyes held a fierce glimmer that was most unsettling. Hannah was easily the most opinionated and outspoken woman he'd ever known, and that meant a lot from someone who lived under the same roof as Aunt Evie, Lizzie, and Rachel.

Gregory stepped toward Hannah and reached out to greet her with a customary kiss on her knuckles. But Hannah folded her hands and looked away, refusing a member of parliament the most basic courtesy. Arnold rubbed his forehead.

Fave gave Arnold a stare that said "tame the chit," but Arnold knew the message went deeper. Hannah didn't fit into his world.

"I've heard about you, Mr. Stone. Written about you, too," Hannah finally said. Her voice was shaking but her eyes were blazing.

Gregory gave a mean chuckle that Arnold knew all too well from their school days. "You have? Only good, I hope," he clearly wanted to get back to business and gave her only basic courtesies.

"I'm afraid not, not at all," Hannah said. She was honest. Painfully and inappropriately so. At all times. Arnold felt a headache rising.

Gregory gave Arnold an annoyed stare, just like the time Doctor Banks had given them a surprise examination in algebra back at Eaton. "Since this is the first time I've met you, Ms. Solomon, what information did you have to write about me prior to our acquaintance?"

Hannah looked at Arnold as if she were apologizing ahead of time. His headache had now brewed into a reverberating thunderstorm.

"I mentioned you in my newspaper," she said.

Gregory's eyes darted to Fave and then to Arnold. "You have a newspaper?"

Now Arnold was annoyed with him. "She's a talented journalist, Greg—" Arnold pursed his lips when he saw Fave's death stare and Hannah's placid smile. He'd wanted to help but was interrupting.

Fave reached for the Community Circular on the desk and folded it into half, quarters, and then eights and put it in his vest pocket.

"I run a weekly paper for the..." Hannah searched for Arnold's support.

He'd resigned. There was no stopping her anyway. She seemed unimpressed by his best glowering efforts.

"I write the Community Circular for the Jews of London," she said primly, folding her hands before her. Her delicate arms framed her slim silhouette. This beautiful girl had a wild wit. "You wouldn't know, of course, it's delivered to Jewish households only." Ouch!

"And where, pray tell, did you find my persona fit for

this"—Gregory waved at Hannah mockingly—"newspaper of yours?"

Arnold shook his head; he knew this would provoke Hannah.

"I'll find a copy for you. You were the feature story last week, a traitor of your heritage to gain political favors." She was in full swing now.

Fave looked at Arnold in alarm, as if Arnold were saying the words that came out of Hannah's mouth. Did he think he could actually tame her? Hadn't Rachel taught him anything about women yet?

"A what-not-to-do example for our community," Hannah said.

"That's enough," Arnold said.

"Have you considered, Ms. Solomon, that I may be the only ally your community has in parliament?"

"No, I haven't," she admitted. As always, painfully honest. It was worse than being a pathological liar, Arnold thought.

"Well, give it some thought then." Gregory sneered. "You never know why people do what they do. They have reasons you might not understand."

"What reason is there to disrespect seven thousand years of history?" Hannah asked.

"What? When did my family ever disrespect Jewish history? It's one of the oldest of religions, the longest track record of—"

"Sacrifice, Mr. Stone. And by renouncing your heritage, you disrespect the sacrifice of your ancestors. You negate their efforts and suffering. Make it all in vain.

Your bloodline ends." She ended her monologue with bravado.

Quite frankly, she took Gregory, Fave's and Arnold's breath away. She was furiously beautiful, clever, and she had a backbone made of moral integrity, strength of character, and willpower. Arnold was shocked how he could be upset about her tirade and yet oh so turned on by her character.

Fave stepped closer to Arnold, and said, "We have business to discuss." He signaled to Hannah that she should shut the door behind her.

"Good afternoon, gentlemen." Hannah pivoted and left the room.

The three men stared at each other in shock.

"I can see how you'd fall for her, Arnold, but she's a piece of work," Gregory said.

Arnold sighed and rolled his eyes. Hannah wasn't one of the many conquests he'd discuss with Gregory. Certainly not one to pass on as they'd done in the past. She was pure and priceless. He wished to keep her safe like an oyster its pearl.

"What happened?" Arnold asked.

"Someone gave my last ship a clean bill of lading." Gregory put his hands on his hips and stretched one foot sideways.

"And why is a clean bill a bad thing?" Arnold asked, readying himself for bad news.

"The ship was empty," Fave said.

"You don't say?" Arnold looked at Gregory.

"And you signed it off," Gregory said.

"Me? I did what?" Arnold blinked. He'd never signed

off on a bill of lading. He didn't like to go to the docks. It was dirty, ridden with criminals, and smelled like fish.

"Here." Fave handed him the document.

Arnold skimmed it. "This is my seal, but not my signature." He strode to the desk, took the quill and a piece of paper and drew a straight horizontal line. Then he signed his name with the A and E flared. "This is how I sign." He handed it to Gregory. "Did you recognize my handwriting?"

Gregory compared the two documents, his eyes darting back and forth. Then he handed them both to Fave.

"What do I do now?" Gregory asked. "Someone is out to get me. It'll cost me the spot at the House. Everything my parents did for me will have been in vain." He sank into the settee.

"It seems to me that someone's out to get both of us, Greg," Arnold said, giving Fave a questioning glance.

"But who?" Fave asked as if the question had to be spoken out loud so that it could linger in the air above their heads like a raincloud.

CHAPTER 42

*H*annah stepped away from the office with a bitter taste. Gregory Stone really irked her. A traitor. A man without integrity. And if Arnold was such a good friend of his, did it put Arnold in a bad light? Or had she made a terrible first impression after Arnold's warm greeting in front of his confidants?

She walked through the hallway past the delicate vases she'd noticed on her first day here. It now seemed worlds away. Laughter and clinking of cups on saucers came down the hallway. Maybe there'd be biscuits. Her stomach growled. Eve's afternoon teas were nothing short of buffets with gorgeous tablescapes, lush flowers, and the most fragrant treats.

The door to the drawing-room opened and...oh no, Allison Thompson stepped out. Hannah was too close already; it was too late to turn around and leave.

"Oh hello, Ms....er...I forgot, something Jewish..." Allison headed straight toward her.

"Solomon. Like in King Solomon." Hannah really couldn't help herself.

"Ah, then you're a princess? Your father is the king?" Allison mocked her with a condescending singsong.

That was enough. Hannah stepped closer and the tip of her nose almost touched Allison's. "You know nothing of my family. Guard. Your. Poisonous. Tongue." Hannah emphasized every word, just as Allison had done before. She hated to lower herself to her level, but it was just one of those days.

Allison blinked at her, stupefied for a moment, but then it seemed as if a wash of evil darkened her eyes. She pulled Hannah into a hug and whispered into her ear, "I'm sorry! I guess you'll just have to be collateral damage."

What was that supposed to mean?

But without explanation, Allison took off, leaving Hannah in the hallway, dumbfounded. She'd never understand the ways of the ton.

Hannah shrugged it off and peeked through the drawing-room door.

"Oh Hannah, do come in." Lizzie rose to take Hannah's arm and led her to the small group of ladies.

Hannah smiled at the chipper group of women in frilly pastel-colored dresses. They looked like stuffed animals having a tea party when little girls were pretending the queen had come to visit.

Rachel poured a cup of tea and handed it to Hannah. "This is my mother, Hannah. Please meet Mrs. Stella Newman."

Hannah smiled at the lady with the same dark hair as

Rachel's. She seemed kind, with round eyes and thin brows. As if her face could tell stories.

"Mama, this is Hannah, I told you about her," Rachel said.

"*Angenem.*" Pleased to meet you. Mrs. Newman said in familiar Yiddish that immediately settled Hannah's temper.

"Evie, Aunt Evie?" Arnold came yelling down the hallway and into the drawing-room. When he saw the ladies sitting around the teascape, he slowed for a moment. Then bowed, "*Meyna Damen, gut nokhmitog.*" My ladies, good afternoon.

"Arnold, come join us? Stella brought rugelach. Chocolate and hazelnut, they're marvelous, darling," Eve said.

"I'd love to Aunt Evie, but I have a pressing matter to attend to, I um..." he looked at the women, all eyes on him.

"What's wrong?" Lizzie asked.

He searched for Eve's signal.

"Speak freely, darling, everyone's family here." Eve gestured around the room.

Arnold's eyes rested on Hannah with a questioning glance. None of the ladies here knew of the terrible display she'd put on for the member of parliament, a token of how little she fit in.

"My seal has gone missing. I wondered whether you might have seen it." Arnold looked at the women and stepped closer. On the table, rugelach and watercress sandwiches were surrounded by platters of sliced apples, grapes, and other berries that Hannah had never seen before.

No, his eyes were going past the food, onto the floor. He was searching for something.

"I shall inform you instantly if I find it," Eve said.

Arnold nodded and as he stepped out, he said to Hannah, "A word?"

His voice caught her like a breeze, carrying her into the hallway.

"Whatever your problem was with Greg, he's a friend." Arnold was close, oh, so close. She could smell his delicious breath.

Hannah frowned. "He's a traitor of our people."

"He's a friend. Can't say that many people want to be my friend these days, so don't scare him off!" Arnold looked like a boy now, young and vulnerable. Hannah could touch his wide shoulders, but he'd lowered his head to hers, so he seemed a little shorter. Less intimidating.

She licked her lips. She tasted the lingering sweetness of the hazelnut and chocolate rugelach.

Arnold's eyes fell to her mouth. "Hannah," he rasped. Closing the distance between them, he brought his hands to her shoulders, then her hair, and her neck. *"Ikh ken nit makhn zinen fun dir."* I can't make any sense of you.

He leaned in, and Hannah closed her eyes. Arnold pulled her closer.

And then *cling*. Something fell to the floor.

They both jerked back.

"What was that?" Hannah asked.

Arnold bent down and took the small metal thing in his hand. He rose and looked at her, his head inclined, hurt written all over his face. The bad expression polluted his handsome features as if with soot.

"Where did you get this?" he asked.

"What?" She reached for the thing, but he snapped it up and closed his fist around it.

"I'll ask you one more time, Hannah, and don't lie to me. Where did you get my seal?" Confusion and hurt shimmered in his eyes as if he did not know how to reconcile his finding with Hannah's presence.

"I've never seen this before. What would I do with your seal?" Anger clouded her mood.

The door to the drawing-room screeched open and four ladies stepped into the hall, Lizzie, then Rachel with Mrs. Newman, and finally Eve. A rush of blood rushed to her face and she felt herself blush and then pale. Was she being accused of theft?

CHAPTER 43

At one o'clock sharp, Arnold and Fave pulled up in front of the Custom House at Sugar Quay in the parish of All Hallows Barking on the Thames. They'd come in a hired hack, better not to come in their opulent carriage with the gold stitching of their initials if someone was forging signatures and stealing seals.

When they entered the Port Authority's big hall, Arnold immediately noticed the large clock, the focal point on the highest point of the back wall. The gathered men screaming for prices much as they did at the markets, which Arnold preferred to drive through—he hated the stench of fish, spirits, and gunpowder.

"Where's the admiral's office?" Fave asked a man in relatively clean clothing, glasses, and a gray hat. He seemed sober enough and was holding a ledger.

The man eyed Fave from head to toe, then did the same for Arnold. Fave took a few coins from his waist pocket and held them out. The man grabbed them and gave them a side nod. "Through the double doors to the left, second door."

Arnold and Fave followed his directions and found a door labeled:

Sir Stuart Murphy
Admiral of the Fleet

"Do you think Prinny knows what kind of man he is?" Fave asked.

Arnold gave a terse nod and knocked. The door was askew and he gave it a gentle push.

"Ah, here we are again. Sharp and spit spat," the Admiral greeted them from his desk. "Tea?"

The irony wasn't lost on Arnold. He didn't want empty crates of tea, he wanted jewels for the competition. To win the competition! "Good morning, Sir. We're here to—"

The Admiral turned over the books on his desk for Arnold to see.

Fave leaned forward and inspected the seal. "That's your seal, Arnold," he said.

Arnold checked the seal. It was his curved P with an uppercase E set off by a curly diacritic mark. "This is my seal but not my signature. I've never seen this ledger in all my life." Arnold's hands turned cold, his shoulders seemed to lose body heat and his knees grew soft.

"Someone's forging your documents," Fave said.

"And you owe the carrier about fifty thousand pounds," the Admiral said, his double chin wobbling like a goat's wattle.

Arnold needed to sit, but there was no chair, so he

leaned a thigh on the Admiral's desk. "Who's delivering these signatures?"

"A young fellow, skinny, kind with a wide-brimmed hat. I met him once or twice. Very high-pitched voice for a lad."

"Is it always the same fellow?" Fave asked.

"No, sometimes, another man comes. Your barrister, I think."

"My barrister?" Arnold asked incredulously, his voice about two octaves higher than becoming. "What's his name?"

"Oh um…Tom…no, um…Mark"

"Marvin Thompson?"

"That's it!" The Admiral shuffled some papers. "He's due here at nine o'clock."

"For what?" Fave asked.

"Delivering the new contracts," the Admiral said.

A young boy in a blue uniform knocked and walked in, probably the Admiral's secretary. He nodded at Arnold and Fave and delivered a few envelopes to the Admiral's desk.

"Jack, please do me a favor. Take these two gentlemen with you when the barrister comes later this morning. Hide them in plain sight, if you know what I mean."

Jack eyed Arnold and Fave and tilted his head signaling for them to come with him.

Arnold stayed behind and closed the door while Fave and Jack waited outside. "Admiral, Sir, I'd like to thank you for your support in this matter." He retrieved a dark brown velvet box from his pocket and handed it to the admiral.

The Admiral grumbled something inaudible as he opened the box. Arnold knew he was going to use it as a bribe to smooth over his infidelities with his wife. Such a distasteful purpose was a waste of the beautiful pearls. Unfortunately, pearls were for sale and at this moment, he was exchanging them for information. He had no choice. He couldn't change the world, just try to make his corner a little bit better. And he knew he needed to do right by the Pearlers. Someone was out to harm them, but he didn't know who.

"This is...my lad" The admiral was visibly moved by the sight of the bracelet. "You have some serious talent for pearls."

Arnold inclined his head and turned toward the door.

"Mr. Ehrlich," the Admiral restarted.

Arnold glanced back. "Yes, Sir."

"It's a tough life for a Jew, but you've earned your place in society. Don't let anyone trick you out of it."

"I won't," Arnold said but a knot formed in his stomach. Someone was trying to trick them out of what was rightfully theirs, a chance to earn their place as the king's jewelers.

CHAPTER 44

*J*ack outfitted Arnold and Fave with blue uniform coats like his. He gave them boxes to carry and told them to stay in the background during the hand-off with the barrister. Fave and Arnold stood under an awning of a loading station, keeping to the shadows. If they were found out too soon, they might lose any leverage they had.

The clock tower rang nine times, and the sun was still low in the sky. A gloomy fog set over the port, but the men around them seemed undeterred by the weather. Everything about this place was rough and ragged, the people, the weather, the humid air, the pungent smell of fish and sweat.

"Ah, Mr. Thompson, good morning." Jack turned his back to Arnold and Fave—smart boy—giving them a better view of the barrister.

Thompson gave no response, so Arnold checked over his shoulder as he bent over one of the crates, pretending to inspect the writing on the side. The man wasn't Marvin.

* * *

1804, Eaton College, Berkshires, England.

Eaton's red brick wall, seeping tradition, aristocracy, and scholarship was behind them. Arnold had always been wary of their secret, fearful they wouldn't fit in. But with his cousin, he never felt alone. Just recently, Fave's best friend Marvin Thompson had started to ask too many questions.

"You never told me why you were excused from classes to go home last weekend," Marvin said.

"Fave, you can't tell him, he's not one of us!" Arnold punched Fave in the arm.

Fave scowled at Arnold. "I'm 13. I'm a man and I know what I'm doing."

It had been their *Bnei-mitzvah*. Rabbi Solomon had brought a Torah to the Pearler's house and the family had gathered ten men, most of them Pavel's sons, plus a few goldsmiths and jewelers whom Uncle Gustav trusted. And so, in a clandestine but dignified ceremony, Fave and Arnold read from the Torah for the first time, their rite of passage into adulthood, an ancient Jewish tradition.

But Gustav had warned them, "Mark my words, sons, you're not adults outside of this ceremony."

Arnold understood, but the ado about their ceremony, and Aunt Eve's proud tears when they returned from the makeshift bimah in the green dining room, it had all gone to Fave's head, and he pranced about like a man of at least eighteen.

"He's my friend!" Fave's blond hair glistened in the sun.

"You don't know that," Arnold growled.

If the school found out they were Jewish, it would spell the end of their gentleman's education. Eaton was known as the cradle of England's statesmen, the gateway to Oxford and Cambridge—and it was closed off to Jews. Uncle Gustav had pulled some strings and made it abundantly clear in the carriage on their way to their orientation that they had to guard their secret at all cost. They'd be expelled immediately if anyone found out they were Jewish. And Fave was about to blow their cover. But Arnold stood firmly beside his cousin, he could never abandon him, no matter how naively or stupidly he sometimes behaved.

"Marv, we went home for an important rite of passage," Fave said.

"Did your father take you to Whites?" Marvin's boyish eyes blinked mischievously. "Did you meet Madame Griselda? Did she and you…? Did she teach you, too?" He made some wicked but uncoordinated flips with his hips.

Arnold grimaced. He leaned his shoulder against the black iron fence surrounding the statute of Henry VI, the founder of the prestigious boarding school for boys, and listened to Marvin Thompson telling his naive blond cousin about his father's mistress.

"Marv, it's more than that!" Fave beamed proudly. Arnold was in awe of how much goodness Fave had in his heart and how he always failed to see the evil in people, their truths.

"What could be better than that?" Marvin's eager tone only served to encourage Fave.

Arnold felt pure agony, like watching a hawk descend on a rabbit back at Brockton house in the summer—a devastating outcome, but he couldn't look away.

"We went back to London for our Bnei-mitzvah. We read from the Torah, and we're men now." Fave said, his back straight, his chin held high as if he'd just won a fencing match.

Marvin's face fell, his cheeks turned pale, but his forehead was red. A vein on his right temple pulsated under adolescent acne while Marvin processed the information. "Y-you mean you...you both...you're Jewish?"

Fave smiled warmly and nodded. The fool.

Arnold propped himself up and took a wider stance. There was no telling what Marvin would do now, but he knew it wouldn't be good. Yet, what Marvin said was even worse than Arnold had expected. It broke Fave's heart. And there was nothing Arnold could do to stop the hawk's grip on the bunny now.

Marvin eyed them both as if he'd seen them for the first time. Odd, since they'd shared the same dorm room for two years. "I don't understand. You're in our uniform!" Marvin pointed at their black tailcoats and black waist-coat, their starched stiff collars, and black pinstriped trousers. "You look...so normal!"

Fave's eyes widened for the first time, and Arnold's heart sank. The bunny was defenseless against the predator.

"Do your parents know?" Marvin asked, obviously puzzled.

Fave's eyes began to glisten. "What do you mean?"

"It's...it's atrocious! It could get you expelled! Don't you know you can't be Jewish around here?" Marvin waved his hand at the despicable word as if he couldn't force it out.

Fave spat on the floor and a small blob of foam landed right at the tip of Marvin's brightly polished black shoe. Arnold had never seen Fave spit before. And he never had since.

* * *

ARNOLD LOOKED at Fave in the blue coat. He knew all too well when his cousin was uncomfortable, and he appeared as awkward now as he did ten years ago in Eaton's schoolyard. Marvin Thompson had a way of getting under his skin. Since he'd betrayed Fave's trust and turned down his friendship, Fave had preferred books. He read Greek mythology with a passion. Arnold was his only friend, his brother. Arnold had often secretly worried that Fave would never find a girl to marry, but then Fave married Rachel. She was just as bookish as Fave, and Arnold liked her. She was pretty, and since Rachel had moved in, Fave had a spring in his step that he'd lost that day at Eaton.

A smallish figure appeared from the shadows and scribbled a signature on the paper. When the person bent over, Arnold thought he saw some blond curls, stiffly glued to...it couldn't be. He nudged Fave with his elbow and Fave nodded without looking at him. He'd recognized her, too.

CHAPTER 45

*B*ack in the carriage, Arnold watched the city reappear as they trotted further away from the smelly port. As if the positive green energy from the trees pushed up from the soil through the city and reached for the sky, he felt replenished as he distanced himself from the corruption he'd witnessed this morning. He closed his eyes and inhaled deeply, wishing he were on a boat on the pond behind Brockton's house where he'd relaxed many days in his childhood, dangling his feet into the water and watching it ripple away from him, washing away his sadness after his parents had died.

"Why do you figure she's doing it?" Fave asked, so innocently Arnold worried for him.

"We did take her home away, exile her mother to the country house, and remove her from society," Arnold said.

"I just don't understand how anyone can be this venge-ful." Fave expected an answer that would explain the world to him, how evil still reigned free. Clearly, Rachel had restored his faith in humanity, and Arnold didn't want to be the one to blow on his house of cards. "Doesn't she see that we've been paying for her life for over twenty years?

"She took my seal," Arnold said. "She planted it on Hannah so I'd suspect her. She…" he made a fist and rubbed his thigh in agony. How could he have doubted his sweet perfect Hannah? How could he have hurt her so?

"Surely, we can challenge the validity of the contracts? A bill of lading is just a sales contract," Fave said.

"We could, but it would take years. Greg needs to get his ships back onto the sea. If we wait for years, Marvin or some other prick could take his spot."

"But if we don't fight the bills of lading, then he owes over fifty thousand and so do we," Fave said.

"Go home. Please tell Hannah that I know she didn't take my seal. I'll explain it all later. I have to make another stop before I come home." Arnold didn't have the heart to bring Fave's spirit down as low as his own. The extent of corruption had profoundly disheartened Arnold. All he could think about was the repair and restoration of an order he hoped he could live with. Allison wielded too much power over him and his family. Fave left the carriage and Arnold rode on to the temple gardens.

* * *

HALF AN HOUR LATER, Arnold jumped out of his carriage, which bore the elegant Pearler family crest with a curly capital E on the side of the cabin to honor his last name, Ehrlich. And "ehrlich" he would be, for it meant earnest. His last name had a meaning, both in German and in Yiddish. Two languages, poles apart, converged in a simple word, the one that positioned him at the axle of his life. He was tired of keeping the antisemitism as close to his heart as the pride in his Jewish heritage. Fed up with the injustice of having to keep his head down or cover his tracks, Arnold knew he hadn't done anything wrong. Society was unforgiving, as if Judaism were a transgression. For the Pearlers and Arnold, it was a privilege. The secret that endangered his livelihood and his family's welfare wasn't even remotely as dark as the many corrupt and criminal activities done by the people who threatened his existence. Enough was enough. He'd always been upstanding. And he was going to stand up for what he knew was right.

He stormed into the barristers' offices and up the stairs to the dusty towers of paper that soiled them.

"Marvin!" he yelled.

Arnold recognized the woman with painted lips from a previous encounter with Marvin's father. She came through a door, left it open, and seemed to stuff her breasts back into her bodice.

Arnold swallowed in disgust and walked into Marvin's office. "Does your new wife know about your by-blows?"

Marvin was putting on his jacket and buttoning his shirt. "She needn't know, and I trust you won't tell her."

Arnold made a fist. It took all of his restraint not to punch Marvin in his smug face. "Well, fancy that, I just saw her at the port." Arnold sat down, spreading his legs as if he owned the place.

Marvin eyed him suspiciously, then erected a wall before his eyes. Arnold remembered this face from the many times he'd been sent to the headmaster at Eaton. It was his tell when he lied.

"You must have mistaken her for someone else," Marvin said as he sat, straight as a menhir in the wind.

"Funny that, I think you're right." Arnold grinned.

Marvin's eyes shot to his. "Arnold, out with it."

Arnold leaned back and took up even more space. He was better built than Marvin and had a stronger presence in the room. He'd always been an alpha predator, while Marvin was nothing more than one of those plovers, the jumpy little birds that cleaned crocodile's teeth. Arnold gave Marvin enough time to realize he was about to snap his little beak off.

"Imagine my surprise when I was going to check on one of my tea shipping contracts"—Arnold pushed his breeches down with both hands and rose from his seat, assuming a wide stance—"when a skinny chap comes to my clerk bearing my seal and signature on a bill of lading." Arnold leaned toward Marvin and pulled his screeching chair with the man in it.

Marvin remained stiff like a meerkat blinded by the sun.

Arnold leaned lower and put both hands on Marvin's armrests, locking him in his desk chair. "Do you know what kind of coiffure the chap had?" Arnold asked.

Marvin shook his head, avoiding Arnold's gaze.

"Tight little blond curls, waxed and oiled. A slick prick," Arnold said with a deeper voice now, purring like a lion on the prowl. "Does this remind you of anyone in particular?"

Marvin remained silent. The vein in his temple pulsated vigorously.

Arnold released Marvin and paced the room. The stacks of paper and dusty treatises were as tall as grass in the savannah. His shoulder blades and hips moved as if in slow motion. This was the moment he'd been waiting for since that day in the schoolyard. Marvin broke Fave's heart then, and he threatened Fave's family now.

"So, you know the bills of lading have to be signed off by a barrister, and bear a seal of authenticity before they can be presented to the clerks at the port?"

Marvin nodded.

"Of course, you'd know. Since you've been called to the Bar." Arnold gave Marvin a sideways glance and noticed a few sweat pearls forming on his forehead. Ironic, the bad kind of pearls. Time to strike.

"What do you think, in your expert opinion, as a newly barred member of the Inner Temple, of a pregnant woman's chances to survive a sentence for impersonating a barrister?"

"What do you mean?" Marvin whispered.

"Well, if she's about two or three months along, and the sentencing takes half a year, she'd be giving birth just in time to see her child on the way to the reformatory…or where is it they send impoverished aristocratic women for legal infractions?"

Marvin looked at Arnold as if he were the sun, blinded by the shock of being found out.

"I'm not the expert here when it comes to crimes but let me see"—Arnold rubbed his chin to drag out the moment—"breaking and entering into a private study, theft of a seal, document forgery, and there is, of course, the matter of *respondeat superior*." The legal doctrine of holding the master responsible for his employee.

"There is no such matter," Marvin said.

"You are mistaken, my friend."

Strike two. Allison had signed Marvin's name, thereby binding him to the forged bills of lading, which served as the sales contracts of the goods.

"A bill of lading has to be reissued with every new cargo vessel, doesn't it, Barrister Thompson?"

Marvin nodded. He was gripping his armrests as if to brace himself for a tornado.

"And explain this to me, Barrister Thompson, when do the rights of a bill of lading vest in the consignee, the buyer of the goods?"

"Upon completion of the transaction," Marvin mumbled.

"And when is that moment?" Arnold asked, enunciating every word perfectly to augment the pain he could finally inflict upon Marvin, who'd tortured his family and endangered their livelihood.

Marvin mumbled something inaudibly.

"What was that?"

"When the seal and signature are affixed," Marvin shouted.

Strike three. Allison had forged the seal and signature for Arnold, thereby making the contracts enforceable.

"Ah." Arnold stood in front of Marvin's bookshelf and skimmed the treatises. "Maritime law, bills of lading, forms...let's see." He set the thick leather-bound book with minuscule text before Marvin. "Find the page," Arnold commanded in his deepest growl.

Marvin lowered his head and did as he was told.

I. RIGHTS under Bills of Lading to vest in Consignee or Endorsee.

Every Consignee of Goods named in a Bill of Lading, and every Endorsee of a Bill of Lading to whom the Property in the Goods therein mentioned shall pass, shall be subject to the same Liabilities in respect of such Goods as if the Contract contained in the Bill of Lading had been made with himself.

ARNOLD LEFT Marvin with the thick book and walked around the office again, strutting like a peacock with his arms behind his back. Why hadn't he thought of this earlier?

"What do you want, Arnold?" Marvin grumbled.

"Nah, nah, don't be so gruff, my old friend,"

"I'm not your old friend," Marvin hissed.

"Now, that's the only true word you ever said." Arnold gave him a dangerous smile with raised brows. If he had the power, he'd have shot fire darts from his eyes. "If I understand the statute correctly, the endorsee—that's you

—is liable for the same contract for the sale of goods as the consignee, me?"

"Yes."

"Aha, so then it really is a shame that those crates of tea had been emptied. We could've made a fortune, you and me."

"I don't do business with Jews." Marvin spat on the floor.

Arnold felt his arms tensing, getting ready to give Marvin a blow to his smug evil face. "Marvin, if you were only so lucky as to do business with me, you'd have made a profitable gamble here. But your wife forged my seal and signature onto the contract that binds you to pay for the empty crates. And do you know, Marv, how much I owe?"

"As much as Stone," Marvin said.

"Well, as much as you, Stone, and I. What's fifty thousand pounds divided by three?"

Marvin remained silent.

"That's what I thought, it's more than you have. More than you'll ever have. But not me. Not Stone."

"You're a rat, nothing but a filthy little Jewish rodent." Marvin's eyes were bloodshot, and he seemed like a ferocious weasel about to jump on a bug, but unable to take on any higher animals.

"The thing about rats is that they're strong, Marv. They swim, they climb, they even live for days without food and water." Arnold stood straight and looked down his chest at Marvin. And with his most condescending tone, he said, "Rats feast upon slimy little eels when they get into deep waters, Marv. And the eel in this story, that's you!"

"What's your problem, Arnold?" Marvin asked.

"My ... my problem? Are you jesting?"

"It seems as though you managed to turn the cards in your favor." Marvin shrugged like a scorpion before closing in for a sting.

"You forged my signature, you bound me to contracts I never made, you tried to remove a member of parliament from his post, your pregnant wife impersonated you, a barrister, and you ask me what my problem is? You stayed our shipments and blocked us from producing—" But he stopped himself before he could give Marvin too much credit. For all he knew, the nasty eel would revel in the agony he'd caused and take it as a compliment.

Marvin smiled menacingly and shrugged again.

"Have you lost your mind?" Arnold asked.

Marvin jumped up from his seat. "Have I lost my mind? No, Arnold, I have not!" He pushed past Arnold and hit his shoulder.

Arnold felt the bony, unshapely body of a do-no-good whose only physical exercise consisted of extra-marital affairs.

"I was going to marry the daughter of a patroness of Almack's. I was going to be tapped into the ton. I was going ... argh," Marvin growled.

"You did marry her! She's expecting your child if I am not mistaken."

"Oh, but you are mistaken, you filthy little rodent."

Arnold stood over Marvin, tall and strong, clean and elegant. He blinked pityingly at the man who cowered and pulled his nasty ringtail between his legs. It was clear that

Marvin was more of a pest than Arnold, who posed as the king of the jungle would.

"I'm stuck with Allison, and she's a witch!"

Arnold spluttered with laughter. They deserved each other. "Congratulations on your nuptials, Marvin. Have a lifetime together and then some!"

Arnold pivoted and strode out of the barrister's offices.

CHAPTER 46

$\mathcal{M}$eanwhile, back at the Pearler's house, Hannah was pouting in her room.

Someone knocked.

"I'm sleeping."

"Hannah, it's Fave."

Why was he here?

She opened the door. Lizzie and Rachel were beside him. Of course.

"Arnold had to run an errand, but he asked me to tell you that he knows you didn't take his seal."

Hannah puffed indignantly. "I've never stolen a thing in my life!"

Fave nodded and gave Lizzie a nudge. "I'll let you ladies be. Rachel, I'll see you later?"

He kissed his wife on the cheek with all the tenderness Hannah longed for in Arnold's kisses but thought she could never have again. He'd implied that she stole his seal. How could he distrust her so? After … everything?

Lizzie took Hannah's wrist and pulled her to the bed. "Sit, we need to talk." She had the same airs as her mother. There was no arguing with her.

Fave closed the door and Rachel and Lizzie sat on either side of Hannah.

"I think you like my cousin," Lizzie said.

Hannah blushed.

"You more than like him, don't you?" Rachel said, clearly the more mature and experienced of the two.

"I can't go back to how I was before I met him," Hannah said.

"Did you ... um ..." Lizzie's eyes were wide and curious.

Hannah nodded. "But also, my home is in shambles, and I am"—Hannah made a hand motion around her hair —"I don't want to look like a kitchen maid anymore." Her voice crackled with tears at the last few words. "You were so nice to me, and I made a mess of things." She heaved with sobs.

"You didn't. It's Alli, she has a certain way to ..." Rachel turned to Lizzie for the right words.

"She's like a curse, leaving a dark cloud of pestilence in her wake, wherever she goes," Lizzie said.

Hannah snorted a strained laugh. "Her baby will be quite a brood."

Lizzie gasped. "Her baby?"

"She's about two months along, close to three probably. She's nauseated by everything, even biscuits, and tea."

"And you know this because you have a baby?" Rachel asked cautiously.

"Yes, but it's not what you think. Ruthie's my baby

sister. She's ten months old. My mother died when I was twenty. She had a seizure when the baby was born."

Lizzie's hand flew to her mouth. Rachel paled and sat closer to Hannah. She put an arm around her and grabbed her hand tight as though she felt her pain.

"Ruthie is my sister, I know that, of course. But she's *my baby.*" Hannah swallowed a tear. "I've never been apart from her for this long. I … I …" she started to weep and gasp for air, "I can't breathe. I want my baby back. And I miss all of them terribly."

She looked and felt defeated. Hannah had assumed her mother's role in the family without a chance to grow up first. She wasn't a wife, she hadn't been with child, she'd never been married, yet Hannah was the mother to seven siblings, and one of them an infant.

"I keep her crib in my room at home. It's cold at night, so I hold her on my chest and keep her warm. She's so tiny."

Rachel's cheeks were lined with tears. "I had a baby sister, too. But she died."

Fave had told Hannah about Rachel's baby sister's tragic death in Switzerland before Rachel and her family came to England.

"And your father?" Lizzie asked.

"What about my father?" Hannah asked, trying to cease her sobbing.

"I think what Lizzie means is that Ruthie is his child, surely, he wouldn't let you keep her when you marry?"

"I'm not marrying. She's my baby. Nobody will have me with a baby. And *Tate* can barely make ends meet. The boys eat more in the morning than the rest of us in a day."

Lizzie gave Rachel a sad look.

"You'll have to live your own life someday," Rachel said.

Hannah gave her a dark stare of rapprochement. "Ruthie is part of my life."

"D-do you like Arnold?" Lizzie asked.

"What's not to like?" Hannah asked, but she couldn't mask her wounded heart. Every time she saw his sultry blue eyes and every time she ran her hair through his soft hair, she felt as if the scabs on her heart were being torn open. Instead of making herself fall out of love, she could barely breathe without Arnold.

"You're not answering my question. Do you?" Lizzie persisted.

Hannah nodded.

"Then you have to find a way," Lizzie said sternly. "I can't imaginee he'd ever hold family against you. He loves children and he loves family."

Hannah turned ashen. "What did I do?" her hands came to her cheeks. "Do you think it's too late to win him back?"

CHAPTER 47

Arnold looked for Hannah as soon as he came home. He wanted to apologize, to make it right. He'd wronged her by even entertaining any doubt that she could have stolen his seal. He was an idiot. Now, she'd leave and not even know that he loved her.

Hannah's door was open, the room empty. Arnold heard voices from Lenny's room, so he approached the door and listened.

"What will happen to us now, *Channi*? Are we homeless?"

"Oh no, my dear, we're not homeless. *Tate* will come back, and we'll simply move to another house," Hannah said, her voice thick with doubt.

"In Birmingham? Do you think he'll come to pick us up?"

"Maybe...but don't worry your little head, my dear. Let me tell you a story," Hannah said.

Arnold leaned back against the wall; he didn't want to be seen or heard. Actually, why not? He took the jewel from his pocket, clutching the pouch in his fist.

"Pardon me," he peeked around the door.

"Arnie!" Lenny beamed.

Arnold liked the nickname the boy had established for him. Hannah smiled, too. Maybe he still had a chance with her?

"Good evening, Lenny, Hannah." Arnold came close and bowed. "I came to see whether there's anything the patient requires."

"I changed his bandage a few times. The wound is healing well." She scooted closer to Lenny on his bed. "We were just going to tell a story, and then get some sleep." Her voice was motherly, mature, and a little dismissive.

"May I join you?" Arnold didn't wait for areply, but sat beside Hannah on Lenny's bed cover.

"There's a girl knight, but she has to go back to the fairy world," Lenny filled him in.

"Ah, I see." Arnold looked at Hannah, but she dropped her gaze. She was holding Lenny's bandaged hand with both of hers. Arnold realized that she felt responsible for her siblings, but it was more than that. She loved them like a mother. She'd stepped into her mother's shoes.

"Did this girl knight slay any dragons?" Arnold asked.

"Oh yes, yes!" Lenny sat up straight.

"And what happened to the dragon?"

"Er, nothing," Hannah said.

"What do you mean nothing?" Arnold smiled.

"You never told me, did he die, *Channi?*" Lenny asked, his eyes wide.

"How was he defeated?" Arnold asked.

"By sword!" Lenny explained.

"Aha, there we have it," Arnold said.

"Have what?" Hannah asked.

"Well, as an avid fencer"—Arnold put his hand on his chest and blinked at Lenny, who gave him a worshipping beam—"let me tell you, a sword rarely kills. That's only in fairy tales."

"But this is a fairy tale." Hannah grew impatient.

"No, it's not. I can prove it." He turned to Lenny. "The dragon was hurt, but he flew home. His home was far, far away … an ocean away. He soared up into the cold air like a bird and through the clouds. But the strain of his wings flapping caused him such pain that he cried." Arnold gestured large flying motions with his arms, careful to keep the little pouch hidden in his palm.

Lenny gasped. "Dragons cry?"

"Of course, everybody cries when they're hurt," Hannah said.

"Even Arnie?"

Arnold cleared his throat. "Sure."

"Anyway, the poor dragon cried, not only because of his injuries, but also because he was defeated. And when a dragon's tear falls into the ocean, and if they're caught by a giant conch shell, do you know what happens?"

"What?" Lenny was on the edge of his bed.

"This!" Arnold took out the pearl from the pouch he'd brought with him. "A rare and magical Melo Melo pearl is formed. This is the only one known to exist in Europe."

Hannah and Lenny both leaned over Arnold's hand to admire the precious pearl. Arnold held it between his thumb and index finger. It was large, shiny and yellow-orange with a speckled pattern.

"How did you get a dragon tear?" Lenny asked, amazed.

"I didn't. My grandfather gave it to me."

"Why?" Hannah asked.

"He never told me why, just that it was meant for me to pass on when time was right. He said I'd know when that will be."

Lenny looked sleepy and rubbed his little eyes, so Arnold waited in the hallway while Hannah gave him a good-night kiss.

"Arnie?" Lenny called from under the covers.

"Yes, little one?" Arnold stood in the door.

"Will you tell me who gets your pearl?"

"Yes, Lenny, I promise to tell you. You have my word."

Hannah blew out Lenny's nightstand candle and came out of the room. She closed the door quietly, and Arnold took her hand. She hesitated but held still.

He placed her hand on his heart. "Hannah, I would love for you to have the Melo pearl."

Her eyes found his. "I don't understand."

"As an engagement present."

Hannah shook her head as if she was protesting the thoughts in her mind. "I wish I could, but I …" She looked at Arnold's feet. "I can't."

"Why not?" Arnold asked, his voice low and sad.

"Because I don't belong here. You welcomed me into your home, and I'll be forever grateful, but I am packaged in your life. I don't even have my own clothes."

"I know how you feel."

"You can't possibly."

"I do, truly. Like an imposter. As if you won a prize that you didn't earn."

Hannah's eyes grew wider.

"I made arrangements with Greg today. I'll fix everything. He's letting me take his fleet to America, and I'll bring back the supplies we need for the competition."

"Is this why you want to go to America? To earn your place in the family?"

Arnold nodded, delighted by the depth with which Hannah could understand him. She saw him for who he was, not who he seemed to represent.

* * *

"I can't burden you with a child," Hannah said.

Arnold looked down along her stomach. "It's impossible," he whispered.

"Oh, oh … oh my, I mean Ruthie."

"Who?"

"My sister."

Arnold stared at her quizzically.

"I'm like a mother for her. I need to see her grow up."

"You said she's your sister."

"She is, my *baby* sister. My baby."

Arnold rubbed his eyes. "If I marry you, you'll have more than enough funds to see her well cared for. I don't understand how Ruthie is an impediment to our love."

"I care for her. I'm the only mother she knows. I can't

give her to a stranger, which means, I can't go with you. I understand your quest to bring the gems for the competition, it's who you are. But you must know who I am."

"I know who you are, Hannah, but I'm not sure you do."

"I know very well! I am Hannah Solomon, the Chief Rabbi's daughter! Everyone knows who I am. And I'm ruined now. Plus, my duties continue, so I basically go on like before, except in disgrace."

Arnold stepped back. "You think I am a disgrace?"

Hannah pinched her eyes closed and sighed. "You know that's not how I meant it."

Arnold stood stiff before her, at a carefully calculated distance.

"She's a baby, she needs me!" Hannah restarted.

"*I need you.*"

At that, she frowned. "You don't." She put her hands on his chest and felt the strength of his youth, the appeal of his heat. "You still have to prove yourself, build a fleet, cross the ocean, find a treasure—"

"What's that supposed to mean, that I'm a child?"

"No, but you're still growing up, Arnold. You're lucky, you *get* to grow up. The day my mother died, when the doctor's assistant put Ruthie in my arms"—Hannah started to cry and swallowed a lump in her throat—"my childhood ended, and I became a mother of seven, an adult."

"My parents died when I was a little boy."

"I know, Arnold, and I'm sorry. But this isn't a competition. Your family loves you, unconditionally. You've been pampered and spoiled. And yet you need to prove yourself because you clearly have nothing else to worry about." Hannah waved for emphasis.

Then she pushed him away, her palms lingering on his chest. "No matter where you go and how far you fall, the Pearlers will catch you. But in my family, I'm the catcher."

She felt so fragile and modest. Meek compared to the stallion that was Arnold.

* * *

HIS FEELINGS WERE HURT, but no matter what she said, he loved her more and more with every passing second. Still, he couldn't restrain her. He had to set her free. But he wasn't sure her understanding of freedom was what was best for her.

It would be unfair to hold on to her, to tear her away from a baby. He wasn't a monster. He'd have to find a way to cure his rage, the thirst for her, his inability to breathe when she wasn't near.

"Hannah, I am going to America for the pearls. For the competition. If I don't go, if we lose because of me … this is our chance to prove our merit."

"I understand. The ton. You need a footing … but if all the money and riches don't matter, who says the appointment to crown jeweler would make a difference?"

"Hannah, how can you be so cynical at one and twenty?" He ran his hands through his hair.

"I'm not. You go on your adventure and treasure hunt. If I'm not round with child when you return, you're free."

"And if you are?"

"I shall release you of your burden."

"You're not a *burden* to me!" He wanted to tell her how much he loved her. But this wasn't the time. She was angry, her heart had closed off.

"I'm not in my elements, I'm a fish swimming in the sand here, Arnold. Can't you see?"

"See what?" he snapped, louder than he should have. "Am I an evil scorpion ready to eat your head?"

Hannah rolled her eyes. "I sleep in your family's bed, I wear their clothes, eat their food, and for what? What can I possibly offer them in return?"

"You don't need to offer them anything in return. You have me."

"That's rich coming from you. They love you like a son, yet you're rebuilding Stone's fleet to travel across the Atlantic to prove your worth. What can I say? I'm an imposter."

"You're not an imposter, Hannah. You're … you're …"

"I'm sorry but I can't. Ruthie needs me … and I need her … to be with her."

Arnold closed his eyes and mumbled, "How very altruistic of you!"

"Yes, actually," she crossed her arms. "I'll be exactly where I am today in twenty years, when Ruthie has gone off with a family and they're all married. In fact, it's my job to see to it."

"No, it's a rut. You're too scared to get out of your own way and make a life for yourself."

Hannah humpfed and turned to leave. She had her

hand on her bedroom door handle, when Arnold said, "Hannah, please come with me. As my wife."

She looked him deeply in the eyes but then disappeared into her room.

CHAPTER 48

*H*annah leaned against her door and sagged down like a rock in the Thames. She'd ruined everything. A prince had kissed her, he even proposed to her, but she rejected him. When *Tate* would see that the synagogue had collapsed under Hannah's care, and Lenny had a cut on his hand from the ice skating blade, he'd never trust her with anything again. For someone who thought she was so responsible, she felt rather careless.

Her eyes fell to the book on her nightstand. Adam Smith's *The Theory of Moral Sentiments*. She opened it to the first page. First edition printed in 1759. She closed her eyes. This book probably cost more than her entire wardrobe. But even that was gone, crushed by the roof that had destroyed her life, as if the burden had been too much to bear, not just for her but her entire community. The collapse of the synagogue and their home was a sign. If only she knew for what.

She clutched the book to her chest and walked to her bed, dropping it on its spine. The book opened on a random page, and Hannah leaned down to read.

THE PRINCIPLES OF THE IMAGINATION, upon which our sense of beauty depends, are of a very nice and delicate nature, and may easily be altered by habit and education: but the sentiments of moral approbation and disapprobation, are founded on the strongest and most vigorous passions of human nature; and though they may be somewhat warpt, cannot be entirely perverted.

When custom and fashion coincide with the natural principles of right and wrong, they heighten the delicacy of our sentiments and increase our abhorrence for everything which approaches to evil. Those who have been educated in what is really good company, not in what is commonly called such, who have been accustomed to see nothing in the persons whom they esteemed and lived with, but justice, modesty, humanity, and good order, are more shocked with whatever seems to be inconsistent with the rules which those virtues prescribe.

SHE WONDERED why Arnold had chosen this book for her. Was she so inflexible in her thinking? Was she so consumed by the teachings of the Torah as to see them only in her orthodox community? If it was true that *justice, modesty, humanity, and good order* could exist in any set of customs, then maybe she'd been blinded by fashions? Was it the packaging that warped her thinking?

Hannah swallowed. Was she as shallow as Allison? Was

it possible that she judged a man like Gregory Stone by his fashions rather than his actions? Had her sentiments been warped to become insensitive to true evil?

She hadn't seen what Allison was capable of. But she was appalled by it. Hannah closed the book and searched for the name of the author. This man, Adam Smith, was really on to something.

Hannah's hand flew to her mouth as she reread the passage. She had to tell Arnold. She had to apologize. Hannah snapped the book shut and took it with her. She ran down the flight of stairs and called Arnold.

A light flickered from the study. She slowed down and knocked on the door.

She found Arnold standing in front of Gregory.

"Good evening, Hannah. Pardon us but we have matters to discuss," Gregory said grimly.

Arnold looked at her with the same pained expression he'd had when she ran away from him earlier that night. She'd rejected the marriage proposal of a prince. She'd been a fool.

"I...I...um... have come to apologize."

CHAPTER 49

*G*regory stood, swirling a tumbler of a dark brown liquid. The liquor left oily hills and valleys on the inside of the glass. Arnold, as usual, was the perfect host but not much of a drinker. He'd told her he didn't like the burn of alcohol and preferred another kind. Hannah was consumed with a burning rage against herself and her circumstances. She wanted Arnold; she didn't want to take the edge off her feelings with alcohol. She wanted to punish herself for letting it all go this far. She'd allowed him to put her up in his palace. She'd been the fairy knight and watched him slay the dragon, Lady Allison, and now she needed to return to her fairy people. And yet her sensibilities had changed, as Adam Smith would have put it.

"Hannah, I have pressing matters to discuss with Arnold," Gregory said again. "Please leave us."

Hannah's eyes darted to Arnold. She couldn't muster polite niceties with Gregory. While she still disapproved of his family's choices, she had to apologize for seeing the world as all black and white.

"I'd like to speak to you, please," Hannah said to Gregory, but she glanced at Arnold.

Greg sighed. "Hannah, I don't have the time to chit chat—"

"—I asked her to marry me, Greg. While I'm awaiting an answer, you can discuss anything freely before her."

Hannah gasped. Arnold was serious.

"I apologize for my ... er ... rash judgments of your family, Mr. Stone," Hannah said as she squared her shoulders before him.

He took a sip of his liquor.

Hannah stepped to Arnold and assumed a wide stance on his side. He took her hand and placed it in the fold of his arm. His hand never left hers.

Maybe he'd still have her after all. Perhaps she could have a prince charming in a castle. Could she rise to the challenge and somehow balance her priorities? She could allow herself to love him without the fear of betraying her siblings. Wasn't more love a good thing?

Arnold looked down at her, and she held his gaze. Before he could turn away, her eyes told him what was in her heart. He glowered at her and seemed to take it all in. They shared a magical connection, being able to speak with their eyes only. Right from the onset back in the synagogue, it had been like this. And somehow, as precious as this connection was, it was larger than either of them alone.

Gregory eyed the couple. "Is this"—he waved an air circle around Arnold and Hannah—"supposed to stick?"

Arnold tightened his arm and pinned Hannah closer to his body. "I hope so."

Gregory sniffed and held silent in thought. Hannah felt as if she was being examined and about to fail an important test.

"The ton's gonna feast on you and rip you apart." Gregory came closer, and Hannah held her breath.

"They might," Arnold said grimly. Hannah was a threat to the Pearler's secret. She'd been so self-absorbed, so focused on what he would do to her life, that she never truly considered his feelings? She was the Rabbi's daughter and surely there was no place for her in the ton. Hannah nearly gagged on her realization. Arnold's arm grew tighter.

Gregory stood right before them like a large pillar. "I hope you know what he's offering you, Hannah," he said with a clear warning ring.

Hannah said nothing. A million thoughts and doubts raced through her mind. She couldn't possibly be deserving of Arnold and his world. The Pearlers...she could destroy their position among the ton with her ties to the orthodox community. Their worlds didn't mix, like vinegar and oil. And their religion would surface when the emulsion wasn't shaken. She didn't understand the machinery of the haute-couture jewelry business, but surely Arnold had ties in his community just as she had in hers.

Arnold's grip was so strong now, that she could sense him steadying her. He was holding her, anchoring her to him regardless of where her mind trailed.

"I'd like to give her my name and my protection," Arnold told Gregory.

The man looked startled and raised a brow. Then he bowed before Hannah.

* * *

ARNOLD REALIZED Hannah wanted to slip away, but he wouldn't let her. Not again. Never. But there was still the problem at hand.

"Let me be the first to offer my congratulations then," Gregory said with a bow.

Hannah flushed. "Oh no, I ... er—"

"So, the fleets are all stranded without contracts, Greg?" Arnold said.

"Indeed, I have fourteen ships in this fleet and nine in the other. Marvin's gotten to them all."

Arnold took this in for a moment. "I was willing to take a small group to import pearls, but I don't know what to do about two fleets."

He felt Hannah's eyes on him. She probably wasn't following the conversation. He liked her on his arm though, her soft small hand warmed him through the layers of his sleeves.

"What are these buttons made of?" Hannah asked.

"Mother of pearl," Arnold said, "but now's not the time."

"I'm not." Hannah started pacing the room. "Can I see the document Allison forged?"

Arnold groaned and went to retrieve it from the desk. The forgery was on the top of a small neat pile of documents. When he handed it to Hannah, she sat down and read it over and over.

"Hannah?"

"Hmmm?"

Arnold shook his head. "It's not just one. Marvin and Allison sabotaged Greg's entire fleet. It's one thing to pay for the outstanding contracts, we can barely manage that, but the ships are stuck at the harbors, and the crews—"

"This says you can't return an empty cargo ship."

"Yes, so what?"

"Then don't."

Gregory turned and poured himself another glass of liquor.

"Hannah, don't you understand? I'm bringing a crew, supplies, provisions … when it's all used up, the ship's empty," Arnold explained.

"It doesn't have to be."

Arnold lost his patience. "Look, Hannah, I appreciate your concern, but I am at an impasse. If I don't bring back the largest and fanciest treasure trove of pearls for the competition, Gustav and Fave won't win the competition. Then I can't pay for the contracts that bear my seal. Allison really put us in a pickle this time. And if she takes Greg's position in the house of Lords for Marvin. And if Gustav and Fave don't win—"

"I know. Then you're not the one who helped them earn their place in court as the crown jewelers."

"Yes."

"Tell me again what will happen when you go to America?"

"I can't go now."

"Let's pretend that you can. Talk me through the steps."

"It's not a step-by-step process like braiding challah."

"Arnold, tell me."

"All right. We get there and purchase carriages. Then we travel to the Ohio river, gather as many pearls as we can, and move on to the Tennessee and then the Mississippi."

Gregory walked to Hannah, the liquid in his tumbler flip-flopping over the edges of his glass. "The passage usually takes about thirty days, but my ships have many sails, so we can do it in twenty-five."

"The competition is set for the end of the year, which gives us May to travel, three months in America, then another month for the return passage. I need to bring back enough pearls for Gustav and Fave to set in October and November, so we can present the jewels in December."

"You expect to go there once, find a treasure trove of pearls, and come back to win the competition?"

Arnold and Gregory stared at Hannah as if there was nothing more natural in the world than a successful pearl treasure hunt. Had they been fooling themselves?

"What happens when you win the competition? And others want pearl jewels from you?"

Her question hung in the air and Gregory and Arnold exchanged a glance. Gregory rubbed his chin.

"You're going at this all wrong, it's not sustainable," Hannah said.

Arnold rolled his eyes. "It's my only chance."

"I have quite a bit riding on this as well, Ms. Solomon," Gregory added.

"Then use the triangle of the rivers," Hannah said. "And a triangle over the Atlantic."

"What triangle?" Gregory asked, obviously at a loss why Hannah wanted to discuss geometry while their family's livelihoods were at stake.

She walked to the desk and took the quill and a piece of paper. "Look." She drew a rough outline of the North American continent. Then she drew some squiggly lines representing the Ohio, Tennessee, and Mississippi rivers."

"We'd set anchor here." Arnold pointed to the approximate position of New York.

Hannah marked the spot with an X.

"I don't have time for the geography lesson." Gregory put down his glass, clearly preparing to leave.

"Hear me out." Hannah's voice was stern. "When you arrive, it'll cost you to keep the ships in the harbor for four months. You won't have enough time to get to know the areas and to rummage each riverbed, or whatever the search is called."

Gregory huffed impatiently, but Arnold asked Hannah to continue.

"You'll need to set up outposts with people you can trust. If you have teams of men traveling along each riverbed, they can load a ship at a time."

"We can't possibly fill a ship with pearls and make it seem loaded," Gregory said.

"Not with pearls"—Hannah smiled—"but with shells."

"Why would we bring the shells back?"

"For me. I'll need them." She felt Arnold's smile growing but kept her eyes focused on the paper on the table. "You create trade routes. There's a small triangle around the rivers, then another larger triangle over the Atlantic. You have two ports to diversify the pearl searches and you can keep the outposts mobile." She drew a star on the peninsula near Boston, another near Florida, then swished the quill straight back to England.

"Hannah, you can't imagine how many shells there'll be," Arnold said. "You may want a few—"

"I'll build a button factory in my community. I'll need lots of shells." She beamed with excitement, enthusiasm, and something else, something new. Entrepreneurship.

Gregory sat down.

Arnold's chest filled with hope, proud to have the smartest girl in England. Well, he didn't have her yet. But almost. "You mean to start a trade route? The fleet will be constantly loading, unloading, reloading pearls?"

"And shells," Hannah added.

"And shells." Arnold smiled at her and then at Gregory. Why hadn't they thought of that? "So, we'll have a steady influx of pearls and gems from the various outposts for our business, and shells for you to manufacture?

"Precisely." Hannah smiled.

Arnold's face lit up. "And where pray tell, will this button factory be built?"

"On the premises of the old synagogue," she said matter-of-factly.

"And where will the new synagogue go?"

Hannah shrugged. "I don't know, maybe closer to St. James." She beamed at Gregory with an implied invitation to bring the matter before parliament. When church and state weren't separate, the state could help to fund the construction of a new temple.

Arnold stifled a laugh. Prinny would have to approve such an endeavor if it promoted the arts.

"I'll find some architects to get Prinny's support," Gregory said.

Arnold couldn't believe his ears. Gregory was on Hannah's side now. "You're quite possibly the most brilliant person I have ever—"

"Ahem, ahem," Gregory cleared his throat. "Yes, she's a much-needed fresh wind. But where does that leave my fleet?"

"Isn't it obvious, Greg?" Arnold took a second piece of paper and laid it next to Hannah's map. He drew dotted lines on his rough sketch of Great Britain. "You have an exclusive contract, a form contract that can't be forged. You'd have a trade route, and outposts. You'd be one of the richest, most influential members the parliament ever had."

Gregory stood and inspected the sketches. He turned the paper. "This map will need a little finessing by my navy officers..."

Arnold laid his hand over Hannah's. They knew they had him.

"You mean this fleet would forego continental Europe and yet allow for a fluid travel from here to New York?" Gregory asked.

Arnold nodded. They all examined the sketches.

"My, my, Ms. Solomon, you may have just solved one of the greatest political and economic impasses—"

"I'd like to ask for an advance on the first shipment of shells and permission to open a Jewish factory." Hannah was brazen.

Arnold's chest filled with sweet pride. Oh, how he loved her. "I suggest you come and get the shells yourself. Then you don't need an advance at all." He grinned.

"I'll personally file a petition for your factory," Gregory added.

"But you'd have to come to get your shells and hire your own men to wash and load them," Arnold said.

Hannah's smile fell away like a leaf from a tree shedding its leaves in the autumn.

CHAPTER 50

The next morning, Hannah was sitting at the small escritoire in her room when she heard a knock on the door.

"*Channi*? Are you sleeping?" Her father stuck his head in.

"*Tate*!" She jumped up when she saw him standing at the open door and fell into his arms.

"My sweet girl." He kissed her forehead and she dug her face into his coat.

He was cold but she felt his heartbeat. Suddenly, she couldn't stop the tears.

"*Oy va voi, zise meydl.*" Oh, my sweet girl.

"*Tate*, our home, the temple..." She sobbed uncontrollably as if the dam of her confusion had shattered the walls of restraint.

"I know, I know."

"I wanted to stay, but the rats and Arnold invited us here, and...and..."

"It's not your fault. You can't shoulder the burden of the community. Gustav said it was the heavy load of snow."

"Oh *Tate*, I saw it. The roof collapsed. All is ruined." Hannah blinked at him through wet eyes. "I'm not even wearing my own clothes. I'm not...I can't..." She broke into the cries that she'd kept in until now. It all bubbled to the surface. Far beyond the last week at the Pearlers' home —the last ten months, the loss of her mother, the burden she'd shouldered with her siblings—it all poured out in the form of salty tears.

"Let me look at you, *meyn kind*." My child. And with his words, Hannah set the burden aside. She no longer needed to hold her stern posture and to be strong for her siblings. When her father was near, she could be a child. He would be strong for her.

"You look...*vi aoyb pild fun di ey*." Like peeled from an egg. Her father beamed proudly at his daughter as if he werepleased?

Hannah felt undeserving. "Mama said I was her good egg, but *Tate*, I wasn't so good while you were gone." She confessed that she'd fallen for Arnold.

Her father's eyes grew darker, sadder, then he closed his eyes altogether. He muffled a silent prayer to himself. Hannah waited in silence.

"I'd hoped something like this might happen, but it seems that you have, as usually, exceeded my expectations, *Maidale*." Sweet girl. His eyes were bloodshot. "I don't know when I lost sight of your happiness., but you should know that you have my blessing to find love and happiness with the boy."

"But he's—"

"He is an apple from a tree I know well. And I was praying that he'd suit you."

"You were?" Hannah couldn't hide her surprise.

"I saw it the day he kissed you. He saw you for you, not for the shul, the children, or me. He saw *you*."

Hannah blinked back her tears and sniffled. That hadn't occurred to her. Arnold had been overcome by the shabby girl in the woolen dress. He really had seen *her* despite it all.

Eve walked in carrying a little bundle. "Someone wishes to see you, Hannah."

"Ruthie!" Hannah shot to Eve and gently took her baby sister in her arms. She held her to her cheek and kissed her soft baby hair. "Oh, how big you've grown!" The baby made some happy cooing noises and grabbed Hannah's nose with her tiny hands.

"Solomon, may we have a word with you?" Eve reached her hand out and signaled the Rabbi to follow her.

Hannah followed, carrying Ruthie lovingly in her arms.

They followed Eve to the study, where Gustav stood before his glass cabinet.

He had his head tilted sideways as if assessing the shelf for the first time. "We removed the shelves and stood the Torah here for the time being," he said as Eve, the Rabbi, and Hannah walked into the room, Ruthie still cooing.

"I'm having drapes sown as we speak," Eve said.

"A temporary solution, until the temple is restored, of course," Gustav added.

The Rabbi stood before the makeshift Torah cabinet, an ark that was even more elegant than the one at the temple. Hannah realized that the Torah had a place of honor at the Pearler's home, a place filled with good people who respected the ancient teachings beyond the scripture. How wrong she'd been before, how closed-minded.

"Rabbi, there's a matter I'd like to discuss with you," Gustav said with a serious tone, although Hannah caught Eve's half-smile.

"Certainly, Gustav, *vos ken ikh ton far dir?*" What can I do for you?

"It's a delicate matter because it involves...shall we say...an episode of blackmail from recent history that Eve and I are keen to put behind us." He glanced at Eve now and she gave him a nod.

"Solomon." Eve approached him as if she was going to put her hand on his arm as she often did when imparting a matter of importance, but she didn't touch him. It wouldn't have been proper for a woman to touch an orthodox man. Eve was ever so polished, and proficient in all aspects of etiquette.

"You have me worried, Gustav." The Rabbi looked expectantly at Gustav, then at Eve.

Hannah shrugged; she didn't know what this was about.

"We had to evict...of sorts...a tenant from one of our holdings here in the city, not far from here actually, on the other side of St. James Park." Gustav blinked at Eve again. "But I'm digressing."

"There is a full staff, and we've been running the household without occupants," Eve said.

"Like a ghost house? Here in London?" the Rabbi asked.

Gustav and Eve smiled.

"Um, no, more like a house that is furnished, staffed, and warm, but has no master," Gustav said.

"It's taken too much of my time to keep it running, Solomon, and I'm spread too thin for my other responsibilities," Eve explained. "And there's the matter with a family friend who's petitioning the parliament to support the construction of a new synagogue closer to St. James, of course."

Warmth crept back into Hannah's heart along with the beauty of lighthearted hope. She hugged Ruthie more tightly. The Pearlers had hearts of gold.

"Seeing how you're on the market to assume oversight of new lodgings, we hoped that you might consider helping us out with this holding of ours," Gustav asked the Rabbi.

The Rabbi glanced at Hannah, and she returned a wistful smile and an incline of her head.

"And this holding of yours, would it fit my family?" the Rabbi asked.

"There are six bedrooms only, I'm afraid, so some of your children would have to share," Eve said, visibly stifling a smile. The six bedrooms were more than they'd ever dreamed of. And the boys were all close in age and could share, as would Esther and Alma.

The Rabbi rubbed his beard. This time, Hannah didn't cringe at the scratchy sound, she'd missed him so much.

"There are servants' quarters and a small office for the butler. His name is Oliver Hinckley. He's quite set in his ways, I am afraid," Eve said.

"Which could be helpful as you learn the ways of this new house, Solomon," Gustav said. "Some of your attention may be diverted by the plans for the new shul."

"Hmmm." The Rabbi nodded. His eyes crinkled as he smiled, and he was obviously trying to suppress the glee spreading in response to his friends' generous offer. "And I'd be your tenant, pay rent monthly?" he asked, holding on to his pride.

"Certainly." Gustav nodded.

"And how much rent did the previous tenant pay?"

Gustav shot another look at Eve. She raised one brow. Hannah already knew that Allison Thompson's mother, Carol Bustle-Smith, hadn't paid anything for years and extorted the Pearlers.

"What did you pay at the temple?" Gustav asked.

"Oh, er, it was an old arrangement, grandfathered in, so to say." The Rabbi rubbed his beard and then his bushy eyebrows. "They withheld twenty percent of my salary to cover the lodgings."

"That's the exact sum we are hoping for," Gustav said as he stepped closer and reached out to shake the Rabbi's hand.

"You see, you're doing us quite a favor since we can't keep staff on if they're not serving anyone. And there's a staff of twelve, four of whom live in the house, so we didn't have the heart to take the purpose away from the poor dears' lives," Eve said as she sat and folded her hands elegantly on her lap.

"And their livelihoods, of course," Gustav added.

"Of course," the Rabbi said as he stared at Hannah. She understood what an enormous gesture this was, more than a token of friendship. The Pearlers were treating them like family.

"I promise I'll see after running the household. And I'm sure my children will keep the servants entertained." The Rabbi smiled and sidestepped Gustav's hand with a warm hug.

Eve came to Hannah's side and put her hand on her arm, her telltale move. "One of the servants is our old governess. She's been wonderful with Lizzie, but since Lizzie is on her first season, we thought she might better move to the house where there'll be children in the schoolroom."

Hannah couldn't blink away her tears of joy as she tried to thank Eve.

"That leaves one matter to settle," the Rabbi said. "I need to speak to Arnold."

Gustav and Eve nodded at him and left the room.

CHAPTER 51

*A*rnold walked into Gustav's study. He'd been told the Rabbi had returned, and his heart ached. Hannah would leave now.

"Good evening, Rabbi Solomon."

The Rabbi waved him in. He sat behind Gustav's desk, commanding the room.

"How is your grandson?" Arnold asked.

"The baby's doing quite well, thank you for asking."

Arnold smiled at Hannah. She was so happy fussing over baby Ruthie.

"A-pooh!"

Hannah crinkled her nose. She was so adorable when she did that. She picked up the baby and turned to leave the room. "We need to freshen up a little. May we be excused, *Tate?*"

The Rabbi gave her a soft, warm look, and she disappeared with the beloved bundle.

Arnold grew uneasy.

"Sit," the Rabbi said. His demeanor had changed. He seemed determined, a little angry even.

"I'd rather stand," Arnold said. This was his home. He hadn't done anything Hannah didn't allow. Or enjoy. Why did he feel as if he'd been called to the headmaster again?

"My daughter tells me that you've grown closer."

Arnold deflated. She'd confessed.

"What are your intentions, son?"

"Rabbi, I proposed marriage. She refused me."

The Rabbi chuckled but then masked his laughter with a fake cough. "She's spirited, shall we say?"

"Stubborn, even," Arnold added. The Rabbi chuckled.

"Arnold, son, my daughter stepped into the shoes of my wife. Her death was a shock and Hannah went into an automatic mode of caring for the family."

"I've noticed that she cares deeply—"

"It's her virtue and her vice."

"I don't understand, Rabbi."

"She tends to take on *a konto tzures*," the Rabbi explained. The sorrows of others. "And she puts her own interests aside."

Arnold sat down after all. This could take a while.

"Do you like her?" the Rabbi looked Arnold squarely in the eyes. Arnold felt as if his soul were exposed. "Tell me the truth."

"I always tell the truth, Rabbi."

The Rabbi nodded appreciatively. "I won't force her upon you if it's not your desire."

"It is. I think I love her."

"You think?"

"I don't know, Rabbi, I've never been in love. But I miss

her when she's not in my arms." Arnold stopped and raked his hands through his hair. He'd said too much. But the Rabbi's look was friendly and soft. Something about the Rabbi made Arnold want to pour his feelings onto a platter before him.

"I can't sleep. She occupies my mind all the time. But when she's near me, my stomach flips and I break into a cold sweat. I mean … er …" Arnold stood and paced the room. "It's so frustrating, Rabbi!"

The Rabbi remained silent, and Arnold continued. "Fave thinks I'm in love, but I think I'm sick. I don't feel like myself. I used to be so self-sufficient and now I can't imagine how the passage to America can possibly work. She won't come with me, you see, because of Ruthie and the other children."

"What passage to America?" the Rabbi gasped in alarm.

"It's for the competition…" And Arnold told him everything.

WHEN HE WAS FINISHED, the Rabbi rose from Gustav's chair and came to Arnold. He stood in front of him and took his head between his hands. Then he inclined his head for Arnold was half a head taller than him. He mumbled something in Hebrew and kissed his forehead.

Arnold looked at him, puzzled.

"I'll tell her not to worry about the children. Ruthie will be here when you both return."

"Re-return?" Arnold caught his words in his throat. "D-do you mean—"

"You have my blessing. I appreciate your honesty, and I

can see that your heart is true. Just promise to bring her back home safely."

Arnold was speechless. It was unlike him, and he didn't know how to handle this dumbfoundedness.

He hugged the Rabbi and ran off to find Hannah.

"Hannah!" Arnold ran up the grand staircase, taking two steps at a time. "Hannaaaaaaah!"

"Shhh! Ruthie just fell asleep!" Hannah emerged from the nursery with her index finger pressed against her lips.

Arnold saw Eve, Gustav, and Lizzie peeking out from the nursery door. Arnold swallowed.

"What's all this noise?" Fave came down the stairs from their chambers, Rachel holding his arm.

Then the Rabbi arrived. Oh good, everyone was here. This would be even harder than he'd thought—but he wanted to stop thinking and get on with it.

"Where are the other children?" Arnold asked his aunt.

"I sent them to Madamme LaFleur, my dressmaker. The poor dears came with one trunk and need to be outfitted." Aunt Eve waved it off as if it were a trifle.

"Why did you come to find me?" Hannah asked.

"It's about the Melo Melo," Arnold said. He didn't see Fave but heard his sharp inhale.

Arnold retrieved a satchel from his pocket and knelt before Hannah. Lizzie took a breath and stood agog. Aunt Eve patted a tear away. Rachel wrapped herself around Fave's arm more closely. The Rabbi took a stand next to Arnold. He felt his hand on his shoulder, a tight pinch of support, then he stepped away.

Hannah saw her father's hand on Arnold's shoulder. Then Arnold looked into her eyes and everything around them went dark. She only had eyes for the depth of his gaze, which spoke of sincerity and love.

He retrieved a velvet satchel, turned it upside down, and shook it. Something shiny fell into his hand. He opened a clasp to rows of pearls with something at the center.

Lizzie gasped somewhere in the background but Hannah's eyes were locked with Arnold's.

A smile overcame Hannah's face and love enveloped her heart in a foggy mist of glee.

"Hannah, I took the liberty of restringing your mother's pearls into three strands. They're exquisitely matched." Arnold held up a collier of cascading rows of pearls with five pendants, the largest in the center.

"I set the Melo Melo in the middle. The most precious one in Europe." He held the luxurious collier up. "It would be an honor to see this on you. I hope you'll allow me—"

Hannah made a funny squealing noise.

"My dear Hannah, my sweet, smart, and complicated love." He smiled; his eyes glued to hers.

Hannah knew there were others around them, but couldn't muster the attention to see them. She never thought Arnold would give her another chance, much less propose again.

"Hannah Solomon, my love, would you do me the honor of marrying me?"

She fell to her knees and into his arms. Somehow, she whispered yes into his ear, and he immediately took her mouth in a searing kiss.

And when they broke the kiss, the family had left.

CHAPTER 52

Hannah sat in the green drawing room at Eve's desk while Arnold and Eve had tea behind her. She'd been given all the paper and ink she needed, but it seemed harder to write her last column than her first.

~~Dear Members of the Community,~~

~~My fellow Community Members,~~

My beloved Community,

For the first time, I am not citing the Torah or Talmud in this column. I have come to understand that there is much to be learned outside our community—but I expect to bring back what I learn to help us better communicate. The philosopher and economist, Adam Smith, wrote, "It is decent to be humble amidst great prosperity, but we can scarcely express too much satisfaction in all the little occurrences of common life." So, I *have tried to bring us all together, one challah at a time, one page at a time. But our community needs something greater. I will embark upon a quest to bring a new purpose to those most in need among us, to help our community thrive in a sustainable future.*

This is a bittersweet goodbye as I will embark upon a terrifying adventure with my new husband. I entrust my family with new and old friends, and I hope to return with elan and purpose to a brighter future for us all.

ARNOLD CAME TO HER SIDE. "Is this your last column?"

Hannah sighed. "I think so. For now."

He picked it up, and she watched his eyes move along the lines as he read.

"You didn't tell them about the button factory?"

Hannah shook her head. "Let it come to fruition first."

"Stop doubting yourself, my dear," Eve said. She took the paper from Arnold. "I'll reach out to my contacts and the haute-couture dressmakers will have a waitlist for your buttons before you return. And your baby sister won't know you were gone, I'll oversee the nanny and help your father, my dear," Eve promised.

Hannah, agog, warmed to Eve even more. It was understandable why Arnold wanted to honor the Pearlers.

"She will look up to you when she grows up, my love," Arnold said. "You're breaking them all out of the rut. You'll be an entrepreneur and build a factory she can be proud of!"

Hannah could only hope Arnold was right. For her,

any time away from her baby was an inexcusable infraction against her code of motherly conduct.

James, the butler, came in and announced, "Mr. And Mrs. Thompson—"

"Yes, they know me, thank you." Allison stormed in, a rumpled skinny man trailing in her wake.

"You!" Allison said to Arnold, her index finger pointing high in the air like a witch's broomstick.

"Hannah, dear, this is Marvin Thompson, Allison's husband." Arnold ignored Allison and introduced the barrister.

"Has your nausea passed, Mrs. Thompson?" Hannah asked, feigning politeness.

Allison growled like a cat whose tail had been stepped on. Her husband pushed her aside and she cowered on a chair next to Eve.

"Ahem, Arnold, may I—" Marvin started, but Arnold waved him off.

"The matter is out of my hands. Greg is passing the forgeries on to the authorities," Arnold said nonchalantly.

"As indeed he has, I am afraid," Marvin said in a low stern voice, "that's why we're here."

Allison railed against Arnold. "You took my house, then you captured my mother in the boondocks, and the police—"

"That's quite enough out of you!" Eve said.

"Arnold, I was hoping you could give us a chance to redeem ourselves," Marvin said, red-faced.

Arnold gave Hannah a look and she said, "Forgiveness is one of the Jewish virtues most find difficult to achieve."

She felt Arnold deflate beside her.

"Yes, Ma'am." Marvin twisted his hat around his hand. "And I suppose you are better people than we are, so I was hoping—"

"Pah!" Allison cried.

Hannah frowned at Arnold. She'd tried, but surely there was a place for lowly criminals like the Thompsons other than here?

Marvin tried again. "Arnold, pardon me, but there is little left here for us. Allison's mother is no longer welcome among the ton, so I have lost my clients. The authorities will find a—"

"What do you want from me, Marvin?" Arnold growled.

"Take us with you to America. Let us work off our debt," Marvin said.

Allison held her breath.

Eve rose from her seat and touched Arnold's arm, giving him a squeeze.

Arnold pinched the bridge of his beautiful nose with his strong fingers and spoke without opening his eyes. "With interest, Marvin."

Allison let out a haughty cry while Marvin fell to his knees.

"Get up, Marvin!" Arnold said.

"Thank you for giving us a second chance. You won't regret this," Marvin mumbled as James and Christoph, James' apprentice, lifted Marvin and turned to escort him and Allison out.

Arnold turned to Hannah, "I'm almost certain that we'll regret this."

"Me too," Eve said.

But Hannah's heart filled with all the joy that a *mitzvah* would bring, for every good deed would call for another in return.

CHAPTER 53

The last few days had passed in a daze, and Arnold couldn't believe he was already aboard Gregory's ship. The wedding ceremony had been held there, and Hannah had cried while her father recited all the Hebrew blessings in his arsenal. During the small family celebration, her little siblings had ducked in and out of her wedding dress as if it were a tent. She'd laughed heartily, although Arnold thought it was odd that she'd allow someone to go under her dress. And yet, her interaction with her siblings were innocent. She'd be an amazing mother. She already was to her siblings, and Arnold knew she left them reluctantly, an immense declaration of love.

The time had come to say goodbye. Gregory had left a selection of French champagne as a parting gift and Arnold intended to make the most of their honeymoon at sea.

"You have the folder with the designs?" Fave asked as he patted Arnold on the back.

"Of course. Only Fibonacci numbers, only the rarest and clearest gems...I know, Cous," Arnold said. They'd never been apart for more than a few days, and Arnold guessed it was as hard for Fave to say goodbye as it was for him.

"Mazal tov," Fave said but his voice broke, and Arnold stifled a few tears himself.

One by one, they said goodbye to their families.

"If I were younger, I'd come myself," Pavel said, "you're very brave to go on this adventure, my boy."

His son, Caleb, stood behind Arnold. He was coming along in Pavel's place. Our families are united in this competition. I'll do my best to make you proud as I would my grandfather," Arnold promised Pavel when he reluctantly hugged his son goodbye.

"AND DID you bring the sun hats?" Lizzie asked when it was her turn.

"Yes, dear. I have the bonnets and this." Hannah let go of Arnold's hand to pat the large white flower hat on her head. Lizzie had outdone herself in the short period she'd had, and Hannah was a most stunning bride. Arnold couldn't wait to untie her dress and peel her out of the layers of fine lace that hugged her curves so elegantly.

* * *

SINCE HER FATHER performed the ceremony, Hannah had asked Pavel to walk her to the chuppah. In her mother's place, Eve had circled Arnold with her seven times, for the seven blessings of matrimony. Hannah couldn't count for she barely saw where she was going through the pools of tears flooding her eyes. Hannah wasn't one to cry much, but the emotions of the day washed over her as if she had to fill the ocean she was about to embark upon.

"I am so sorry, *Tate*," Hannah told her father as he held her in a tight hug.

"Don't be, *Maidale*. You're not leaving us." He gave Arnold a stern look. "You will bring her back safely, Ehrlich!"

"*Meyn Ehrenvort.*" On my honor. Arnold bowed.

"*Maidale*, wherever you go, you will take the love for our faith, our traditions, and all of your knowledge with you. Carry us in your heart," her father whispered. "Not just us, all the Jews!" And with these words, he left along the thin walkway to the dock.

"Byyeee," her little brothers waved and jumped on the dock. Fave, Eve, and Aunt Rifkah held the boys' collars so they wouldn't fall into the water. Baby Ruthie was in her father's arms.

Hannah clutched her chest as the ship swayed gently. She stood beside Arnold but couldn't make herself look at him. She knew she'd shatter from the pain she felt at taking her leave.

"Do you think Ruthie will remember me?" Hannah asked when their friends and families were mere specks on the horizon. "Your aunt said that the girls will look up to me when my button factory creates jobs and brings affluence to the poor—"

"How could anyone not?" Arnold said as he wrapped his strong arm around her. "You are the Pearl of All Brides."

THE END
Rate this Book
Goodreads
BookBub

GET FREE Receipe Inspiration from Regency London (including a tutorial of how to braid challah like Hannah) when you sign up for Sara Adrien's VIP Newsletter at https://SaraAdrien.com.

ABOUT THE AUTHOR

Sara Adrien writes hot and heart-melting regency romance with a Jewish twist. She is a prolific legal scholar and professor by day and author of the series *Infiltrating the Ton* and *Diamond Dynasty* by night.

Some of her law textbooks, published under a different name by the world's most renowned publishing houses topped Amazon's international charts. She has taught graduate-level law and policy across the globe and always enjoys learning something new herself. Her hobbies are everything food-related, painting, and reading. She speaks six languages and loves to travel.

These days, she is homeschooling her sons with the help of her beloved parents and husband in their multi-generational Boston home. Sign up for her VIP newsletter to be the first to hear about new releases, audiobooks, sales, and bonus content. Just cut and paste into your browser: www.SaraAdrien.com.

AUTHOR'S NOTE

Our story takes place in 1813 London at a time when the world was in an uproar. The US was at war with Great Britain since June, 1812. Although peace terms were reached in December, 1814, at the Treaty of Ghent, the war did not officially end until the peace treaty was ratified by Congress on 17 February, 1815. What became known as the French invasion of Russia, when Napoleon forced Russia back into the Continental blockade of the United Kingdom, also occurred in 1812, further complicating matters among the Western world powers. Even though the perspectives of Jewish merchants at the time are limited, it is likely that the isolation of the European continent had an effect on Jews in Britain. This is where I have allowed my imagination to fill in the blanks and create a trade route between London and New York, for Arnold to direct Gregory's fleet and achieve glory for the fictional family of the Pearlers in London.

Around the same time, in the Ohio, Tennessee, and

Mississippi river basins, the British truly searched for pearls, virtually depleting the freshwater mussels and oysters. Arnold and Hannah may have been some of the first British citizens to search for pearls while most of the American settlers were preoccupied with agriculture and the wars. The Tennessee Washboard mussel produced a variety of nacre colors that gave the pearls special allure. It was also well-documented that Native Americans wore pearl jewelry from the Ohio River. Mississippi River pearls were found years ago during the pearl button rush in Muscatine, Iowa. They were large and often turned into brooches or buttons, just like the ones Hannah wants to produce in London when she brings the shells back. However, the British exhibited most of these jewels and the treasure trove from the North American continent in the late 1800's, long after my story here ends. As such, it is entirely plausible to consider Arnold and Hannah's mission to find pearls in America as spearheading the effort to restore trade routes that did not lean on human trafficking. To this day, we can admire pearls from the American continent in the Crown Jewels of the Tower of London. King George IV has been said to have made great contributions to the art world, and it is a figment of my imagination that he may have allowed Jewish jewelers to earn a place in history with their exquisite designs.

Finally, there are several well-documented Jewish families who were baptized and converted to Christianity to complete their assimilation, like our character Greg Stone. My story slightly predates the decades during which baptized Jews were awarded baronies and joined the House of Lords, but who is to say that Gregory's family couldn't have done this secretly before it was a more established practice? Unfortunately, to this day, Jews find it necessary to forego their beliefs as they seek acceptance of their families. Let us remember that there was no State of Israel in 1813 and no safe haven for Jews. As an author of Jewish fiction, it is my hope, however, to stretch people's imagination to a place where Jews are able to hold on to their traditions while prospering in the society of their choice.

MARGINS OF LOVE

Infiltrating the Ton Book 1

Fave's Story

Elusive haute-couture jeweler, Fave Pearler, has to put his beloved Greek mythology aside to face an arranged marriage suiting his family's dynasty while all of London is on the quest for the biggest, rarest gems for the king's competition. Meanwhile, his mother's meddlesome frenemy threatens to reveal their secret and her blackmail is driving good-natured Fave mad. But when the evil gossip catches him with Rachel Newman, he has to fight for the love of his life and the family's business...

Rachel Newman only wants one season before resigning herself to a wedding her father has arranged, and golden boy Fave is off-limits. When he rattles her principles, she's determined to protect her family's true identity—but she cannot resist Fave's kisses. How can Rachel reconcile romance and family tradition?

Bestselling author Sara Adrien's Regency Romance with a Jewish twist will leave you gasping for more. Find out how the smart and strong heroine overcomes impossible obstacles of the period? Join Rachel and Fave on their journey to find true love in a time when Jews were not welcome among the ton. Immerse yourself in a time where the difficulties that minorities faced were similar to the present and yet delivered differently. This is not a fairy tale, it's real-life packaged in a delightful love story filled with vivid descriptions, geopolitical depth, and charming characters.

Praise for Margins of Love

"One of the Best Regency Romance Novels in 2022 . . . a Masterful Combination of Historical Romance with Jewish Fiction"
-Yahoo! News

"The new bestselling voice in Regency Romance and Jewish Fiction"
- Pittsburgh Post Gazette

"The *Infiltrating the Ton* series [i]s an "exquisite page-turner" and "a remarkable debut." Readers praise Adrien's "vivid depictions of how complex love stories could have been in the previous centuries" and cherish the geopolitical currentness and depth of her books."
- FOX40

"Jewish history romance? Yes please!
This book was all about the power of love. The hero is talking about how Rachel's love for him is his power. It's a beautiful scene and set up. Overall, I liked the book a lot. . . The love between those two characters is so strong."
- Sally on Goodreads.com

"What a Great Story!
As someone who enjoys reading, I was immediately hooked and drawn into the writing. As the daughter of Holocaust survivors, I appreciated that the author described what it means to be Jewish, through the concrete experiences of two families at one point in time. The issues, however, are timeless."
- Barbara M.

"Lovely and Interesting!
Not only is Margins of Love well written, it immersed me in a world I never would have known about otherwise. I've read plenty of Regency romances but the addition of the Jewish angle made it especially intriguing to me…"
- Denise D.

"If you need your Bridgerton itch scratched, this book will def do that. And getting to see this period from a Jewish perspective is really exciting to me - something new! Also, just solid writing and story-telling. This is a joy."
- Hudlocke on Amazon.com

ALSO BY SARA ADRIEN

Margins of Love (Fave's Story)
Infiltrating the Ton Book 1

A Kiss After Tea (Lizzie's Story)
Infiltrating the Ton Book 3

Jewels and Love (Izaac's Story)
Infiltrating the Ton Prequel

Stay tuned for the **Diamond Dynasty Series**
Launching in 2023